Louise Croft lived for 10 years with her husband in a small village in the Tarn on the borders of the Aveyron River in France. Their home was 300 years old. "It was a life-changing experience, speaking French daily, absorbing the customs of country life, and making local friends," describes Louise Croft. Details of the various markets, fetes, and vide greniers (bric-a-brac), hunting in the forests, and shooting the rats (loires) described in this novel are real events that she shared.

She has had the opportunity to live in 7 countries and work in 16. She emigrated alone from England to Australia in April 1989 with the Government Business Migration Scheme. She established an IT consultancy providing document management services for mining, engineering, oil and gas industries, as well as the federal and the State Governments.

She wrote and self-published her first novel, 'The Edge of Life', in 2020. It is based on the real experience of an Italian woman living in Puglia during World War II.

In commemoration of the villagers of Le Riols, including the mayor with whom we shared 10 eventful and happy years, 2008–2018. We will never forget their kindness and acceptance of 2 étrangers in their daily lives and their support during difficult times.

Le Riols survives unscathed and is truly 'Un Village Sympathique'. To my loving family, Simon, Ben and Sam, Adam, Alyssa, Ryan and Liezl, and my sister, Elaine.

Louise Croft

A Village Betrayed

AUSTIN MACAULEY PUBLISHERS™
LONDON * CAMBRIDGE * NEW YORK * SHARJAH

Copyright © Louise Croft 2023

The right of Louise Croft to be identified as author of this work has been asserted by the author in accordance with sections 77 and 78 of the Copyright, Designs and Patents Act 1988.

All rights reserved. No part of this publication may be reproduced, stored in a retrieval system, or transmitted in any form or by any means, electronic, mechanical, photocopying, recording, or otherwise, without the prior permission of the publishers.

Any person who commits any unauthorised act in relation to this publication may be liable to criminal prosecution and civil claims for damages.

This is a work of fiction. Names, characters, businesses, places, events, locales, and incidents are either the products of the author's imagination or used in a fictitious manner. Any resemblance to actual persons, living or dead, or actual events is purely coincidental.

A CIP catalogue record for this title is available from the British Library.

ISBN 9781035801862 (Paperback)
ISBN 9781035801879 (Hardback)
ISBN 9781035801893 (ePub e-book)
ISBN 9781035801886 (Audiobook)

www.austinmacauley.com

First Published 2023
Austin Macauley Publishers Ltd®
1 Canada Square
Canary Wharf
London
E14 5AA

To my beloved husband, Ian Allison, for thirty years of encouragement and support for my aspirations and adventures.

Table of Contents

List of Characters   11

Vichy France 1943   14
    Resistance   14

Vichy France Spring and Summer 1942   19
    Broussac   19
    Spring   26
    The Boar Hunt   31
    The Summer Fete   35
    A Mother's Grief   48
    The Storm   58
    The School Teacher   65

Vichy France Autumn and Winter 1942-43   71
    Harvest Time   71
    Intrusion of War   76
    Refuge on the Farm   80
    Hardship   83
    Oppression in Cahors   90
    Rescue by the Maquis   97
    Deprivation   102

Vichy France Spring and Summer 1943   108
    Suspicion   108

The Maire's Opposition	*111*
Child Evacuees	*116*
Support for the Maquis	*124*
Germans in Cahors	*128*
Sabotage	*141*
Summer Hunting	*144*

Vichy France Autumn and Winter 1943-44 — **147**

Disintegration of the Village	*147*
Winter Suffering	*149*
Malignant Forces	*153*

Vichy France Summer 1944 — **157**

Maquis Attack	*157*
Escape Route	*161*
Reprisal	*165*

Aveyron Summer 1995 — **170**

Memorial to Brutality	*170*

Vichy France Historical Notes — **176**

Broussac and the Aveyron	*176*
German Reprisals	*178*
The STO Releve	*179*
STO Refractaires	*179*
The Maquis	*180*
Evacuation of Children from Paris	*181*
Local Villages and Towns	*181*

Bibliography and References — **183**

Glossary French to English — **184**

List of Characters

Madame Britt Ziegler—School teacher. Widow of a German officer. No children.

Liliane Damour—Wife of Jean-Jacques, Boulangerie. Two sons-Armand (aged 17) and Louis (aged 15). One daughter Rose-Marie (aged 11).

Josette Favel—Wife of farmer Alain. Two married daughters. Two sons-Martin (aged 17) and Gilles (aged 16).

Paulette Vidal—Owns the cafe with husband Jean-Luc. Two sons-Jean-Paul (aged 17) and Michel (aged 16). Two daughters Louisa and Maria (aged 15 and 14).

Nicole Lacroix—Wife of Albert, skilled cabinetmaker and forester. No children. Cousin to Josette.

Marie-Francoise Michelet—*Propriétaire of La Chene* café in *Villane-le-Foret*. Her husband died at the beginning of the war and her son was a German prisoner of war.

M Bertrand Danton—Village Maire, married to Pierrette. Two married daughters living in the next village and two sons living in Rodez.

Michel Duroux—Deputy Maire, married to Chantal. Teenage son called Claude, friend of Armand, and two married sons in Rodez.

Jean-Paul and Pierrette Latour—Large landowner owning two herds of dairy cows and two herds of beef cattle. Two young sons-Pierre and Luca, friends of Guillaume Damour. Daughter Chantal is a friend of Rose-Marie.

Joseph Lanzac—Widower and soldier of the Great War. Friend of Michel Favel and Bertrand Danton.

Michel Favel—Father of Alain Favel, married to Mauricette. One married son-Claude.

Madame Pellier—Widow with two married daughters. Son is a gendarme.

Madame Royal—Widow. Her husband died in the Great War at the age of 21. They had no children.

Madame Ricard—Widow. Her husband was killed in the Great War.

M Compiegne—Lives in a sheep hut. Soldier of World War 1.

Regis Duval—Plays an accordion. Lives in wooden house at the edge of Broussac and looks after his grandchildren.

Antoine and Claudine Ricardo—Antoine is the lively village handyman. They have two adult sons-one married who lives in a nearby village and Matthieu who is not married.

Friends of the Maire—Paul Gauthier, farmer. Alain, husband of Josette. Armand Laron, farmer. Martin Robert, retired blacksmith, brother of Madam Ricard. Armand du Bosc, farmer.

Amedee and Paulette Cantou—Run the local Post Office. They use a radio transmitter stored in their cellar.

Pierre Dalmain and wife—Quarrelsome neighbours of Liliane and Jean-Jacques.

Madame Ponthier—Owner of small terrier with bull-fighting instincts.

Vincent Lefevre—Owns a farm producing olive, sunflower and maize to make into cooking oil. Friend of Antoine Ricardo. Son is **Serge Lefevre**.

Albert Larzac and Jules Durfour—Live in Broussac.

Monsieur Pascal—Village priest.

Alphonse Germain—Owns Broussac hardware store. Married with one son who works in the shop.

Pierre and wife Simone Lasalle—Cousins of Liliane who live in Cahors. Three children-one boy, Hugo and two daughters-Paulette and Chantal.

Louise Duprey—Granddaughter of Liliane Damour.

Vichy France 1943

Resistance

Liliane Damour pedals rapidly along the narrow country lane lined with tall oak trees. Her cotton dress is tucked into her belt and her feet pushed into heavy wooden clogs that grip the metal pedals. The bike shudders over the brown rutted track, the morning sun creating slats of shadow and light as it filters through leafy trees. Bread bounces in the front and back paniers attached to the bike and she breathes in the aroma of freshly baked dough. She feels excited and nervous as she cycles to the village café in *Villane-le-Foret*. She is determined to fight against the German invaders but must keep her actions secret to protect her children. A scrap of paper is hidden inside a baguette made that morning by her husband, Jean-Jacques. She received a sealed coded message from her cousin in Cahors brought by Madame Cantou who runs *La Poste* in Broussac. It's essential Liliane delivers it to the pre-arranged *rendezvous* with the *maquis* hiding in dense forests north of the village. She pauses to listen to the birds trilling in the tree canopy to calm her nerves. She smells the damp earth and fallen leaves and sees the paw prints of a fox.

She pedals uphill until she reaches the hamlet of *Villane-le-Foret*. Gasping a little with her effort, Liliane leaps off her bike and leans it against a café table. She hauls the bread out of the paniers and walks into the café. Marie-Francoise, the *patron* looks up from making coffees for customers sitting outside and points to a space on the kitchen table. "*Bonjour, Liliane. Qu'est que ce passe?* What's happening?"

"*Bonjour, cherie. J'ai une rendezvous avec le Maire. Je suis pressé.*" Liliane says she's in a hurry and kisses her friend on both cheeks. She waves to the café customers and mounts her cycle to head further into the forest. Perspiration beads her forehead and her dress clings to her damp back. The air has become humid and the sun is hidden behind heavy dark clouds. It looks like a thunderstorm is brewing.

She pushes her bike into a thick bush and slides through the tree trunks to a rough wooden hut. She knocks and a large calloused hand pulls her through the door as it partially opens. It's dark inside except for a few chinks of sunlight threading through the gaps in the wooden walls. She smells unwashed bodies and feels her way to crouch in a small space on the earth floor. "*J'ai une message de Cahors,*" Liliane whispers to the shrouded bodies.

"*D'accord. Merci. Allez. Allez rapidement.* Go quickly." A deep male voice rasps the words, a shadowy hand takes the message and pushes her through a gap as the door is opened slightly.

Liliane emerges into the shadowy glade of oak trees to see a brown deer spring lightly in front of her. She shivers a little, glad to mount her bike and return to the *Boulangerie* before the storm hits. Two brilliant flashes of forked lightning slash between the stormy black clouds as she pedals furiously down the hill to the crossroads. A large uniformed man is standing by the stone cross, his outline stark against a threatening sky. A sudden ray of sunlight reflects off his brass buttons and epaulets. He stands with legs spread, his feet pushed into heavy soled boots and is blocking the lane. He holds up his gloved hand for her to stop. It's *Gendarme Pellier* from the *Milice*, the German replacement for the local police force. As Liliane skids to a halt a few feet away, she can smell sweat and see white dog hairs spread liberally on his dark military uniform. He's a tall obese man with bushy black eyebrows, a large nose and a slack mouth which is twisted into a smirk. Liliane knows his family well as his mother is a customer at the *Boulangerie*. She keeps her right foot on the pedal for immediate escape and her sweaty hands clench nervously on the handlebars. She takes a deep breath and smiles at him, "*Bonjour, Gendarme Pellier. Tout va bien.*"

"*Ou va tu?*" he growls at her, rudely inquiring where she's been. He rifles through the empty paniers with his gloved hands. He can see they are empty except for a few crumbs. He places both hands on her handlebars and leans into her face, his breath a foul mix of chewed meat and rough red wine.

"*Je fais la livraison a Villane-le-Foret comme d'habitude,*" she replies tartly, her foot pressed hard on the pedal. "I deliver bread to the village *café* as usual. *Excusez-moi, je suis pressé.* I'm in a hurry."

Gendarme Pellier sneers and releases the handlebars. Liliane rapidly cycles away, turning back briefly to see him still standing in the lane, backlit by a frightening fork of lightning slashing down to the village. This is the second message she's delivered from her cousin to the *maquis* hiding in the forests of the Aveyron. Has *Gendarme Pellier* followed her? Is he spying on her? Anxious thoughts tumble around her brain. She props her bike in her backyard and walks up the stone steps into the kitchen. The door is propped ajar by a large rock.

Jean-Jacques sits in his favourite chair, elbows resting on the wooden arms, smoking his pipe. The homely aroma of tobacco, fresh bread and woodsmoke calms her nerves. "*Tout va bien?* All well?" He asks with a smile as Liliane kisses both cheeks.

"*Oui. Je doit visiter le Maire*. I must see the *Maire* before I cook lunch." Liliane runs out, across the yard and up the steps to the *Place de la Mairie*. She knocks on the door of the *Mairie* and puts her head round the door. "*Tout va bien.*" She tells him.

"*Sois prudent*, Liliane. Be careful."

Liliane walks past the café and stops to chat with her friend Paulette and some of the customers. Broussac is a friendly village, *tres sympatique* the locals say proudly with a laugh. The conviviality of the café revives her spirits and she returns home, picking a few herbs from the front yard. She's cooked chicken stew with the remaining bones and skin of an old *poulet* that's stopped laying eggs. She takes a deep breath of relief before walking back into the kitchen where her husband has placed pottery bowls and fresh bread on the scrubbed table for the midday meal with her three offspring, Armand, Louis and daughter Rose-Marie.

Liliane sits quietly, savouring the delicious stew and fresh baguette. Her sons chatter and squabble amicably as usual but Jean-Jacques looks across the table and raises his eyebrows. His wife seems anxious and smiles distractedly at the family. They eat fresh cheese and fruit, then Rose-Marie returns to school and the youths to their work. Liliane wipes her chin of fruit juice and leans against the wooden chairback. The door creaks with the breeze and Liliane frowns at it before rising to close it.

"*Alors, ma cherie. Qu 'est que se passe?*' What's the problem, Liliane? Please share it with me." Jean Jacques moves his chair, so he can place his arm around her shoulders. He can feel her shaking and see her hands tightly clenching a cotton serviette.

"*Gendarme Pellier* stopped me at the crossroads on the way home from Marie-Francoise's café. He searched my panniers even though he could see they were empty. He's a nasty man and I felt threatened." She shudders and leans into Jean-Jacques' shoulder for comfort, thankful that she got home before the thunderstorm hit the village. The rain is lashing against the kitchen window and the room is brightly lit by a harsh flash of lightning. The wind howls round corners of buildings and snatches up dead leaves heaped in the lane outside.

Jean-Jacques gets up to pull the wooden shutters half-closed and hugs his wife. "Liliane, are you taking messages from your cousin in Cahors? It's dangerous to help the *maquis* and there could be repercussions on our family and the village." He frowns but tightens his embrace, worried for her safety. He hears unpleasant stories in the *Boulangerie* of *gendarmes* threatening to denounce people to the Gestapo.

"*Pas du tout, mon amour*. Not at all, love. Only a message for Madame Cantou. *Pas de probleme.*"

Liliane lights a kerosene lamp and washes the dishes in the stone sink, placing them on a metal tray to drain. As she fills a metal coffee pot at the sink, she gazes abstractedly out the window through the gap in the shutters and sees *Gendarme Pellier* stepping out of the *Maire*'s office, a satisfied smirk on his face. She notices he is wearing a gun holster strapped to his belt which he pats as he descends the steps. He looks at the *Boulangerie*, then walks across the *Place* to his mother's house behind.

Liliane retreats out of sight and stirs two spoonsful of *ersatz* coffee grounds into the coffee pot and places it on the wood stove to boil. She made the coffee grounds that morning from crushed acorns and roasted grain. Pure coffee is impossible to buy since the war started.

She sits at the kitchen table and thinks about the threat of *Gendarme Pellier*. He has always been a meddling officious policeman inclined to threaten people he decides are breaking the law. He is enjoying his mandated authority to search village homes for hidden crops and food secreted from the Vichy Government to avoid government regulations. Liliane is not sure where the *Maire's* loyalties lie—with the Vichy Government and the *Prefecture* who pay him, with Marshal Petain under whose command he fought in the trenches of the Great War or to his villagers. Bertrand is well liked as a *Maire* and his efforts to erect a memorial to the village dead of the Great War has won him many supporters and friends in Broussac.

Liliane twists her hands in her lap, aware that she is at the beginning of a dangerous venture, passing messages between different *Resistance* groups in the *zone libre*, free France. She is fiercely patriotic and hates the capitulation of the French Government to the Germans although she tries to understand the reasoning of Marshall Petain. She pours herself a mug of scalding coffee and ponders on the risks she runs if she continues as a *Resistance* go-between.

She needs local support and considers whether to involve Britt Zeigler the school teacher who has important connections in Paris or Joseph who hates the Germans with a deep-seated bitterness after losing his entire family to them. She finishes her coffee and takes it the sink, opening the window to cool her face. Of one thing she is positive—she will not involve her family in her *Resistance* role. Jean-Jacques has no idea she hides messages for the *maquis* in his bread. Liliane hears angry voices outside and sees *Gendarme Pellier* striding away from his mother's house, his face red with pent-up anger and his hands clenched on his gun holster. Madame Pellier stands on her terrace waving her fists at her son. "*Allez. Allez*. Go away," she screams at him, then marches inside her home and slams the door.

Vichy France Spring and Summer 1942

Broussac

After the long cold winter, the villagers of Broussac welcomed the first days of spring when the sun was warm and the mild breeze carried the perfume of wild hawthorn, chestnut flowers and apple blossom. Birds of different sizes and colours flew between houses and fields, chirping and trilling. Chaffinches perched on tree branches sporting bright breasts, glossy blackbirds and red robins sat on gate posts singing melodiously. Doves gathered on the slate roof of the church. Bees flitted from flower to flower and cats snoozed on scrubbed doorsteps.

The weekly Saturday market was held on the *boule* ground in the centre of the village and the *Place de la Mairie*. It was an occasion to meet with neighbours, friends and family, and the café was always busy. Locals arrived on bikes carrying baskets and paniers filled with items to sell which they parked in the *Place de la Mairie*. Farmers drove in vans or tractors with carts attached which they parked in a nearby grassy field.

Children in hand-me-down clothes and battered boots escaped to play in lanes and fields. Women called out greetings from open doors and windows, hair tied in cloth scarves, clothes looking worn and faded. They had an attitude of stubborn cheerfulness despite the shortage of many essential goods. Men and women clumped around in wooden clogs, others wearing scuffed leather boots with nailed soles as they shook hands or kissed neighbours and friends. *Ulysse*, the former *Maire*, parked his ancient yellow van in the lane and wandered around greeting people. He was short, tubby and friendly with a beaming smile. He was very popular and had been *Maire* of Broussac for twenty years before retiring five years earlier.

Liliane removed the flower-patterned overall she used when delivering bread and tied a bright cotton scarf over her curly dark hair. She took two baskets that were hung on hooks on the kitchen wall and packed in some homemade goods. She slipped her feet into clogs and walked briskly across the cobbled yard from her house to the *Boulangerie* where there was the usual queue of gossiping neighbours. Liliane was tall and slender with a small nose and wide smile. She was a kind and loving person who adored her three children and enjoyed participating in village life. Her eldest son, Armand, was seventeen and worked on a nearby farm. Louis, was fifteen and apprenticed to a local carpenter. Rose-Marie was ten and attended school in the village. They were a popular and respected family.

"Bonjour, Madame Royal. Comment allez vous? Bonjour, Madame Ricard. Bonjour, Madame Pellier. How are you ladies? Spring has finally arrived and I see lots of flowers in your gardens. I'm off to the market. *Au revoir*." Liliane kissed each old lady on their soft wrinkled cheeks then firmly kissed her husband Jean-Jacques on his mouth before skipping down the stone steps and walking across to the *Place de la Mairie*.

"*Bonjour, Bonjour*," she called gaily to the other stall holders who were spreading out their goods on wooden trestle tables. She set up her table beside the cheese van of Pierrette Latour, spread out a white linen cloth, unpacked her baskets and laid out the items. "*Bonjour, Bonjour*," she nodded to Pierrette who stood inside her van with her husband Jean-Paul. Pierrette was pretty and wore a smart navy dress, white cotton apron and black beret pressed firmly on her thick dark hair. Jean-Paul was a tall handsome man, always clean-shaven.

The couple used the back of their Citroen van to sell cheese products; a soft sharp goat cheese and a hard cheese made from dairy cows, similar to that produced in the Cantal region to the north. A master cheesemaker visited monthly from Roquefort bringing the specialised blue veined product made at their premises south of Rodez and matured in underground *caves.* The pungent aromas mingled with the sweet smell from market stalls selling fruit picked today from orchards and gardens. This was overlaid by the stink of animal dung and the scent of fresh straw laid between stalls.

"*Bonjour.*" Liliane nodded to the women in the queue by the cheese van who were gossiping as usual. Madame Dalmain was talking loudly, her arms folded over her large breasts. She wore a flowered cotton overall and a dark blouse and skirt. "Have you heard that Claudine fell over in her garden and broke her arm? Says she fell over a log on the path but I think her husband pushed her. *Mon Dieu,* that man is bad-tempered."

The other women nodded their agreement and muttered to each other but replied '*Bonjour*', to Liliane. Pierrette finished serving Madame Dalmain and she stomped away. Pierrette shook her head, *"Pauvre femme.* Poor woman." Liliane ignored the gossip of her neighbours and concentrated on serving her customers. She was not interested in malicious gossip or talking with bitter widows who'd lost husbands in the Great War and dramatized their loss.

"*Bonjour, Gendarme Pellier et Gendarme Gauthier."* The women simpered at the tall handsome policemen, leaning forward so their soft wrinkled cheeks could be kissed. *Gendarme Gauthier* obliged but *Gendarme Pellier* ignored them and glared at the market stalls. He was immaculately dressed, his uniform buttons glinting in the sun, black boots glossy with polish and a cap placed firmly on his head with the visor hiding his eyes. He held one hand on his gun holster and the threat was evident in his erect posture and tight-lipped mouth. His family had lived in Broussac for generations. His attitude of officiousness contrasted dramatically with the warm friendly greetings and chatter of market stallholders.

Liliane briefly glanced at him as he commenced his *promenade* inspecting the market stalls for illegal goods. She shared a stall with her friend Josette selling homemade jams and bottled fruit. She also made savoury tartlets and Josette made chutney. They kissed each other and then concentrated on selling their produce. Rationing of food and fuel by the Vichy Government had resulted in less people travelling from local villages with their products. Women sold vegetables grown in their kitchen gardens, *potagers*, and wild berries and salad greens from the hedgerows.

Their market stalls glowed with the brightly coloured vegetables, red, yellow and green capsicums, sweet-smelling tomatoes, pungent garlic, leeks and onion, aromatic bunches of herbs tied with twine, earth covered potatoes and orange carrots. In summer, colourful sunshades were erected to protect punnets of fresh red berries, purple and yellow plums, golden apples and pears, white and red grapes. Farmers' wives carried cane baskets of eggs, covered with a linen cloth, pats of homemade butter and small jars of fresh cream and yogurt.

Stalls were selling a range of items made by families during the long dark winter months, knitted and handsewn scarves and gloves, cane and wire baskets, wooden bowls, boards and spoons. Used clothes were heaped on a trestle table with outgrown children's wear. Another stall stocked sewing thread, needles and scissors.

The Lefevre family, Vincent and Serge sold their olive and canola oils, including olive oil infused with chilli and another with rosemary. Before the war, local farmers had herded flocks of geese and ducks to the market, and shepherds had brought sheep down from the rocky plateau, *la causse*.

Albert Compiegne had parked a battered rattling tractor, its wheels coated in dung on the *boule* ground. He used an ancient metal machine with a weight sliding on a bar to weigh vegetables placed on a balancing metal tray. Pierre Dalmain had a wooden box by his cellar with old woodworking tools for sale hoping to earn some beer money.

Jean-Jacques Damour had a stall for his baguettes and patisserie, the selection now limited by government rationing. The local vineyard sold red, white and *rose* wine in pottery jugs and small barrels. Alain, the vintner siphoned wine from large wooden barrels stored in his Renault van into customers' wooden casks or glass bottles. On sunny days, he serenaded people sitting at café tables with his accordion.

Florent Gatti, the butcher from St Martial, parked his van in the *Place de la Mairie* and opened a hatch in the side to sell to customers. He wore a white canvas apron, soon splattered with blood and a black beret. He was a cheerful man and liked to tease the women queuing for their meat. He responded to their greetings of, "*Bonjour. Comment allez vous*? How are you," with a shrug of his shoulders, saying, "*Impeccable.*" He sold fresh chickens, rabbit and guinea fowl that were hung on hooks inside his van. Portions of beef, pork and lamb were laid on trays behind the hatch. Women queued for a long time to buy the rationed meat but they gossiped about family and neighbours to pass the time. Marie-Francoise Michelet stood in the queue as she needed to buy meat for her café in Villane-le-Foret. She tapped her clogs as Florent Gatti served Bertrand, the *Maire* first. *"Ca va, Bertrand? Tu as des nouvelles de Rodez et les Allemands? How are you, Bertrand. Do you have news of the Germans?"* The gossiping women stopped instantly to listen to the reply.

Bertrand nodded as he put a large *poule* with its head and feet dangling into a straw basket. *"Oui.* I have fixed a notice to the door of the *Mairie* with the latest news from the Vichy Government." He walked away before he could be accosted by the villagers. He was short and plump with a patch of dark hair clinging to the edge of the shiny bald patch. He cultivated an ostentatious moustache which he carefully groomed, the ends dipping in sharp points over the corners of his full mouth. He had heavy-lidded eyes, sparse eyebrows and a pink bulbous nose. Today, he wore a black worsted suit, a white shirt with a cravat and highly polished black pumps, his normal Sunday attire.

Madame Ricard sat with Madame Royal on their terrace sipping coffee, enjoying the conviviality of the market. They had both been widowed in the Great War and been friends since childhood. "*J'ai mal de tete*. I've a headache." Madame Ricard sighed gustily, patted her forehead and glanced up at her friend, hoping for sympathy. "*Prends des comprimes*." Madame Royal patted her friend's hand. "Take some tablets or more wine," she replied mischievously, filling her friend's glass.

The café was packed and Paulette brought out extra tables and chairs. People stood in groups, chatting and laughing. Paulette's daughters dodged between them carrying metal trays full of cups of coffee and chocolate, glasses of wine and chasers of cognac.

Children raced around, yelling greetings to school friends and neighbours. The radio in the café was playing a selection of French songs—*Bonjour les Demoiselles* and the patriotic *Le Chant de Partisans*. The songs had been chosen in a national contest to give French soldiers something to sing while they marched to war. The two *gendarmes* sat at their regular table drinking black coffee in large china bowls. They expected Paulette to give them free croissants as they were on duty. The villagers acknowledged their presence with a nod or a shrug but few stopped to chat. Since the German invasion, they were the appointed officials of the Vichy Government and not to be trusted.

Men gathered by the bar smoking, sipping *pastis* or beer, exchanging news, guffawing at jokes, tipping their caps or berets at the women, their faces shiny with freshly shaved cheeks and chins. They wore their Sunday clothes—thick cotton trousers in faded black, loose calico shirts and woollen jackets. Pierre Dalmain joined them to complain to the captive audience. "*Mon Dieu. Je n'ai pas du carburant pour ma tracteur*. I have no fuel for my tractor. How can I get around?"

"*Achetez une velo*! Buy a bicycle." Michel Duroux, the deputy *Maire* replied with a smirk, nudging his friend Paul Gauthier, a local farmer. The men gathered at the bar chortled and stamped their clogs to emphasis the comment. Pierre Dalmain wasn't liked in the village. He was suspected of hiding his crops and vegetables from the *gendarmes* who visited the village to collect the quota designated by the Vichy Government.

Three musicians walked into the café and sat at a table. Claude Flaviens carried a guitar, Antoine Michelet had a wooden recorder and Paul Gilbert held an accordion. Claude wore a red checked shirt, yellow woollen scarf slung casually round his neck and navy corduroy trousers.

Antoine and Paul wore traditional clothes, black gaberdine trousers, white calico shirts and navy berets. They were greeted with cheers and clapping, especially when the local musician, Regis, brought his accordion to join them. Regis had a ginger bushy beard and wore corded trousers and a cotton jacket with a patterned scarf. The quartet played lilting, rhythmic tunes. The audience tapped their feet and clapped in time. Small children crouched on the cobblestones, enthralled by the players. They were taught folk songs at school and Britt Zeigler, the school teacher moved to sit with them and join in the clapping and singing.

At mid-day, the villagers queued hungrily to fill pottery bowls with vegetable stew or *aligot*, the local speciality of mashed potato, cheese and bacon *lardons*. Food was served hot from large copper and metal cauldrons placed over stone fire pits. The aromas of steamed vegetables mingled with tobacco smoke and wafts of dung from the farmyards. Trestle tables and benches were set up in a grassy field shaded by plane trees and children scrambled to find a place beside their parents.

For the next two hours, the village resounded with chatter and laughter and the excited calls of small children playing. Wood pigeons strutted between table legs scrabbling for crumbs, a donkey brayed and yard dogs howled for food as the tantalising smell of cooking drifted around.

Living in a close-knit village provided few opportunities for aggression and neighbours helped each other when needed. Naturally, there were a few families who caused problems, the *Dalmains* and *Pelliers* but their wives tried to keep the peace. The villagers shared tractors and other farming equipment. There was no spare money for these or essential repairs to the crumbling ancient houses.

Life was governed by the seasons and only fierce storms, flooding and shortages of basic foods or animal feed interfered with rural routine. The hardship and destruction of war in northern Europe had not reached this village, isolated on the edge of an unpopulated plateau and protected by dense oak and chestnut forests. News of the invasion of France and Paris by the Germans two years earlier was discussed at the village café by the Maire and his officials. They knew the *Aveyron Departement* was now administered by the Vichy Government which was led by *Marechal Petain*, a hero of the Great War and they expected him to protect them.

Broussac had prospered during the mid-eighteenth century when the owners used the chateau for hunting parties and minor Royals seeking a taste of country life and aristocrats travelling from Paris for the winter.

An imposing *Mairie* had been erected in a prominent position on the village *Place* at the same time. A *notaire* providing services to the chateau owners had built a large stone *maison de maitre* on the opposite corner and several local farmhouses had been extended and modernised.

Wide stone steps led to the ruins of the chateau built on a rocky escarpment overlooking the river Aveyron with its thickly forested gorge and to the north the bleak limestone plateau, *la causse*. Lichen and weeds hid the ravages of fire when a band of Revolutionaries in 1790 had taken revenge on the aristocratic owner's chateau and taken over the fertile farmland. The aristocrats had lived a life of ease and luxury whilst the peasants, *les paysans*, dwelt beside the river in mud and wattle huts. Three generations of a family had crowded into basic shelters, scavenging what morsels of food they could find. Farmers toiled on land leased to the *Comte de Broussac* and lived in stone cottages provided while the farmer lived. It had been a feudal environment.

Broussac had once been surrounded on the southern slopes by prosperous vineyards which had now been abandoned. The furthest parts of the village were uninhabited with ruined buildings overgrown by nettle, bramble and ivy.

Window and door frames hung loose where wild winter weather had prised the metal fittings from the stone walls. Stone steps leading up to entrances were cracked and crumbling with the frost and inhabited by spiders and lizards. In backyards, ramshackle rabbit and chicken hutches leaned against wooden fences and unpruned fruit trees flourished.

Spring

It was late April; the sky was paintbox blue and cloudless and the sun hot. Wild primroses bloomed in the hedgerows as Britt Zeigler took her normal morning walk through the village and down to the river, enjoying the translucent light and tranquillity of the countryside. It had been raining over the past week and there was a perfumed freshness in the air. She stepped over muddy puddles in the lane leading down to the river bank. She felt the warm sun on her shoulders and through the sleeves of her cotton shirt. She meandered past the square stone houses with shutters of pale blue or grey, many now opened to let in the soft air. Several *chasse* dogs barked at her but they were firmly tethered in backyards. She stopped to smell the creamy hawthorn blossom in the hedge bordering the lane and listened to a glossy blackbird carolling from an oak tree which spread its branches thick with dark green leaves. She picked a few wild flowers from the verge-golden buttercups, scarlet pimpernel, buttery cowslips and purple vetch, and the frothy white flowers of Queen Anne's lace. She usually placed a vase of fresh flowers on her desk in the schoolroom. She walked past a fallow field bright with golden buttercups and scarlet poppies, and aromatic orchards with fruit trees planted in rows, their branches filled with frothy white and palest pink blossom.

Britt reached the river bank and sat on a metal bench in the shade of a flowering sweet chestnut tree, its creamy candle-like blossoms perfuming the air. A soft breeze caused the trees hanging over the water to sway gently. She spied small birds perched on the banks and fluttering in the bushes edging the river, beaks in the air shrilling their different songs. A grey heron stood poised and alert on a gravel mound looking for fish. A small brown dog barked with delight as it tried to catch a branch thrown in the water by his owner. She could hear the distant rumble of a tractor and children shouting with joy. On a south facing slope on the opposite bank of the river, a narrow tractor was ploughing between orderly lines of vines that were sprouting pale green shoots. They had been pruned in the winter months and the pliable branches trained over arrow straight lines.

Britt watched four youths, clad in cotton vests and pants attempting to cross the swiftly flowing river using projecting rocks. They were challenging each other to jump over the weir and leap across the stones at the top. She taught their younger sisters and brothers and knew their parents well.

Armand, Martin, Claude and Jean-Paul were school friends celebrating the start of the Easter holidays. They had left school and were working on the family farm or learning a trade. Their families had lived in the Aveyron *Departement* for centuries and the youths were expected to follow the work of their fathers, growing crops and managing cattle or working as carpenters, roofers or builders.

"*Allez, allez,*" Martin shouted. "Go, go." He lithely jumped from rock to rock. "*Venez, venez mes copains,*" he beckoned to his friends to follow him across the river. Armand stepped off the bank, then waded to the other side before clambering out and wiping his feet in the grass. "*Encore, encore,*" Armand called as he jumped back into the water and pretended to swim upstream. He swerved round a family of brown ducks paddling downstream using the flow of the river and nearly lost his balance.

The ancient church bells ringing at mid-day reminded the youths to return home clothed and clean to share the mid-day meal with their family. Leaping and splashing each other, they reached the river bank, used their clothes to wipe off excess water and ran home across the fields.

Armand ran lithely up the stone steps to the *Boulangerie* owned by his father, Jean-Jacques Damour. He said, "*Bonjour,*" to the waiting customers. He kissed his mother, Liliane, on both cheeks before walking through the back door and across the yard to their home. His younger brother Louis and young sister Rose-Marie were washing their hands at the stone sink set in the wall of the kitchen. "*Bouge, bouge, ma petite soeur.*" Louis pushed his sister away. Rose-Marie scowled and flicked water at her brother. Armand pushed open the door, patted his brother on the back and kissed his sister. Then he nudged his brother out of the way and put his hands in the water. The siblings jostled as they moved to their chairs at the kitchen table.

Liliane hurried into the kitchen, took off her floury overall and placed five pottery bowls on the patterned oilcloth with fresh bread, metal spoons and thick water glasses. She used a piece of sacking to lift an orange metal casserole pot that had been bubbling on the wood stove and put it on a metal grid set on the table. "*Bon appetit, mes enfants,*" she said smiling fondly at them as she ladled the aromatic chicken stew into their bowls. "*C'est les pieces de poule et des legumes.*" Jean-Jacques sniffed appreciatively and sat at the head of the table, reaching for his bowl of chicken stew. Liliane sat beside him and the family bowed their heads and murmured thanks for the food.

They ate in silence, listening to the normal village sounds of tractors rumbling past, donkeys braying and dogs barking.

"*C'est bien a la riviere avec tes amis?*" He asked his father. Armand nodded vigorously as his mouth was full of stew.

"*Maman. Je voudrai inviter ma copaine a la Fete.* I would like to invite my girlfriend to the summer fete. Her name is Yvette and she's the daughter of Gilbert Flaubert who owns the farm where I work. She's very pretty." Armand dipped his head as his face blushed with embarrassment. "She would like to meet you and *Papa.*"

Louis sniggered behind his hand and nudged his sister. Armand gave a mock punch to his brother's arm and he spilt potatoes onto the table.

"*Bien sur, Armand. C'est important pour Papa et moi.*"

Jean-Jacques agreed and finished his meal, and left to open the *Boulangerie* for afternoon customers. Liliane and Rose-Marie washed the dishes and Louis joined his friends kicking a football around the *boule* ground. "*Au jardin, ma belle fille,*" said Liliane, taking her daughter's hand as they walked out the back door, collecting garden tools to spend the afternoon planting and harvesting in the *potager*, the vegetable garden.

Martin arrived home to hear his parents arguing in the kitchen about the shortage of diesel for the tractors and the battered farm truck. "*C'est important j'ai le tracteur,*" his father Alain Favel was stating loudly to his wife, Josette. She protested that she needed the truck to go shopping in St Martial, a large village five kilometres north. As usual, his father won the battle and his mother quietly served pork stew while her family seated themselves in grumpy silence at the kitchen table.

"*Tout va bien, mon fils?*" Martin sat next to his younger brothers Gilles and Luca. Martin nodded and continued eating his lunch, aware of the tension between his parents. His father was a dominating person who insisted his meals were provided at set times. Alain was a good farmer, so the family lived comfortably. He had a dozen beef cows and ten beehives and traded honey with local farmers for cattle food. Josette managed a large vegetable garden and kept ducks, chicken and pigs which she sold live at the weekly market.

Jean-Paul sauntered across the *Place de la Mairie,* dodging through café tables to get to the family kitchen at the rear. His mother Paulette was serving *le plat du jour* (today's lunch) to their customers.

The village *Maire,* Bertrand Danton, sat at his favourite table surrounded by his colleagues including Michel Duroux, the Deputy Maire and local farmers Paul Gauthier and Armand Laron. Jean-Paul politely said, *"Bonjour,"* to them and kissed his mother who winked at him. His father Jean-Luc Vidal sat at the kitchen table his wooden leg held out in front of him. He greeted his son, gestured to the large metal pot steaming on the wood-burning stove and carried on eating his lunch. *"Tout va bien, mon fils?* All well?" He asked between mouthfuls. *"Oui, papa,"* replied Jean-Paul and ate his lunch with gusto. His mother was a superb cook, inventing tasty dishes out of limited ingredients. Paulette joined her family to eat lunch then washed the dishes.

Jean-Luc returned to his workshop to continue making wooden fencing for Alain. Paulette picked up her knitting and talked with her son for ten minutes before returning to the customers requesting dessert, *mousse au chocolat or tarte citron.* The customers were serenaded by a blackbird and two grey-plumed wood pigeons cooing from the church roof.

Liliane walked to the schoolhouse in late afternoon to meet Britt Ziegler. She politely acknowledged the chattering women outside the *epicerie.* She saw sly looks and overheard gossip about her in the village *epicerie,* usually about her age as she was five years older than Jean-Jacques. She had spent her childhood in Cahors, a town to the north west of Broussac and was not totally accepted by older villagers who had lived in the village for generations but the younger families whose children played with Liliane's were friendly to her.

"Bonjour, chere amie." Liliane greeted Britt cheerily, giving her a warm hug.

"Bonjour, Liliane," Britt kissed her friend on both cheeks and offered her coffee and *madeleines* placed on a China dish. *"Tout va bien avec ta famille?* All is well?"

"Oui. Il y a les nouvelles de Paris? What news have you heard from Paris. I heard two wives in the *Boulangerie* discussing the shortage of flour?"

Britt Zeigler was an elegant Parisienne, well educated and well off. The villagers had been suspicious of her when she came to the village in December 1941 to teach at the school. She was circumspect about her background but explained she had married a German officer in December 1940 in Paris. He had been working with Otto Abetz, the German Ambassador chosen by Hitler. She'd been a school teacher in Paris at an international school and left when her husband was killed.

Britt received letters from friends still living in Paris and she discussed the disturbing progress of the war with Liliane.

"Marie-Francoise reports there's a shortage of transport fuel due to rationing but collaborators can obtain most things. She wrote there are a few resistance groups, mostly Communists since Germany invaded the Soviet Union last year. Ordinary Parisiens are losing their trust in Petain. Those that have relatives in the country are leaving the city. I fear for the soul of France with the Germans controlling Paris and the northern cities. My friends say there are uniformed Germans everywhere—in the cinemas and theatres, restaurants and hotels. There's increasing persecution of Jews who are losing their jobs and must wear the yellow star of David on their clothes. It has become difficult to live in Paris unless you're rich or a collaborationist. I'm glad to be living in a rural backwater where families have been living peacefully alongside each other for generations." Britt took a breath and shuddered, reaching over to squeeze Liliane's hand. "The villagers are kind to me. In Paris, before I left, people were becoming afraid of acknowledging their neighbours for fear they were Jews or collaborators."

"Britt, we're fortunate to have you teaching our kids about life outside the farms. I've sorted out more books to put in the school library. I enjoy teaching dressmaking to the girls and I've brought a dressmaking book given me by my mother to use with them. They know how to darn their father's socks and worn table cloths but making a blouse from an old dress is beyond them. There are few market stalls selling new clothes and material now. I've redone one of my dresses for Rose-Marie for the summer. Pity, we can't get Jean-Luc to give the boys carpentry lessons. Paulette says he has so much work locally due to the shortage of men after the Great War." The friends chatted for another hour before Liliane left to prepare dinner. As she hugged her friend, she noticed how thin she was becoming, feeling ribs beneath the thin blouse. Britt was obviously worried for her friends in Paris.

As she walked across the village, she could hear the peaceful sound of cattle lowing in the distant fields and the church bell from St Martial drifting on the soft air. A hazy mist was settling over the river as it meandered through the pastures. She could see two red kites soaring on the thermals rising above the distant limestone gorge.

Jean-Jacques was smoking his pipe and sat in a wooden chair with his eyes closed. She kissed him on the forehead, inhaling the musty smell of tobacco and the sweet odour of yeast clinging to his clothes.

"*Tout va bien avec, Britt*?" He asked with a smile. Liliane nodded and started preparing a vegetable soup for a stew, tossing in grains of barley to thicken it. She spread a flowered plastic cloth on the table, bowls and cutlery. Their three children pushed in through the kitchen door, shoving each other to get to the sink.

"Did Britt have news from her friends in Paris?"

"*Oui*. All Jews must wear a yellow badge on their clothes and many are losing their jobs. It's not good. I hope the Germans stay in the north and don't dictate how we should live in the south." She shivered a little, then concentrated on serving dinner and talking with her family.

The Boar Hunt

The woods rang with the sound of axes chopping trees to replenish woodpiles depleted by the harsh winter. Fuel was needed for cooking and warmth on cool evenings until mid-May. Tractors towing loaded trailers rumbled down the lanes shedding loose branches as they brushed against stone walls and thick hedges. Pairs of hunters had been searching for the lair of wild boar and deer in the thick oak and chestnut forests surrounding Broussac. The *Maire* had agreed to organise the last hunt of the season to supplement the meals of the villagers existing mainly on vegetables that had survived the frosts. Broussac and the Aveyron area had experienced a bitter winter with heavy snowfalls blocking lanes, frost blackening plants and lying thickly in ditches and ruts. Most villagers had killed and cooked rabbits kept in hutches and most of their hens, so fresh meat was a rare commodity.

On the first Sunday of May, a group of twelve men, dressed in tough dark overalls and thick jackets gathered in the *Place de la Mairie*, their shapes blurry in the dawn light. They stamped about in worn leather boots to keep their feet warm and carried hunting rifles. The *chasse* dogs were muzzled but leaping around in anticipation of the hunt. They were tethered by a leather leash or strong twine fixed around their muscular necks. They were semi-wild and had not been fed for two days to sharpen their hunting sense.

The rest of the village awoke to the normal sounds of cows mooing to their calves in the milking shed and the hiss of milk into tin buckets, and the last hens clucking as they scratched for seeds on the ground. A single donkey brayed in Mark's field and several cats slunk down dark alleys in search of a breakfast rat or mouse. Houses were banging open their shutters and gusts of wood smoke rose from stone chimneys as cooking fires were kindled. Kerosene lamps glowed on unshuttered window sills. Church bells chimed the hour of seven and doors slammed as workers left for the fields.

The *Maire* was dressed in black corduroy trousers, shiny leather boots and a sturdy tweed coat. He stood at the top of the steps of the *Mairie* in the shadowy light, checking the wind direction. Two large hunting dogs sat on their haunches by his side. They turned their heads, sniffing the air, their intelligent eyes alert to the movements of the *chasse* dogs.

"*Bonjour*. The wind's gusting from the east, so we need to be careful how we approach the animals. I must remind you that we only shoot boar, not hare. I should have got permission from the *Prefecture* but I'll take responsibility so control your dogs and follow orders. *Bon chasse et bon courage, mes amis,*" he shouted. The huntsmen gathered round as Bertrand descended the steps to join them. They removed their gloves to shake hands with him and shouldered their hunting rifles and rucksacks. The cold north wind made eyes water and they tightened the scarves wrapped round their necks and pulled cloth caps lower on their heads.

"Is that a new rifle?" Michel asked Alain, regarding the shiny weapon with envy and hiding his rusty gun under his arm.

"It's English and double-barrelled. I bought it two years ago on a visit to Toulouse. I hope to shoot a large boar, *un sanglier*." He handed it to Michel who admired it before passing it to Jean-Paul Latour, owner of two large farms with a herd of dairy cows and another of beef cattle.

Bertrand held up his hand for attention and called out his instructions.

"*Alors. Messieurs. Attention.* Joseph, you take one group up the Roman Road. Armand, you can guide your men into the forest. I'll take the beaters across the large fallow field by the river. Pierre, you take the road to *Villane-le-Foret*. We should get enough game by midday. *Allez, allez.*"

Joseph turned to face his group and said cheerily, "*The vent est trop froid pour le printemps. Les sangliers se cachent dans la foret. Bon chasse, mes copains. Suivre-moi.* The wind is cold for spring. The boars are hiding in the woods. Follow me. Good hunting, my friends."

The huntsmen charged through the village, holding their leashed *chasse* dogs tightly and plunged into the lanes and forest using different routes. Joseph and his group headed to the ruined *chateau* perched on a rock overlooking the village. On a clear day, it was a perfect lookout for surveying the countryside. The faint outline of the Pyrenees could be seen in the distance, mountain peaks snow-covered at this time of year. The *chateau* had been built in the twelfth century as a fort but had been blown up during the French Revolution. One tower had been repaired and was the home of a reclusive relative of the owner. It was built of pale limestone with a slate-tiled roof. The ground floor had a beaten earth floor and was used to house cattle.

Joseph reached his designated post beneath a huge chestnut tree and leaned against its wide trunk, instructing his men to hide in the surrounding trees. Some were devoid of branches as they had been hit by lightning. He remembered hiding as a boy in the *chateau* ruins one hot summer when a violent storm crashed over the area, thunderbolts hitting the tallest trees, showering them in sparks. He had sheltered with two school friends by the *chateau* walls, hands pressed to his ears and eyes firmly shut as the elemental rage of the storm battered the forest and huge hailstones clattered against broken stone walls. He shivered as a strong gust of bitter wind caught him unawares. He could see the shadowy silhouettes of his men and dreamed of standing with them in front of a blazing log fire with a bowl of hot mulled wine.

He pictured the other huntsmen sneaking across fields and through the forest, fanning out to their assigned positions then releasing the hounds. He waited for the howling of the dogs as they picked up the scent of the animals that heralded the start of the hunt. Joseph knew boar, hare and foxes always followed the same tracks year after year. He was renowned as one of the best local hunters.

"*Mon Dieu. Qu' est que se passe?* What are they doing?" Joseph muttered to himself, stamping his feet. He could see Antoine standing behind an old oak tree, smoking and shuffling his feet. Two other men were whispering as they crouched in a thicket a few metres away. They looked cold and disheartened.

The harsh yapping of hounds alerted Joseph and he gave the signal to his men to release their dogs, ensured his rifle was primed and ran after them. The *chasse* dogs had unearthed a den behind a huge granite rock covered with wild vegetation and flushed out a female and two young ones. The hunters ignored these as they hunted only male boar. Soon, the *chasse* dogs were howling like wolves as they picked up an acrid animal scent. A group of eight or nine animals crashed out of the thick woods, heading for the concealed hunters, blunt noses sniffing the air.

The lead boar dodged and weaved but Joseph could see several dogs had leapt up, teeth bared to bite into the animal's neck. The huge animal lowered its great head and speared the belly of the nearest hound with a thick pointed tusk hurling it backwards. The dog crashed to the ground, dragging its crippled bleeding back legs and was trampled by the raging boar. The yapping and barking of the excited hounds distracted the group and several small males broke away, racing for the shelter of the trees.

Joseph primed his gun, knelt and steadied his arm against a tree trunk aiming for a head shot at the lead boar. It crashed to the earth with a mighty thud, its long tusks and bristly coat red with blood. He approached his quarry from behind, gun primed and crouched to fire the killing shot to the heart. The hounds jumped over it, eager to tear the flesh from the heavy belly and chest. Blood poured from the mouth and snout and the hounds greedily lapped it.

A second animal thrust its muscular shoulders through the undergrowth and charged towards the huntsmen. It shuddered to a halt, baring its long canine teeth and snarling. Two *chasse* dogs were clinging to the thick neck with their teeth. Joseph glimpsed the *Maire* positioning his gun, steadying his balance and calmly shooting the animal in its rump, causing its hind legs to collapse. The beast opened its great mouth and roared its fury as the huntsmen and hounds encircled it.

Two headshots completed the kill and the men cheered wildly, slapping each other on the shoulders. Several ran across the field to help Joseph heave the lead boar onto its back. They selected hunting knives from leather belt pockets and cut into the beast's neck then opened the belly to take out the entrails which they threw to the yapping hounds. The *Maire* blew his hunting horn to signal the end of the hunt. The excited *chasse* dogs snarled as they feasted on the bloody steaming insides of the boar. After a few minutes, the dogs were dragged off the dead boar, leashed and hauled across to be tied to the carts, now loaded with killed prey.

The huntsmen trudged down the hill with the carts to the *chasse* hut on the edge of the village. They lowered each animal onto forked metal stakes erected over a fire pit. The *Maire* took a small metal trumpet hitched to his trouser belt and blew a dozen triumphant blasts alerting the villagers of a successful hunt and a feast for all villagers. *"Venez, venez, il y a beaucoup de viande pour tout. C'était une bonne chasse,"* the *Maire* shouted cheerily. "Come on, there's plenty of meat for all. A good hunt."

Wooden trestle tables and benches were brought out of the hut and placed around the roasting boar. Small casks of local wine were set on the tables and everyone brought their tin cup, cutlery and plate. The mood was joyous and celebratory, small children ran around, snatching morsels of meat and bread from the tables. The feasting continued all afternoon then empty plates were cleared into sacks. Regis played traditional songs on his accordion and people sang boisterously with the children clapping the rhythm.

The sun sank to the horizon and the first stars twinkled in a navy-blue sky. The breeze was cool, birds were carolling their evening song. Small brown bats circled the buildings, squeaking softly. House martins flitted to and fro emitting little cries as they returned to their nests in the eaves. The *chasse* dogs were silent lying on the ground with full bellies. A woodpecker could be heard tapping in the depths of the wood. It was an occasion to remember by all. The successful hunt was celebrated the next day by a mass in the church followed by lunch in the *salle de fete* for the older people who had not participated the night before.

The Summer Fete

Liliane woke before dawn when her husband kissed her on the lips before he descended the stairs to the *Boulangerie* to make bread for the village *Fete*. She lay still for a few precious minutes, wriggling to avoid the mattress lumps and listening through the open window to the birds rustling in the eaves of the stone cottage and in the walnut trees outside. Liliane loved the moment when the first rays of sunlight sneaked through the half-open wooden shutters and she could hear the birds starting the dawn chorus. The liquid notes of a lone blackbird serenaded the summer morning. House martins and swallows swooped round the eaves, flying through clouds of insects swirling in the gentle breeze. The heady scent of the old wisteria clinging to the house walls mingled with the soft perfume of climbing roses. The aromas almost masked the farmyard smells of animal dung and inadequate sewage. The timeless idyllic moment was interrupted only by the rumble of ancient tractors driven along farm tracks as farmers sought to harvest their hay and summer crops.

At 7 am, Liliane heard the church bells chiming to remind the locals on weekdays that it was time to start work in the fields, the barns and the forests. She pushed back the blue-painted wooden shutters against the wall and fastened each one with a small ornate metal latch then opened the windows wide so she could lean out to gaze at the fertile fields glowing yellow with sunflowers and ochre with maize and out over the red clay roof tiles of village houses. She felt content with life and looked forward to enjoying the fun of the village Fete, the wine, music and dancing, gossiping with friends and neighbours.

She washed quickly in a stone *evier* set into the wall. She chose a green cotton dress from the closet which she knew matched her eyes, tied on a flowered overall and slipped wooden clogs on her bare feet. She put on a smear of homemade lipstick coloured red with beetroot juice and clipped her long brown curly hair behind her ears, humming under her breath.

Jean-Jacques, her beloved husband, called to her, disturbing her reverie. "*Venez, venez vite.* Hurry." She skipped down the stairs, thinking over the jobs for the day. Before the German invasion, Jean-Jacques would be preparing trayloads of patisserie—*tarte citron, gateau au chocolat, pain au chocolat and pain au raisin*. Sunday was a day for patisserie treats in rural France. Now with wartime rations, he barely had enough flour and fat to make loaves of bread and croissants.

As she crossed the yard to the *Boulangerie,* she noticed the summer sun had risen quickly and silently over the ancient village and was painting a golden glow on the fertile countryside and gilding the church steeple. It shone on the painted wooden statue of Jesus in the *Place de la Mairie*. The metal weathervanes fixed to the roofs of the old stone houses were creaking as they turned in the morning breeze. The ancient village huddled up the side of a steep rocky escarpment, surrounded by hills densely cloaked in a mixture of chestnut and oak trees home to wild deer and boar. The sunlight tinted the river in the valley below, changing it into a flow of rippling blue-green silk with golden flecks.

It was the last Sunday in August and preparations for the annual village *Fete* had been going on for weeks. Women baked cakes and fruit tarts and a pig and several chickens were prepared for the communal feast. Sadly, war rations had affected the quality and size of the livestock. A special carillon of church bells at 8 am heralded the start of the *Fete*. Since early morning, the *Place de la Mairie* had been blocked by wooden carts, their shafts propped up against stone walls. Crowds of locals entered the village from different directions.

Instructed by their wives, the men had shaved and dressed in clean shirts, jacket and flat cloth caps with jaunty cotton neckties. The women pulled out their Sunday best clothes from the armoire the day before to air them of the smell of mothballs, and decorated their hats with wild flowers and bright ribbons. They had prepared baskets of homemade produce to sell and sat outside their homes or in the *Place de la Mairie*.

Downstairs in the *Boulangerie,* Jean-Jacques stoked the fire in the brick bread oven. It was damped down overnight using a few carefully placed logs left smouldering on a thick bed of ash. She took her bike out of the shed and propped it against the wall, emptying the baskets of yesterday's crumbs. She could hear Jean-Jacques humming as he pounded the dough for different types of loaves in the battered wooden trough fixed on a stand, which had been handed on from his father and grandfather. The shapes varied with the seasons and saints' days but with war rations the loaves were smaller and mixed with poorly milled flour.

Jean-Jacques was a strong taciturn man who enjoyed his work and had inherited the business from his father. He and Liliane had met twenty years ago at the large Sunday market in a nearby town, chatting over his bread and patisserie stall. Jean-Jacques had wooed his wife over several months with his delicious pastries and quick humour.

Liliane pecked his floury red cheek before piling the fresh loaves into her baskets and into the small trailer hitched behind her bike. She longed to join her children playing and swimming in the river but must deliver the bread for her neighbours' breakfasts. Their children had left at daybreak to run down to the river and meet their friends. They would be splashing and swimming, chasing each other with rusty tins filled with water or throwing a ball. The river was shallow at this time of the year, trickling over stones and pooling on the edges where trees cast their shade. Birds were calling from oaks and birches that spread their leafy branches over the water and sheltered nests of wild duck, moorhen and coot in their sunken roots. Occasionally, there was a flash of brilliant turquoise as a kingfisher swooped off a branch and into the water, rising effortlessly with a fish in its beak. Small wagtails hopped over the rocks, their tails waggling up and down showing the yellow feathers underneath. A tall grey heron sat on a rock, surveying the river searching for fish.

Liliane drank her *café*, ate a fresh *croissant,* then collected her laden bike to set off round the village, leaving the bread in string bags hanging on door knobs or slipped into baskets placed on front steps amongst the geraniums. She had tucked her dress into a belt to avoid the bike wheels and her brown shapely legs worked with accustomed ease.

Her customers called out, "*Bonjour*," or waved as she delivered to their homes. Madame Ricard thrust a small bunch of roses through her open door. "*Bonjour. Je vous remercie pour du pain*, Liliane. Thank you for the bread. *C'est pour la Fete.*" Liliane skilfully avoided Madame Ponthier's small grey terrier which always sat in the middle of the road and snapped at passing vehicles trying to bite the tyres. The dog manoeuvred swiftly, dodging Liliane's wheels like a bullfighter avoiding a mad bull. She kicked out and swivelled into a gateway throwing a lump of bread to distract it. "*Allez, bête stupide!*"

Liliane didn't deliver to the far end of the village where a deserted stone house stood in large unkempt grounds. Rumour whispered that an old soldier, badly wounded in the Great War, lived there in seclusion but no one had seen or met him. The shutters were always closed, and the paint on them was peeling. Undergrowth and weeds choked the driveway and the formal gardens round the house. Three fierce *chasse* dogs roamed the grounds behind locked heavy wrought iron gates. Monsieur Compiegne visited at dawn and dusk to feed the dogs. Their howling and barking echoed round the village at night.

Liliane rode into the *Place de la Mairie* as Josette Favel pushed open the blue wooden shutters covering her bedroom window, looked across the village street and waved. Paulette Vidal looked up and called, "*Bonjour*," as she swept the house steps and pushed out the family cat before closing the front door behind her. Antoine rode swiftly by on his bike, whistling tunelessly, fresh vegetables piled in the basket on the back. "*Bonjour. Ca va?* Ok?" He called to the girls. "*Oui, ca va bien, merci*," replied Paulette with a grin. "*A bientot.* See you soon," Liliane called.

The *Maire* stood on the steps of his office wearing a bright checked shirt with blue cravat and black trousers that bulged with good living. The *Mairie* was built of cream stone like the rest of the village and Bertrand Danton lived on the premises with his wife, Pierrette, who was also his secretary. He had been the village *Maire* for five years. He enjoyed the social side more than the administration work. Many locals thought he was nosy but kindly. He had erected the French flag on its pole at the *Mairie* entrance and stone pots on the front steps were filled with colourful flowers. He called, "*Bonjour*," to Liliane.

Liliane rode back to the *Boulangerie,* parked her bike in the garden shed at the back and ran inside to collect the keys of their old yellow Renault van. She hugged her husband ignoring the flour on his canvas apron. Jean-Jacques handed her a second batch of loaves that had been piled on the central wooden table which she placed in two deep straw panniers to carry out to the Renault van. She laid a clean tablecloth on the van floor then placed the bread on top. She made a daily delivery in the van to the next village, *Villane-le-Foret*, which had no bakery. "*A toute a l'heure,*" she shouted to her husband as she deftly manoeuvred the van into the lane.

She drove carelessly down the farm track that ran from Broussac to *Villane-le-Foret* and parked outside the small café in the *Place de la Republique*. It had a few battered wooden tables and chairs but was popular with the locals for its *potager des legumes* made by the *propriétaire*, Marie-Francoise. It was usually served at noon with Jean-Jacques' fresh bread. The café served red wine from the nearby vineyard which locals declared 'made them stronger'. It was poured from a pottery *pichet* into small thick water glasses, was a deep red colour and almost as strong as claret. Later in the year '*Vin Nouveau*' was available, a lighter red made from the first vintage of the year.

Liliane opened the van doors and lugged the paniers to a table in the back of the cafe. Marie-Francoise kissed her friend on either cheek. They'd been friends for a long time, having gone to school together in Cahors and met their husbands at the town market. Marie-Francoise placed two expressos on the table and sat with Liliane to exchange news and views.

"*Tout va bien avec ta famille, ma chere amie*? All well with your family?" She asked as she pushed a tiny piece of homemade cake towards Liliane before going to serve a customer. "*J'arrive a la fete apres midi,*" she called over her shoulder.

"*Oui, merci. Tout va bien.* The youths are having fun in the river," Liliane replied with a smile, munching the cake. "*D'accord. Je doit chez moi.* I must go home. *Merci pour le gateau. A toute a l'heure.* See you later."

Liliane stopped to kiss a young woman on the cheek as she left the cafe and shake the hand of her husband. "*Bonjour, Claudine et Matthieu. C'est la Fete de Broussac.* I must hurry." She smiled at the other patrons, walked briskly to her van and drove home.

She parked the van in the back yard, entered the *Boulangerie* and hugged her husband again. "*Je t'adore, mon cheri,*" she whispered in his ear, then ran up the stairs to change into a flowered cotton skirt. She matched it with a frilly white shirt and plain black shoes. She collected a few baguettes before walking to the café. "*Bonjour, mes amis*," she shouted cheerily to the patrons sitting at the tables. Paulette grinned at her as she served steaming coffee in tiny cups or bowls and adjusted a large ragged shade to shield the morning sun from the tables. A mix of metal and wooden tables and chairs spread out across the *Place*.

Liliane nodded to the *Maire* who sat with several colleagues at his favourite table drinking coffee from a flowered china bowl held between his soft white hands. They were discussing the weather and the harvest.

"We'll have a thunderstorm later. The air is heavy and humid," declared Paul Gauthier. He slapped a mosquito on his arm, waved a fly from his coffee bowl and continued vigorously stirring sugar into it.

"*Non, non*. July is the month for bad storms not the end of August. I think we'll have another week to get the corn harvested." Alain, the husband of Josette, spoke decisively, crossing his fingers under the table. He owned a large farm in the area, growing hay, corn, sunflowers and maize.

"The best way to forecast weather is the behaviour of farm animals," said old Armand grumpily. The *Maire* nodded and listened as he was not local to this area. His father had been a stonemason working in the Lot.

Old Michel and Joseph sat at their usual table arguing amicably over an expresso and a small brandy each. Joseph's terrier sat by his side hoping to catch a few crumbs as his master dunked a large croissant into his tiny cup. The *Maire's* wife sat at a round metal table, dressed up for the fete in a be-ribboned straw hat and a flowery dress. Her friends sat around, dressed in their best frocks and hats, munching croissants and swapping gossip. Paulette avoided them but flirted a little with the old men, swishing her skirt and swaying her hips as she walked past their table. "*Bonjour, ma cherie*," said Joseph with a wink. "*Comment allez vous?*"

Michel spoke more formally to her, "*Bonjour,* Madame Vidal." He wore a dark peaked cap and dressed smartly in a tweed jacket, dark trousers, plain shirt and tie. He had fought in the Great War and still retained his military bearing and was kind and courteous.

Paulette was pretty with long dark hair tied back with a fraying ribbon, sparkling hazel eyes and a mischievous smile. She wore a black knee length skirt and white shirt when working and black flat shoes. She ran the bar/café with her husband Jean-Luc who had a wooden leg and worked as a carpenter. The Vidals had managed the café for ten years and knew everyone in the local area, their characters and idiosyncrasies. Paulette knew that Joseph liked to dunk his croissant in his tiny expresso cup, leaving crumbs and drops of coffee scattered on the tabletop. It was a minor crime if the regulars were served coffee in the wrong cup or the croissants or baguettes were less than fresh.

Paulette, Liliane and Josette were close friends with Nicole and Pierrette. They ran the village patchwork and sewing group. Josette was petite with dark curly short hair and a limp caused by a childhood illness. Her husband, Alain, had inherited the farm from his father. It had a rambling stone house with many attached barns stretching along the lane out of the village. Farming was deemed to be a reserved occupation so his father hadn't fought in the Great War and Alain had not enlisted for this war. They had four children, two daughters both married and two teenage sons, Martin and Gilles who worked with their father.

Nicole Lacroix was married to Albert, a handsome forester and a skilled cabinetmaker. They lived with Albert's aged parents in a large stone house near the river. She was cousin to Josette and there was a strong family likeness as both were petite with masses of dark curly hair. Pierrette Latour was married to Jean-Paul, the owner of an extensive farm breeding Limousin beef cattle, heavy white-grey beasts.

The rough wooden door of the public urinal opposite the café was squeakily swinging on its hinges, a mangy cat prowling around searching for mice. Old Armand was descending an old handmade wooden ladder in his slow and erratic way after extinguishing the rusty gas lamps placed on the wall outside the urinal and the *Mairie*. A lone donkey brayed loudly from a nearby field and a late cockerel welcomed the morning. *Chasse* dogs barked as people walked by the yards where they were tethered. Wooden clogs and hobnailed leather boots with thick soles clattered on cobblestone paths as the villagers walked through carrying produce to barter or sell, small children clinging to their mothers' skirts.

Paulette closed the café at 9 am, changed into a smart tailored navy dress and dark sandals, and tied a flowered scarf over her hair. Josette, dressed in a yellow and white cotton skirt with white shirt and sandals, ran over to the café to meet Nicole and Liliane. The four women sauntered arm in arm down the hill to the fete, shouting *Bonjour* or *Ca va?* to neighbours as they walked by.

Their husbands congregated by the temporary bar drinking *pastis*. They whistled appreciatively as the girls passed them. Liliane and her friends waved but went to sit with their sewing friends on a wooden bench under a large chestnut tree. Josette was complaining because the Vichy government had issued a formal directive that the traditional right of the *paysan* to hunt in local forests and fields—*la chasse*—had recently been declared illegal.

"My family needs meat because farm work involves hard physical work and long hours. My sons are growing taller but are so thin, their elbows and knees stick out as there's no flesh on their bodies. I worry all the time that they won't develop properly," Josette complained.

"I'm finding it hard to clothe my growing kids. I have to alter old pairs of Jean-Jacques' trousers to fit Armand and Louis," Liliane replied thoughtfully. "I used to visit the town market to buy second-hand clothes."

"My problem is that Jean-Luc wears out one leg of his trousers more than the other because of his wooden leg! Still, we're lucky to be living in the country and grow our own food and…" Paulette put a finger to her mouth and quietly whispered, "Set traps for small animals and birds to cook in stews."

"*D'accord, mes amis. Nous n'avons pas rien a plaindre.* Stop complaining and enjoy the *Fete* as it's only held once a year!" Liliane got up from the bench and sauntered across to the bar to get a cup of wine. Her friends joined her and their husbands, exchanging local news they'd heard from family visiting from other villages.

"It's very difficult to get tractor fuel. I used the last to finish reaping the hay crop. Now, I'll have to oil the old scythe to harvest the wheat and that will take weeks. *Merde a la guerre!*" Jean-Paul Latour complained swigging a metal cup of red wine. He had inherited a large farm growing a range of crops, two herds of dairy cows and a herd of beef cattle.

"*Oui, oui. J'ai la meme probleme*," responded Alain grumpily. Josette, his wife nudged his arm. "*Arrete a plaindre.*" She wandered over to look at the woven cane baskets filled with vegetables and homemade pots of plums and berries that grew in the hedges. Men were grouping round the gravelled square used for *boule* games. There would be a competition in the afternoon and they were practising tactics on patches of flat ground. Children were playing with balls or practising for the burlap sack race.

Trestle tables made from planks of chestnut were hauled by on a trailer by Antoine and Vincent for the midday meal and set up on a stone slab near the bar. Farmers' wives gossiped as they stirred huge steaming cast iron cauldrons using long wooden and copper ladles. Each region in France had its specialities—in the Aveyron, Tarn and Garonne the pots usually contained a *ragout* of Toulouse *saucisses* and beans with *aligot*. Wooden and metal carts, pulled by dogs or women, held milk churns or barrels of wine which were placed next to the tables so the locals could help themselves. A pig was roasting over a log fire burning in a stone hearth. There was little meat available now only rabbits nurtured in garden hutches or old chickens. Poachers were threatened with the death penalty but die-hard hunters stealthily searched at night, hiding their catch in underground pits in the thickest part of the forest.

Bertrand Danton strolled around, acknowledging his villagers with a handshake for the men, a chaste kiss on the cheek for the women and a smile for small children running excitedly between them.

Punctually at noon, when the church bells rang, the *Maire* walked to the steaming cauldrons and tipped a large ladleful of the aromatic casserole into a china dish and sat in his usual place at the head of the tables. People helped themselves from the cauldrons before sitting down. The only sound was the chattering of people and children, even the dogs were quietly drowsing in the hot midday sun. Shrieks and laughter came from the youths playing in the river that echoed from the high banks. The rumble of a tractor could be heard from fields across the river.

Wine in stone jugs sat at each end of the cloth-covered tables offering a choice of red, white and rose. Alain du Menerque, who ran a vineyard south of Cahors, had brought several bottles of the light fruity red Malbec of the region. Plates of local goat's cheese and fresh fruit were set out in the middle of the tables. After an hour or two, empty wine containers were collected and put into an old wooden cask. Personal China and metal plates were briefly dipped in a bucket of water before being wrapped in serviettes to take home. People rose to take tiny cups of steaming black coffee from the bar. Liliane and her friends got up to dance to the lively music of Regis' accordion, laughing and calling encouragement to the others. Old Joseph thought he was a smooth dancer and circled Paulette, tapping his hobnailed boots and catching her hands.

A group of men and women got up to perform a clog dance and Regis speeded up the music so the noise of clattering and stamping grew louder. They received a boisterous applause and shouts of *encore, encore*. People were circulating, greeting friends and relatives, exchanging news and gossip but many had worried frowns and there were a few angry comments. They had heard the Germans had introduced the *Service de Travail Obligatoire* (STO) which was the mandatory provision of French labour services. All young men in a defined age group must register with the local *Maire*, including the unemployed, unless they were engaged in vital war work. This conscription did not currently apply in Vichy France but the villagers were extremely worried about their sons.

By mid-afternoon, people were going home for the afternoon siesta, when a military jeep with no markings or insignia roared up the main street lined by pollarded plane trees and halted by the bar. Two *gendarmes* alighted, ignored the locals and wandered around the village. They wore smart dark uniforms and peaked caps, and carried a gun each in a holster. They inspected the village then walked across to the *Maire* and acknowledged him with a Nazi salute.

The *Maire*, sipping his third glass of red wine, stood up looking stunned and returned the *Heil Hitler* salute. The *gendarmes* stood to attention as they spoke briefly with him. He was visibly nervous, shaking his head but responded quietly until he suddenly lifted his head and shouted, "*Non, non, non. Ce n'est pas possible.* It's not possible." He wiped his mouth and gulped some wine, his hand visibly trembling. The *gendarmes* saluted him again, grabbed a cup of wine each, cheese and bread, sauntered across to their jeep and drove away.

The villagers looked around nervously and whispered to their neighbours. Pierre Dalmain, bristling with outrage, pushed his chair back and was prevented from marching angrily across to the *Maire* by his wife hauling on his shirtsleeve. "*Tais-toi. Assieds-toi*," she hissed, "keep quiet," as she made him sit down. They all stared with fear and distrust at the *Maire* as he drank the last of his wine. The old men at the bar shuffled across and leant over their wives demanding to know what was happening. The jovial festive atmosphere had changed to one of unease and suspicion.

Michel, the deputy *Maire*, left his seat and sat down to talk quietly and seriously with M'sieur Danton for a few minutes before he stood up and banged a spoon on a glass for attention.

"*C'est une catastrophe*. The *gendarmes* have issued orders for the young men of our community to register at the *Mairie* within a week for work in Germany. We knew this was happening in the north but not here in Vichy controlled France. The *Maire* explained that our young men must stay to harvest the crops and meet the quota ordered by the Germans. The *gendarmes* were adamant. The men must work for the war effort." Michel slumped down next to the *Maire* and put his head in his hands. He had a teenage son. Men sitting at the tables looked horrified and their wives buried their faces in their arms. Liliane clutched her husband's arm and leant onto his shoulder. "They'll take Armand and Louis?"

Josette looked aghast at the *Maire*. "We need Martin and Gilles to work in the harvest. The Germans can't take them away. *M'sieur,* you must do something. Go to the *Prefecture* and complain."

Michel stood up again and declared passionately, "They can't do this without warning us. The Germans have ordered us to meet crop and food quotas determined by the Vichy Government, based on the agricultural survey of farms carried out last month."

"The loss of our fit young men is a bitter blow. The survey was an intolerable intrusion into our lives and requisitioning of animals and crops is a heavy burden. We must send a delegation to the *Prefecture, Monsieur le Maire.*" He sat down suddenly. It was the first time in his life he had spoken so fiercely.

People stood up to go home. Antoine, Vincent and two other men dismantled the tables and lifted them onto a trailer. Flies were gathering on discarded scraps of vegetables and empty cauldrons. The sun shone brilliantly through the waving leaves of the pollarded plane trees and birds flew down to snatch crumbs from the tables. Without warning, a crowd of yelling wet children rushed past the dismantled tables and headed for their parents. It was difficult to understand what they were shouting and why they seemed so terrified.

"*Maman*, two *gendarmes* took Armand away in a truck with his friends, Claude and Jean-Paul. Yvette took her bike and rode away." Rose-Marie screamed at her parents who were helping to stack chairs. Tears were cascading down her cheeks. *"Arretez-les, arretez-les*, Papa. Stop them," she gasped. Liliane grabbed her daughter and gazed in horror at her husband. She looked across to Josette and Paulette and saw the fright on their faces. "Did you recognise them, *ma petite*?"

"*Non, non, Maman.* Caps hid their faces. They waded into the river and grabbed the boys who kicked and screamed but were pushed back with their guns. Jean-Paul tried to run but a *gendarme* tripped him. I think it was *Gendarme Pellier* and *Gendarme Gauthier*. They put on handcuffs and threw them into the back of a truck and tied the flaps down. We could hear them kicking the floor."

Liliane clutched her daughter to her chest then sat down, overcome with horror. She looked at Jean-Jacques who was frowning as he regarded his frightened daughter. "*Bien sur*, you couldn't stop the *gendarmes*. I'll go to the *Maire*. He must have been warned as he's responsible for the villagers." He kissed his wife and daughter then angrily strode over to the *Maire's* office.

"*Non, non, non,*" stuttered Paulette. "How could the *gendarmes* take our boy without warning? Where will he be taken? We may never see Jean-Paul again if the Germans send him to work in their labour camps." She was panicking and turned to her husband, Jean-Luc, shaking his arm. "They took your leg and now they've taken our son! I can't bear it." She put her head on his chest, tears pouring down her cheeks.

Jean-Luc pulled Michel, his other son, to him and hugged him tight. He angrily shouted at the *Maire* who stood at the bottom of the *Mairie* steps. "You could have stopped this. We need our sons to help with the animals and the harvest. You must go to the *Prefecture!*"

Josette looked at her son in disbelief as he was standing in front of her. "Why didn't the *gendarmes* take you?" Martin was clearly terrified but replied, "Because I ran into the woods with Louisa and Rose-Marie. We hid in the bushes until the truck left. I saw it drive towards Rodez. Louis dived into the weir and was swept away down the river. I hope he's safe."

Liliane had just walked over to her friend's house to ask if she had seen her son. "*Mon Dieu*. Louis escaped in the river? Where is he now?" She cried out in despair, wringing her hands. "Jean-Jacques, we must get a search party to find our son; he could be drowned or captured."

The *Maire* held up his hands which seemed to be shaking, whether with fear of the Germans or reprisals, no one knew. "*Mon Dieu.* The *gendarmes* threatened to take our youths as they did in the Great War but I told them to wait for the harvest to be completed. I'll find out from the *Prefecture* where your sons have been taken. *Je suis désoler*. I'm sorry. I meant to warn you that the *gendarmes* said next week is the deadline for compulsory enlistment. *Quelle catastrophe!* I'll lead a search for Louis with a group of men to search both banks, upriver and down river of the weir. *Bon courage, Liliane.*" He took Liliane's shaking hand. "Can he swim?"

"*Oui, bien sur,*" replied Jean-Jacques. Antoine, Michel, Joseph and Victor formed two groups and set off immediately with Jean-Jacques and the *Maire*. Liliane trudged home across the *Place de la Mairie* to reassure her daughter that her brother would be found. After an interminable hour peering out the kitchen window and keeping her front door open, she heard a scrambled cry. Louis struggled down the lane, assisted by his father. His clothes were saturated and dripping pools of brown river water on the front step and fronds of green weeds were clinging to his soggy shoes and trousers. His face was deathly pale, his lips blue and he was shivering uncontrollably. Liliane ran down the steps and clutched her son in her arms, wiping his wet face with a tea towel. "*Mon cher fils. Je t'aime. Je t'aime.*" She pulled him into the kitchen and gave him towels to mop the water and a blanket to put round his shoulders then rushed upstairs for dry clothes from his bedroom.

Jean-Jacques sat next to his son and tugged the blanket more tightly round his son's thin body. Liliane returned with clean dry clothes and turned her back as Louis pulled off his soggy trousers and shirt. She placed clean items on a chair and put a pot of milk on the stove to warm.

"*Dites-moi. Qu'est ce que se passe? Raconte-moi doucement.* What happened? Tell me."

"I was sitting on the bank dangling my feet in the river and saw movements in a willow tree nearby. It looked like dark uniforms. I shouted a warning to the other boys but they were splashing each other across the other side. I jumped into the water and swam fast to the weir, trying to keep afloat as the water pulled me down. The current was strong and carried me a long way down the river, round the bend near *Villane-le-Foret*. I caught hold of a tree branch and hauled myself out and crawled across the bank to a wooden shed in a back garden. I waited a long while inside before I peered out and saw no one. I crept back home through the fields using the hedges for cover. Then I saw Joseph and knew it was safe to go home." Louis sat exhausted and shivering, clutching his cup of hot milk. He raised his head and asked about his brother and friends.

"*Les gendarmes avons les capturer.*" Jean-Jacques bowed his head in despair and hugged Louis tightly. "*Tout va bien avec, Rose-Marie. Elle joue avec ses amis.*" Liliane moved her chair closer and they sat together, arms round each other until Rose-Marie returned home. Jean-Jacques embraced her and gently explained the events of the afternoon. She sobbed and sobbed, frightened for Armand who had always looked after her since she was a baby.

Furious and frightened, the mothers had given *Maire* Danton a look of despair and disgust, as they returned to their homes, clutching husbands and tugging their children. It was a bright mid-summer evening and the seven o'clock church bells had not rung yet house shutters and doors were locked and barred and the village became silent as the local cemetery. There was an abnormal calm, an unbearable silence that felt threatening and oppressive. Farm and yard animals were silent as if stupefied. Inside the ancient houses, families relived the traumatic mobilisation for the Great War when youths had departed in a state of hysteria and excitement leaving their parents stunned as the lifeblood of the village departed.

A Mother's Grief

Liliane was awake and restless throughout the night, grieving over the capture by the *gendarmes* of Armand. She felt overwhelmed by an intense sadness that her beloved firstborn child had been dragged away to an unknown place where she could not protect him. Anxiety unsettled her stomach and her brain churned ceaselessly with unanswerable questions. Would Armand be ill treated? Would he be fed properly? Would he be given more clothes than he had been wearing at the river? Where would the *gendarmes* take him—to an internment camp in France or to a German factory? Or, worse still, would he be ordered to fight for the enemy against his own countrymen?

She sobbed in Jean-Jacques' strong arms, needing answers to questions he could not give. How could they help him, how could the *Maire* help? Who had informed the *gendarmes* so they could capture the young men in the river yesterday? Was it *Gendarme Pellier*? There were no solutions and Jean-Jacques fell asleep after a few hours, exhausted by his long day baking bread and helping with the early closure of the *Fete*.

A full moon shone brilliantly through the partly latched shutters as Liliane slid out of bed. She dropped a soft kiss on her husband's cheek, noticing the deep cleft of worry on his forehead and shadowy lines fanning out from his closed eyes. She paced the room from wall to wall in bare feet, oblivious of the roughness of the wooden floor boards. She hugged her body, her bare arms tucked in her armpits, her fists clenched. She made no attempt to mop the tears dropping from her cheeks onto her feet. She was a strong woman who managed family and business with calm and purpose. Now, she felt deeply vulnerable and couldn't imagine a future without Armand's visits, sharing jokes and confidences. She had noticed the affectionate glances and gestures between Armand and his girlfriend at lunch yesterday, and like any loving mother looked forward to hearing about wedding plans and having grandchildren.

A rosy dawn light tinted the white bedspread as Jean-Jacques rose from bed and dressed. He held her tense shoulders and looked into her face, wiping away the tears with a blunt finger. *"Bon courage, ma cherie.* Why don't you work in the garden before you start the delivery round? It will be calming." Jean-Jacques knew she felt lethargic from her sleepless night. Liliane gave him a bleak smile and sank into the comfort of his arms. The homely odour of freshly dough and baked bread clung to his clothes and soothed her.

Liliane nodded, grateful for his support. She washed her face and neck in the stone basin then dragged on an old skirt and shirt. She descended the stairs to the kitchen, donned her garden boots and unlocked the back door. She could smell the mingled perfume of climbing wisteria, roses and honeysuckle and hear the drone of large black bees searching the flowers for pollen. The peaceful hour passed quickly and she packed her garden tools in the stone shed and walked to the kitchen. Jean-Jacques had laid the table and provided breakfast for his daughter and younger son. Rose-Marie left to walk to school with her friends. Guillaume was pedalling down the lane to work for an hour with Jean-Luc before going to school.

Liliane took a few deep breaths and realised she was fortunate to have a supportive husband and two other children. She washed the dirt off her hands, rubbed her gritty eyes, and put on a work dress and overall, then trudged across the yard to the *Boulangerie.* Jean-Jacques looked up from kneading dough in the wooden trough with heavy lids and tired eyes. He smiled at her.

"*N'inquiete pas. Armand, est un jeune homme fort*. Don't worry, the capture could be a mistake as our son and his friends are younger than the proscribed *Releve* enlistment age. When I've finished making bread, I'll talk to the *Maire*. Come with me as he may know more or can find out from the *Prefecture* in Rodez." He switched off the dough mixer and hugged Liliane, kissing her wet cheeks. "*Croisez les doights, ma cherie*. Cross your fingers."

Liliane loaded the fresh bread into the panniers and trailer fixed to her bike, inhaling the wholesome aroma of freshly baked baguettes. The beauty and bounty of the countryside soothed her as she stopped to listen to a glossy blackbird singing lustily while perched on a hawthorn hedge. The fertile fields glowed with colour—yellow canola flowers, golden wheat sprinkled with bright red poppies, ochre maize ripening for harvesting. Neighbours seemed kinder as she delivered their bread and sympathetic with her distress. The tough farm women bending almost double over the public stone *lavoir*, scrubbing their clothes and household linen with hard muscle-bound arms knew about the young lads who had been taken by the Germans and shouted words of encouragement to Liliane as she cycled past. "*Bon courage. Tu n'est pas seul. Ils reviennent*. They'll return. You're not alone."

Jean-Jacques was cleaning the *Boulangerie* when she returned home to make lunch. It was a subdued family lunch as they missed Armand's lively chatter and hearty laugh. Sensing his wife's continued distress, Jean-Jacques suggested she walk to the river and sit there for a while. He knew the soothing ripple of water as it splashed over the weir had a calming effect. Liliane kissed his cheek, *"Merci, cher mari. C'est une bonne idee."* She picked up a leftover crust of baguette and tucked a blanket under her arm then ambled to her favourite section of the river. There were iron benches set on the grass but she preferred to sit on the bank and dip her feet in the cool water.

A family of brown speckled ducks paddled laboriously up river against the current flowing from the weir, avoiding a grey long-necked heron standing perfectly still on stalk legs on a patch of river gravel searching for tiny fish to spear. A pair of black and white wagtails flew from the opposite river bank to land effortlessly side by side on a large wet rock. The heat of the sun was wafted away by a light breeze that made the feathery fronds of the willow trees sway in an elegant dance. She listened to the soothing sounds of the flowing river and inhaled the damp earth smell of the river bank, the faint scent of tiny wild daisies in the rough grass and wood smoke from cooking fires.

She leant back on her elbows and felt her anxiety lessen a little. She looked up at the deep blue sky and watched a few fluffy clouds drift across. Her eyes closed and her body relaxed as she lay down on the blanket. After a sleepless night, she was dozing when a shadow darkened the river bank. Startled, Liliane sat up, shielding her eyes against the sun.

"Bonjour, Liliane. Comment ca va? How are you?" Joseph's deep rough voice was friendly and concerned. He lowered himself onto the grass beside Liliane and took her hand in his calloused one. "Your son is brave and will survive. *Il est fort et courageux. C'est possible les Allemands font une erreur.* It could be a mistake. Go with Jean-Jacques to *M'sieur le Maire* and ask him to find out. He's a good man." Liliane could see the worry lines etching his rough weathered cheeks and was touched by his empathy. He too had suffered intensely from the Germans as they had massacred his family living in the north of France during the Great War.

Joseph's kindness released some of her tension and she wept for the heartrending loss of her eldest son of whom she was so proud. Joseph's terrier, sensing her grief, sat quietly at her side, his brown eyes shining with compassion. After a few minutes, she calmed down.

Joseph proffered a piece of cotton for her to wipe her tears. "*Merci beaucoup, mon ami,*" she whispered to Joseph.

"*Avec Plaisir,*" he replied and squeezed Liliane's shoulder. "*Bon courage.*" He whistled to his black and white dog and walked home to his lonely dinner. Joseph was a foreigner to Broussac like Liliane. He always dressed smartly in black trousers and white flax shirt, kept his luxuriant moustache neatly trimmed and wore a cloth cap.

Liliane sat for a few more minutes, grateful for Joseph's kind words. She lifted her face to the sun and felt the balmy breeze dry her tears. She had no close family to support her as her parents had died before this war started. Joseph had become a mentor to her. Her father had owned a hardware shop, *une quincaillerie*, on the Boulevard Gambetta in the centre of Cahors. Liliane and her parents had lived in an apartment on the top floor. As a child, she had loved helping her father, running excitedly between wooden shelves packed full of treasures and items used in kitchens, gardens and house repairs. She had clattered up and down the wooden stairs between two floors, peering and poking at objects in boxes or trays. She'd been endlessly fascinated by the items produced by her father in response to customer questions. "Do you have a spare lid to fit this casserole dish? Do you have any screws this size? Do you have staining oil, or a small hammer? Can I buy a mouse trap?"

The capacious cellar had stored old and rarely used articles, some bought or made before the Great War. Liliane had occasionally crept down the creaky wooden stairs, brushing the cobwebs aside, sniffing the dust and oil cans. Once she startled a tiny grey mouse sitting on its haunches washing its face. Outside the shop, her father had placed sacks of sand, cement and animal food. Wooden wheelbarrows were tilted again the wall and garden tools stacked tidily alongside.

She was an only child and had benefitted from the devotion of her parents. On Sundays when the shop was closed, Liliane went with her parents to the weekly open-air market in the *Grande Place*. She'd played with the children of stallholders and customers sitting at café tables under bright parasols, sipping coffee and hot chocolate, munching pastries or pieces of bread.

Liliane had firmly closed a door on later childhood memories when her father had returned from fighting in the trenches of the Great War. She had been ten years old and terrified of the broken disfigured man who walked into the shop and tried to embrace her mother.

He hopped on one leg using crutches to propel himself along, his empty trouser leg pinned to his waistband. As he came closer to Liliane, she could see the horrific burn scars that had partially destroyed his face and one eye and twisted his mouth. She remembered her mother stifling a scream by holding a hand firmly across her mouth. "*Bonjour*," the man mumbled the simple greeting as he tried to manipulate his scarred lips.

"Claude, Claude. *Qu'est que ce passe*? What's happened to you. How you must have suffered." Her mother took one slow step towards her husband and gently touched his uniformed arm as if even that simple gesture would cause him pain. She looked into his one eye and saw the pain and suffering in them and a solitary tear drift down his scarred cheek.

"*Assieds-toi*." Her mother turned away to the sink as Claude manoeuvred his body onto a kitchen chair, placing his crutches on the wooden floor. She handed her husband a glass of water and sat down opposite him, lifting Liliane onto her lap. "*C'est ton papa, ma cherie. Il est retournee*."

Liliane hid her face in her mother's shoulder, feeling a tremor shake her. After several minutes of complete silence, Liliane's mother told her in a whisper to go up to her bedroom. After the trauma of her father's return, she kept away from him, hiding in her room or the attic or playing outside. She and her mother endured this tragic situation for two years until one bitter winter's day Liliane came downstairs to the kitchen for breakfast and saw her mother hunched over the table, sobbing with a broken heart. Two neighbours stood next to her, ineffectually patting her shoulder and arm. "*C'est meilleur*," one said and her friend nodded. Both women wore black and had tears trickling down their soft cheeks.

Her mother tried to run the *quincaillerie* alone for a year but Liliane could see her growing thinner and a web of worry lines creasing her face. "*Ma chere fille*. You must go to live with your cousin's family and I will close the shop and live with your aunt Leila. I'll need to share the only bedroom in her tiny apartment in Cahors so there's no room for you. *Je suis desolee, ma petite*. I'm so sorry, my love. I'll pack a case of your things and Uncle Stephane will bring his cart and collect you tomorrow."

Her aunt and uncle were kind to her and she shared an attic room with her cousins, Pierre and Jeanne but her mother seldom visited and gradually Liliane adjusted to a changed family life. Reflecting on these sad memories, Liliane watched a flotilla of brown ducks waddle out of the river and up the bank. They crowded around hoping for pieces of bread.

She could hear children shouting and laughing as they were released from school and boys yelling as they kicked a ball on the *boule* ground. A group of 10-year-old girls, including her daughter Rose-Marie, came running down to the river to paddle at the edge and splash each other. Two young boys followed, leaping straight into the river to kick water around and scare a family of ducks placidly swimming past. Their antics and exhilaration brought a soft smile to Liliane's lips. They seemed untouched by the intrusion of war into their lives. She waved to her daughter and walked home, passing Britt Ziegler shutting her gate.

"Would you like a coffee and chat, Liliane?" Britt asked with a smile. "I have a small piece of fruit cake we can share." She could see her friend was unhappy and had red eyes from crying over her son's capture. Liliane lifted her head and gave a slight smile. "*Oui, merci ma chere amie. Je suis tres triste et inquiete.* I am sad and worried."

Britt unlatched the gate, put her arm around her friend's shoulders and led her into the school house kitchen where an aroma of coffee brewing on the stove drifted around. Liliane pulled out a wooden chair and sat at the kitchen table, dabbing at her damp eyes. "I don't know how to help Armand. We'll ask Bernard to find out from the *Prefecture* where he's been taken. There's been talk that the *Releve* was set up to exchange French youths for our prisoners of war. He could be sent to Germany to work in their armaments factories."

"The *Maire* will help you and the other mothers as he's a kindly man. He's been very supportive of me over the past two years. He received no advance warning of this capture. He's in an awkward position having to concede to *Prefecture* demands yet protect his villagers."

Liliane nodded, "Maybe the *gendarmes* are mistaken."

"I had hoped that living in Vichy France, I would be spared the intrusion of the Germans. I still have contacts in Paris with German officers through my marriage to Karl. He came to Paris in November 1940 as an Aide to Otto Abetz who was appointed ambassador to Vichy France by Hitler. He and Karl worked to establish good Franco-German relationships by promoting cultural exchanges. I met Karl at a classical concert. He was organising the safeguarding of public and private works of art. We married last May. We were only married a few months before he was shot. They told me he was a traitor. I can try to contact Karl's colleagues."

"*Merci. Merci, mon amie.*" Liliane kissed Britt on both cheeks then briskly walked home, changed her clogs to a pair of flat shoes, told Jean-Jacques she was back and would visit her friends for a while at Josette's house. They talked until it became acrimonious with recriminations and despair.

Liliane opened a bottle of homemade plum wine she had brought to drink with a few macaroons in an effort to cheer them up. "I saw some *chanterelle* mushrooms under a chestnut tree as I drove to *Villane-le-Foret*," she said brightly. "I was looking for nettles and wild garlic to put in our soup for dinner. Jean-Jacques makes croutons which we add to the soup with walnuts and goats cheese to make it more filling."

Paulette rose from her chair and embraced Liliane and Chantal, wiping away her tears before leaving to open the café for the evening customers. "*Bon courage et bonne chance.*" Josette left shortly after, hugging Liliane, whispering, "*Bon courage, ma chere amie.*"

Liliane hurried home to make dinner, walking past the open kitchen window of Pierre Dalmain who was sitting upright in front of a dresser full of flowered China plates and reading a newspaper, his glasses perched low on his nose. Every few minutes, he raised his right hand to smooth his luxuriant moustache. His wife had fastened back a white net curtain and was watering a flowering plant in a tin container placed on the stone windowsill with a pottery jug, her grey hair tightly pulled back tightly. Liliane muttered '*Bonsoir*' as she hurried past, not wishing to hear her husband's perpetual whining.

Louis and Rose-Marie were squabbling at the kitchen table over whose turn it was to wash up. "It's women's work," complained Louis. "Men work on the land." He stood up and held out his hands which were grazed and rough with dirt under the fingernails. "I don't want lily-white soft hands that blister when I drive the plough for Guy de Lamont." He flexed his broad shoulders and pushed up his sleeves to flex his muscles.

"*Assieds-toi, Louis*. Rose-Marie is teasing you. She and I will wash up tonight but do you think your papa is not a man because he has clean soft hands and works inside?" Liliane asked with a smile as she spooned hot garlic and nettle soup into thick pottery dishes, adding a sprinkling of fresh walnuts and crumbs of goat's cheese. Louis shrugged, took a large chunk of his papa's bread and noisily slurped his soup in protest. Liliane looked over his head at Jean-

Jacques who sat down at the head of the table. He winked back and spooned up his soup. "*Delicieux, ma cherie,*" he said loudly looking at his son.

"*Jean-Jacques, parles-toi avec le Maire?* Can he help us and find out where our boys have been taken?" Liliane's recent self-pity had changed to a driving need for action as she cleared the table and swilled the soup dishes under the tap.

Jean-Jacques had moved to the hearth and started whittling a small piece of wood. He looked up at Liliane, assessing her mood and how best to answer her questions. "*Oui. J'ai parler avec M'sieur Danton. Il ne sais pas pourquoi les gendarmes ont pris les jeunes hommes.* Bertrand couldn't find out why the *gendarmes* took our boys." Jean-Jacques dropped his whittling wood into his lap and rubbed his hands over his face in distress. Liliane put a comforting hand over his spread fingers, noticing the residue of white dough in his finger nails, a true sign of her husband's concern as he was usually meticulously clean.

After Rose-Marie and Louis had gone upstairs to their attic bedrooms, they sat for a while in the soft light of the oil lamps, holding hands and talking of pleasant memories of their life in Broussac, glad to have shared happy and sad times with friends and neighbours. Liliane remembered her excitement when Armand was born at home, helped by the local midwife.

She could remember Jean-Jacques gently holding the tiny newborn baby in his hands with a huge grin on his face. She remembered Armand's first steps and words, his thick dark hair sprouting upright and his wet kisses and constant energy. She was proud that he had found a good job with a farmer nearby and enjoyed the physical outdoor work. He loved to swim in the river and had come to the *Fete* at her insistence so he could share the family dinner that evening. Yes, he was strong and brave but would that be enough to sustain him away from his family for a long time? Liliane continued to worry about Armand but she succeeded in hiding her emotions from Rose-Marie.

She knew Jean-Jacques was gripped with anxiety too, and as each week passed with no news about the captured young men, it reinforced their conviction that they had been taken to work in German factories. Liliane started lighting a candle for Armand in the church each evening. She knelt in front of the altar praying for the safety of her firstborn son. Silently, she shared her memories of him from babyhood to teenage years with the statue of Jesus on the cross behind the altar. Some nights M'sieur Pascal was preparing the church for Sunday mass and she felt comfortable in his presence as he was a pious and patriotic man who cared for the locals with dedication.

He had lived his whole life in the *Aveyron Departement*. He helped the refugees passing down the lanes, many sadly undernourished and clad in dirty rags. He found beds for them in barns and cowsheds, even putting mattresses on the floor of the *salle de fete*, the village hall. He discretely helped the local *maquis*. The changed circumstances of war and the impact of the *STO Releve* had impacted local priests whose role was to offer sympathy and support to wives and mothers praying for captured sons, nephews or cousins.

The brutal enforcement of the *STO Releve* had interfered with the clergy's moral leadership and often resulted in their support for the *maquis who* hid the *refractaires*, defectors, in their camps in the hills and forests of the Aveyron. In some areas like the mining industry around the town of Carmaux, the clergy became priests for the *maquis* and the parish.

To an outsider, the conviviality of Broussac markets and seasonal *Fetes* portrayed a tranquil village but beneath the façade, there was a strong feeling of anxiety with the decisions and actions of the *Prefecture* in Rodez and particularly with Marshall Petain and his position of conciliation with the Germans. The villagers lived in the shadow of the invasion of Paris and the north of France and feared for their future. A constant anxiety weighed on the families of the young men who had enlisted in 1939 to fight for France.

The intrusive quota system applied to farm crops emphasised German control over Vichy France and significantly impacted agricultural life. With each passing day, *les paysans* felt their ordered rural life was disintegrating beneath the formidable control of the enemy who seemed invincible and powerful. L*es paysans* had been rooted in their land for generations and were struggling to harvest crops and manage the animals after the terrible slaughter of young men in the Great War. During the past twenty years, many fields had remained fallow and farm buildings left to deteriorate. Every family had suffered when sons, brothers and husbands had enthusiastically departed to unknown parts of Northern France. They had joined the French Army fighting desperately in the trenches and lost limbs, lives and sanity in the savage bombardment. A war memorial carved in local stone had been erected on the north corner of the *Place de la Mairie* with the names of the dead and missing etched into its harsh façade. Families placed flowers to commemorate their lost loved ones on 11 November each year when a service of remembrance was held in front of the memorial stone and in the church.

Jean-Jacques and Liliane had both lost elder brothers in the Great War. Liliane's cousin Francois had been an ace pilot flying an observation bi-plane over the trenches and had died in a horrific crash. Jean-Jacques' brother Gilles had fought in the trenches and been blown apart. Joseph had lost his home in Picardy and his family who had farmed in the north of France for generations until trench battles in the Great War devastated their land, home and buildings, killing his parents and young sisters whilst Joseph was fighting for his country. He had travelled south to the Aveyron to start a new life and had established a carpentry business in Broussac.

Albert Compiegne suffered so badly with shell shock that he came to Broussac seeking solitude and safety. He chose to live alone in an isolated stone hut in the middle of a field called *Champ des Fleurs* where colourful wildflowers proliferated, fertilised by grazing cows. The hut provided basic living, the floor was beaten earth and he slept on a wooden shelf using a rough blanket for warmth, and cooked outside on a wood fire. It was rumoured that he washed once a year in a stone manger filled with water for the cows. He had few teeth and arthritic hands but cultivated the best *potager* in the village. He kept three scrawny *chasse* dogs in a fenced pen who barked ferociously when anyone approached his hut.

The village war memorial and ruined *chateau* were the only evidence of these tragedies. No monuments stood in the hills around Broussac that told of the bravery and martyrs of Broussac over the centuries. Madame Royal visited the grave of her husband in the village cemetery once a week to place fresh flowers. "*Il a mon coeur*. He still has my heart," she said poignantly to her friend Madame Ricard after each visit.

When the Germans invaded and occupied France in September 1940, they had taken full control in the north, establishing their headquarters in Paris. The Vichy regime was set up by Marshal Petain to administer the South, *le zone libre*, in collusion with the *gendarmerie*. One and a half million French soldiers had been captured by the German Reich as prisoners of war before France surrendered and signed the armistice. In June 1942, Pierre Laval was forced to agree to the *Releve* with the German Minister of Labour.

This enabled the occupation force to increase their control by threatening that all workers could be seized for compulsory work in Germany, the *Service du Travail Obligatoire*-STO. This scheme required the exchange of fit agricultural workers for French male prisoners of war.

Country people deeply resented this enforced capture of young men to labour in German factories because they were deprived of crucial labour, yet were legally obligated to meet set quotas of food at imposed prices.

The Vichy government had incorporated all municipal forces into one state police, the *Milice* with authority to carry out the orders of the Germans. To resist was a dangerous choice but many local *gendarmes* attempted to warn people who could be arrested. The *Prefecture* were obligated to report signs of agitation among the population, eliminate doubtful elements, and denounce people not complying with German decrees. Rationing had caused shortages of electricity, food, animal foodstuffs and vehicle fuel.

The Storm

One week after the summer fete, in the turgid heat of late afternoon, ominous black clouds crowded the sky over village and forest. Vicious forks of lightning streaked across the horizon and thunder threatened and growled round the forested hills. A vicious wind tossed dead leaves piled in corners and made tree branches sway, their leafy branches reaching to the ground and scratching on stone walls. Strong gusts snatched items on clotheslines and flung them around the lanes. A white tablecloth wrapped around a tree in Paulette's backyard. Forked lightning jabbed down on village houses and with a sudden bright flare of electricity hit the spire of the church creating a ragged hole in the roof tiles.

Icy balls of hail were flung from the black clouds, obscuring houses and lanes, thickly coating stone steps and pathways. Hailstones clattered on rooftops, spattered in the fields and frightened cattle into stampeding. The hail battered against unshuttered windows, breaking fragile old glass. A violent wind tore through the lanes, lifting loose tiles on cowshed and barn roofs and slinging them into the fields. Trees bordering the river were uprooted and flung into the water, blocking the flow and causing flooding. Ripened crops were blasted flat and fruit torn off trees in orchards and hedgerows.

The villagers were deafened by continuous cracks of lightning as it forked down into the fields, following the river as it meandered through the rocky gorge. The growling of thunder increased as it roared directly overhead. Secure inside their shuttered houses, women placed tin buckets under ceiling drips and used towels to soak up rainwater leaking through badly fitting old window frames. Men dashed between lightning streaks into their barns to check the condition of farm animals.

Joseph, Michel and Armand, soldiers of the Great War, shuddered inside their homes with the tremors of remembrance. The clattering and rattling of hailstones on slate roofs sounded like German gunfire and images of the shattered bodies of their dead comrades filled their minds.

At the height of the storm, Alain's terrified mare pulled its tether in the stall so hard, it snapped. It crashed through the unlatched wooden door and galloped out into the farmyard. Alain, alerted by the unusual noise, ran out of his kitchen and started to chase but slid on the icy cobblestones and thumped onto his back. "*Arrete*! Stop!" He shouted loudly but the fierce wind tore away his words. Josette came hurtling out of the kitchen and helped her husband to stand up.

"*La jument est sortie le grenier. Elle est en colere.* The mare has escaped from the barn and is angry. She will hurt someone," Alain shouted as he held onto the barn door for support. "*Faites bien attention a les grelons. C'est glissant.* Be careful, the cobblestones are slippery with hailstones." He stumbled over to the shed where he housed his tractor, gripping his coat tightly as the wind whipped it open. Josette ran back into the kitchen and donned heavy farm boots and a waterproof coat. "I'll check with the neighbours while you drive the tractor round the lanes. *Elle est vieille et tres fragile*. She is old and weak."

The ferocity of the storm had decreased slightly by the time Alain and Josette captured the mare, checked she was uninjured and tethered her firmly in the barn. Thunder rumbled and lightning continued to spark in the distant hills, flashing along the river for another two hours. By sunset, the storm had subsided, the hailstones ceased and a watery sun coloured the grey clouds a soft rose as it edged down to the horizon. The villagers unbarred shutters and doors and walked outside to examine the damage.

Heaps of icy balls blocked cellar and kitchen doors and were shovelled to the side of the lane. Dead chickens lay in backyards and rats were already feasting on them, pushing through the *chasse* dogs for fresh meat. Wooden fences and hedges were strewn across the fields and a few cattle lay on their sides killed by lightning. A massive chestnut tree had been struck and lay across the main route out of the village, blocking access to the next hamlet, *Villane-le-Foret*.

Mark's donkeys, *Alphonse* and *Petit*, had chewed through their tethering ropes and jumped a gap in the hedge that fenced them in and out to the lanes. The animals had devoured the vegetables in Mark's *potager* and left a steaming pile of dung outside his kitchen door. Mark and Victor, the local handyman, chased the animals across the *Place de la Mairie* towards the edge of the village.

The donkeys' hooves clattered over the cobblestones and their braying resounded round the village as they became more agitated. They were strong well-fed beasts used to pull farm carts and carry loads of firewood or hay sheaves. The donkeys headed down a lane to a harvested hay field.

Jean-Paul Latour was rumbling along the lane in his tractor, towing a cart full of dung to fertilise his fields. He pulled up sharply as the donkeys charged around him, narrowly avoiding them but causing his cart to shunt into the rear wheels of his tractor. It tipped over onto the road, spraying the hedgerows and Jean-Paul. "*Merde, merde. Bêtes stupide. Hommes stupides,*" he swore loudly.

The stink filled the village causing Bertrand to tug open his front door and yell, "*Quelle catastrophe. L'odeur est terrible et les fleurs sont mort.*"

Dung had been flung over the stone flowerpots that the *Maire* was so proud of and covered the steps of the *Mairie*. Villagers hung out of their windows and stood around in the *Place*, hiding their laughter with their hands. The donkeys finally halted and were drinking noisily out of a water trough outside the *Salle de Fete*. Mark whacked both donkeys on their backsides with a stick which he had been angrily brandishing.

"*Il y a une grande probleme, Bertrand.*" Victor yelled as he ran past and disappeared down an alley leaving Mark to face the angry *Maire*.

"*Allez, allez,*" Bertrand shouted, waving his fist as Mark picked up the rope halters trailing from the animals' necks. He noisily berated them as he viciously tugged them down the lane and shoved them into his barn. He heaved the wooden doors shut, briskly rubbed his hands of dried dung and stomped back home to eat a late lunch.

Jean-Paul and two villagers pushed his cart upright and he checked the metal attachment to his tractor. His clean overalls and trousers were covered in dung. Pierrette, his wife, had walked to the *Place* to see what the commotion was about. She shouted at her husband to come home and change. "*Non, non,*" he retorted, looking over his shoulder. "I must fertilise my crops today." He continued, muttering angrily to himself. "*D'accord,*" answered Pierrette with a shrug and wandered over to the café where she shared a laugh with Paulette. She had been organising the unloading of wooden barrels of wine into her cellar and seen the whole miserable incident. Her customers hastily finished breakfast and departed home to avoid the stink.

The *épicerie* was open and the owner was stacking outdoor shelves with baskets of vegetables and fruit. He tied a handkerchief over his mouth and nose.

Madame Ricard walked past the café with her black poodle on a lead. She was going to meet friends for lunch at the cafe but waved at them and hurried past, her hand over her nose.

Bertrand gingerly walked down the steps, avoiding the splatters of dung and marched across to the café for his regular bowl of soup. His friends were at their usual table laughing and joking about the accident. "Shovel up the dung to use on your flower pots and your garden," Michel, the Deputy *Maire* said with a grin. Antoine grimaced as his wife Claudine came marching over from their house, angrily asking what the terrible smell was.

The *Maire* instructed Victor to clear the mess and he'd returned with an old handcart and a shovel. "*C'est bon pour mon jardin*," he said with a cheeky grin. He rarely washed his body or his clothes.

The setting sun sent gleaming golden rays onto wet roofs and cobbled lanes as the villagers gathered later at the café to discuss the damage to their homes. Many had flooded cellars in houses located near the river that left a thick glutinous coating of mud on stone slabs. Frightened *chasse* dogs howled as they were chained outside.

"The river is rising fast and is blocked in places by fallen branches and debris," shouted Michel, the Deputy *Maire* as he hurried into the cafe. "I heard it roaring under the bridge as I walked here. Luckily, we have a new house, so no roof or window damage but the barn door was ripped off and flung into the field opposite. What damage have you seen, Antoine?" Antoine had cycled to the café from his home with two shovels strapped to his handlebars. He carefully leant his bike against a table and looked around the *Place*. "*Beaucoup*," he responded tersely.

Madame Ponthier, who lived opposite the *Mairie*, stood in her doorway, her terrier jumping up and down in a barking frenzy as it was tethered to the door handle. She had dressed hastily and wore black socks and slippers, an apron hung over her shabby dress. She looked down at the pile of melting hailstones on her front step and grimaced, muttering to herself, "*Quelle catastrophe!*"

Antoine joined Michel, saying, "Jean-Paul and Pierrette Latour are still trying to round up three dairy cows that stampeded across the ditch and on to the road. He said some slates had blown from his barn roof and the bonnet and roof of his tractor was peppered with holes from the hailstones. I popped in to see Madame Ziegler as I cycled past her house because the schoolhouse roof is in need of repair. She was scared by the ferocity of the storm and her washing was torn off the line but no house damage. Madame Royal told me she has broken windows."

Liliane left the *Boulangerie* and walked to Josette's house to ask about damage to their crops. "The *Boulangerie* is intact but we have two broken windows in the house. Pierre Dalmain's *chasse* dogs were howling in fear. I saw a chicken lying in the road. What's the damage in your fields?"

"The mare escaped the barn in fright but Alain captured her. The corn is flattened but the maize is still standing because it's sturdier." Josette sighed, "I think many of the sunflowers will be bent over but we can harvest most of the seeds. The roofs of our barns are undamaged."

"A few slates broke as they crashed to the ground." She continued angrily, "I suppose the Germans will still expect us to meet their crop and food quotas. We're struggling and the storm damage makes it worse."

Men gathered outside the *Mairie* in the growing dusk shouting for the *Maire* to help them. They felt they had suffered enough from German food restrictions and the loss of fit young men because of the forced enlistment by the *gendarmes*. Bertrand Danton walked to the *Mairie* steps and raised his hand for silence. He spoke forcefully, taking responsibility for managing the devastation. "Tragedy has struck our village with the worst storm damage I've ever seen but we have good artisan skills in the village. Pierre, will you check what windows are broken? Jean-Luc, can you sort out the carpentry repairs? Michel, will you arrange help for farmers? I'll meet with Pascal to discuss building repairs."

"That's not good enough. The government agricultural survey has recorded the numbers of our animals and the quantity of crops to be harvested. Have you seen the damage to these? Have you walked outside the village or are you cowering inside your office?" Leon Allegre shouted angrily. "I've been ordered to provide the government with a set quota of cows, calves and sheep as well as wheat, corn, maize and hay. My neighbours have received the same orders. We're struggling to do the harvesting with a shortage of fit men and to battle the Vichy Government." Leon stormed away, pushing his way through the villagers.

There were hearty nods of agreement and loud mutters of discontent among those standing in the *Place*, raising their arms in despair. "*Mon Dieu*. How much more do they want to take?" Alain shook his head.

"We share harvesting equipment as we have little money and the prices have risen since the Germans invaded," furiously declared Guy de Lamont who owned a large farm in the area. "We harness our wives to the threshing machines and our children miss school to work in the fields."

"You've been offered compensation for the provision of crops and food quotas, although at a price lower than market value," retorted the *Maire*, stung by the animosity of the villagers.

"A disgustingly low price based on 1939 values and if we don't deliver on time, we're fined. My cousin told me the fines could be up to twenty times the actual value. It's a rip-off." Another local farmer shouted, raising his fist. "What have we gained from fighting in the Great War? *Rien*, rien. Nothing, I tell you."

Bertrand Danton was irate, his face blooming red as he tried to make himself heard over the angry villagers. "Don't be stupid. You must comply with the orders of the Vichy regime or there will be repercussions on the village. I've heard reports the Germans shoot French people who resist." He turned away and went into his office, slamming the door behind him, disgusted with the men and deeply concerned about his position and any repercussions on his family.

"I'll cheat and hide crops rather than support the Germans. My eldest son was killed by them in the trenches of the Great War." Pierre Dalmain threatened and left. His neighbours could hear his wife berating her husband for telling others about their plan. He pushed her aside and stormed into their house on the corner, setting their *chasse* dogs barking furiously. The villagers left the *Place* and hurried to the relative safety of their homes.

Liliane anxiously talked with Josette about the amount of bread her husband, Jean-Jacques must supply each day. "It's almost impossible with the rationing of flour. We'll have to buy on the black market."

"Ssshhhh." Josette whispered in her ear. "*N'inquiete pas*. We haven't harvested our corn yet and I'm sure we can supply you direct to supplement what you are allowed. We can declare less due to storm damage. You'll have to grind it yourself but my cousin in the next village has a water mill and may help if I ask him quietly."

"*Merci, ma chere ami*." Liliane said, hugging her friend.

The church bells were ringing at seven the next morning when gunshots echoed round the village, bouncing off the stone buildings. Shutters opened with a clatter and heads popped out of the windows. A group of local farmers were brandishing rifles at the roof of the church and the *Mairie*. "*Bonjour, c'est les loires et les rats*," yelled Joseph. "The river's flooded so the rats are running wild through the village."

"*D'accord*, ok," a few voices replied and shut the windows.

The dead rodents were collected in sacks and strung on a wire across the end of a fallow field. They attracted the crows who carked loudly as they pecked at the eyes and flesh. The village rang with the sound of hammering as broken windows were boarded up and slates replaced on roofs. From the fields, there was the clamour of frightened cows as they were herded down the lanes and into barns for protection.

By noon when the church bells rang again, the village seemed a more peaceful place except for the rushing sound of the river. After lunch, local tradesmen visited the villagers who had storm damage to their houses and made a list of materials required.

That evening, the sun set in a sky of vibrant red and orange. A few heavy clouds were edged with golden rays as they drifted on the soft evening breeze. The air smelt of fresh crops and piles of ripened fruit lying on the ground. A lone blackbird perched on the damaged church spire and sang tunefully and mournfully until dusk blurred the buildings. The bird lifted his head so the notes sounded bright and sharp as they issued from his orange beak. Swallows gathered on the wires or swooped at clouds of insects, and the clucking of ducks rose from the river. The *chasse* dogs were silent, slumbering with their bellies filled with nourishing meat from dead rats. Two young owls swooped out from a barn and alighted silently on a high roof, perched closely together as they breathily communicated.

Next evening, local farmers met with the *Maire*, Michel and Joseph. "It's important we help harvest field crops for families bereft of males in this community," Joseph said. "Corn and maize must be threshed and grapes picked before winter ploughing starts. When we've finished our fields, it's my opinion that we old men should go to local farms and offer assistance." Joseph continued forcefully. "We can start with urgent tasks such as threshing and ask the women and children to stack the sheaves, bring them into the cellars and barns."

The *Maire* nodded his head. "Michel, can you make a note of that please? I'll contact the *Prefecture* in Rodez to check if the Aveyron *Departement* is providing assistance for repairs. The storm damaged many villages and farms, especially those on the *causse*. The track to *Villane-le-Foret* is blocked so there is no access to Rodez."

Antoine helped to chop down damaged trees and carted them on his tractor trailer to the edge of the forest to dry out for next year's firewood. He pruned and tied up the wisteria climbing the front of Madame Royal's house and mended a garden shed for Madame Ricard. Britt listed the repairs needed to the roof of the school and schoolhouse for Jean-Luc and Antoine to fix. The wooden statue of Jesus in the *Place de la Mairie* tilted to one side as rainwater had undermined its foundations. The priest enlisted the help of Victor to sort it out. Alphonse Germain in the *quincaillerie* hardware store did a roaring trade selling jars of nails and screws, glue and wood paste.

Because of the serious damage done by the storm, the villagers worked together on repairs, even children assisting with washing slate tiles as they were removed and repaired. An emergency kitchen was set up in the *Salle de Fete* and women took turns to cook and provide lunches for the tradesmen.

Bertrand quickly recovered his equanimity and assisted where he could, offering money from *Mairie* funds to help the widows in the village. Jean-Jacques delved into his declining store of flour to make extra bread for the workers and women brought baskets of vegetables for lunchtime.

The School Teacher

Britt woke early on Saturday and listened to the usual sounds of the village as it started the day, *chasse* dogs howling for meat, a donkey braying and cows mooing as they were moved from milking shed to field. Locals were arriving in the *Place de la Mairie* for the weekly market and the clamour of voices mingled with the clattering of stalls being assembled in the *Halle*, the covered stone market place. Britt could hear the clucking of hens and ducks as they were marshalled off a cart and into a wire enclosure. The engine of the cheese van belonging to Pierrette and Jean-Paul stuttered as it was manoeuvred into its space beside the *Mairie* steps. Children's cries reverberated on the stone walls and a cat screeched as it was kicked out of a house.

She looked out the window at the paintbox blue of a Midi summer sky with wisps of woolly clouds drifting in the gentle breeze. She could smell animal dung mixed with the sweet scent of roses and purple wisteria climbing in thick clusters on stone walls. She chose a cool plain cotton dress and slipped on a pair of black pumps, briefly remembering the shops where she had purchased them in Paris two years ago. Her husband Kurt had had a day free of officer duties and they had decided to enjoy the enticing pleasures of Parisien life—pavement cafes, one famous for its jazz quartet, a patisserie with the aroma of freshly baked croissants. They had peered in smoky bars with old men huddled together drinking *pastis* and seen entwined couples walking along the banks of the Seine. She sighed and wiped away a stray tear.

Kurt had walked smartly into her life when she was ushering a class of school children around the Louvre. She was describing the paintings of the *Impressionists* but the children were more interested in the sight of two uniformed German soldiers standing to attention in front of a large Monet painting. They were talking quietly in German and pointing to the skilful paint strokes and the mingling of soft colours. Britt was sitting on an upholstered bench in the middle of the gallery as the Germans moved to stand in front of her. She waited a few minutes to see if they would move to another painting but they remained in place, intensely discussing the painting technique.

"*Pardon, messieurs*," she said standing up and touching the shoulder of the taller soldier. He had short blonde hair, was clean-shaven with pale blue eyes and sculptured cheeks, his military cap tucked under his arm. He turned around and smartly saluted her before apologising in excellent French. "*Pardon, madame, je suis desolee.*"

"*De rien*, it's nothing," Britt replied standing statue-still. She gulped and felt her stomach flip over, drawn to his Aryan good looks and courteous, friendly manner. She was thirty years old and had led a quiet almost celibate life working as a school teacher in the southern suburb of *Bourg-la-Reine*.

"*Bonjour, je m'appelle Kommandantur Zeigler,*" he removed his leather glove and held out his hand. "I work with Otto Abetz, the German Ambassador to Paris."

Britt avoided his hand and replied, "*Mon plaisir.*" She turned away and gathered the school children around her for protection. Her hands were shaking and drops of perspiration dampened her face. She turned slightly to look at him and saw he was regarding her with admiration and warmth. Kurt walked slowly across to his companion officer but the warmth of his smile lingered with Britt for several enchanted moments before the clamour of the school children broke her reverie.

"*Allez, allez, mes enfants. Nous allons chez nous.*" She told them briskly, pushing them together in a close-knit group as she marshalled them across the road and along the *Boulevard Saint-Michel* to get the train back to Bourg-la-Reine where they lived.

The next afternoon Britt was required to supervise a class of senior children on a return visit to the Louvre. She was a *professeur* of history and art at a *Lycee*, a high school in Bourg-la Reine. The exhibition of Impressionists was soon to be re-housed for safety in a private chateau in the Loire region. The newly arrived German authorities were keen to restore some semblance of cultural life in Paris and had re-opened the Louvre Museum in September 1940, several months after their army had marched into the city. France had declared war on the Germans on 3 September 1939 and the French Government had decided to ensure the most valuable art works were packed into crates and taken to secure locations in rural France. Some 3,690 sculptures, paintings and decorative *antiquities* were driven south by truck, joining the crowded convoys of refugees leaving Paris at this time.

Many of the galleries and viewing rooms in the Louvre had been emptied and Britt wanted a last chance to gaze on the glorious French paintings of the late nineteenth century. She patiently endured the slow train journey from *Bourg-la-Reine to Place-St-Michel*, the train station opposite Notre Dame Cathedral built on the *Ile-de-Cite* in the Seine.

Britt had intended that the children get off the train and walk round the *Jardins de Luxembourg* before visiting the Louvre but the train took longer than usual as if the engine had run out of fuel. She marshalled the children across to the Louvre, ran the gauntlet of armed German soldiers standing guard at the entrance and hurried her group to the Gallery of Impressionist Paintings. To her embarrassment, the tall German soldier was sat on the bench gazing intently at the Monet.

He heard the chattering of the children, saw Britt encouraging them to enjoy the paintings and stood up, giving an automatic salute. Britt felt her face grow pink with embarrassment and tried to avoid touching his hand which was politely being offered to her. "*Bonjour, Madame Professeur,*" he said with a smile lifting the corners of his thin lips.

"*Bonjour Kommandantur. Je suis pressé aujourd'hui.*" Britt told him she was in a hurry but the children stood fascinated watching the German soldier and refused to move. Britt had ignored the soldier's hand, noticed it was immaculately clean with neatly pared nails. She looked down at his polished black boots, afraid to look him in the eye.

"*Tout va bien avec les enfants, Madame?*" *Kommandantur* Zeigler asked quietly. He could see Britt was embarrassed to be spoken to by a German officer and wanted to avoid exchanging further conversation. His French was impeccable and his manners courteous. "*Vous etes tres belle*," he whispered softly. "*C'est possible nous prenons un café demain soir?*"

Britt breathed in, twisting her hands as she debated taking the risky step of agreeing to meet a German officer. "*Oui, le café Saint-Michel*," she replied then placed herself in the centre of the children and marched them away.

Returning home after school had finished, she pondered her hasty decision to meet the Kommandantur. She had no intention of becoming a traitor to France but hoped she might gain useful knowledge of German intentions in Paris that she could pass on to the Resistance. She spent a restless hour pacing her small kitchen.

The next day, she nervously selected a plain dark dress and a black hat with a lace veil which she could pull down to disguise her face. It was a balmy evening, so she took the train to the Boulevard St Michel. She walked through the *Jardin de Luxembourg*, the air perfumed by colourful flowers planted in the formal areas. Mothers were walking with their children and smart ladies dressed in couture fashions held the leads of small lapdogs.

It appeared that normal life continued despite the obvious presence of uniformed and armed German soldiers. Britt arrived at the café a few minutes early and saw Kurt sitting at a small wrought iron table set against the café wall. She was relieved to see that he was not wearing his uniform but was casually dressed in cream tailored trousers and an open neck shirt. He was sipping a glass of *vin rouge* and dipping into a bowl of olives. She thought how handsome he looked and her heart somersaulted in her chest and her palms felt damp. She'd had several short-term affairs, *cinq-a-sept*, the French expression for men and women who met their lovers after work before going home to their family. None of her lovers had flipped her heart over and created butterflies in her stomach like this smart German officer was doing unknowingly.

Kurt saw her and smiled and waved her over to sit at the table. He beckoned to the smartly dressed waiter who responded and stood to attention at the table, his metal tray held shoulder high in one hand.

"*Bonjour, monsieur, madame. Qu'est que vous voulez?*" He was very formal with an expressionless face that could have masked his disgust at a French woman sitting with a German invader.

"*Nous voudrons du champagne, s'il vous plait.*" Kurt smiled as he spoke politely in impeccable French.

The waiter nodded and walked over to the wood-panelled bar where he placed their order. Judging by the whispered conversation punctuated by many shrugs as the bartender looked over at Kurt, he was resigned to serving a German. However, as the waiter poured the champagne into fluted glasses, he managed to spill a small amount with each drink, so when Britt and Kurt lifted them, drips of liquid spilt on their clothes. The waiter smirked and turned away abruptly with a pretentious smile as he took the orders of a French couple on the next table.

Britt felt embarrassed and her face blushed pink but Kurt appeared to take the rudeness in his stride and took a perfectly laundered white handkerchief out of his breast pocket to wipe the bottom and stem of a full glass to give to Britt. "*De rien*," he said quietly with a smile. "It's nothing." He raised his glass to Britt, saying, "*Salut.*" There was a long silence between them until Kurt started a polite conversation.

"It's a beautiful summer evening and I'm pleased you accepted my invitation. I'm not a combat soldier as I work for Otto Abetz, the German Ambassador. I was a university professor before having to enlist and taught classic literature and art."

Britt sipped her wine, aware of the disagreeable glances sent her way. Fraternising with the enemy was almost seen as treachery to La France. She leant across the table and said, "Let's walk through the Tuileries Gardens. I feel out-of-place here. I'm a truly loyal French woman yet I feel guilty meeting you." Britt bowed her head, finished her wine and stood up to leave the café. Kurt paid the bill and followed her across the road.

"I'm sorry to have embarrassed you. I've never met a lady who attracted me so much. Let's find a bench in the Gardens and I will properly introduce myself."

Britt nodded assent and walked briskly along the gravel path to an ornamental iron bench shielded between two flowering bushes. Kurt chose to sit at the opposite end and leant back to give the impression to passers-by that they had met by coincidence. "Britt. I was forced to enlist due to my age. I'd hoped to be exempt as a school teacher but Otto Abetz, the German Ambassador to Paris is a long-term friend of my parents. He knew I'd studied fine art and architecture at the Sorbonne and requested I join his staff as an officer and provide expert advice and assessment of the Old Masters works held in Museums throughout Paris. My parents pushed me to accept his offer as they didn't want their only son to fight in the trenches. Now, will you tell me about you and why you love art and Impressionist Paintings?"

Britt and Kurt talked for a long while, watching the sun set over the city, the most romantic city in the world. Britt rose to leave as the shadows deepened and Kurt held out his hand to help her. She leant on his shoulder, entranced by the evening and his company. It was a *coup de foudre;* love at first sight. They met regularly for the next few months in backstreet cafes and finally took the train to Bourg-la-Reine where they made passionate love.

They married and shared a few months of blissful marriage before Kurt was shot. They told Britt he was a traitor.

Vichy France Autumn and Winter 1942-43

Harvest Time

Repairs to storm damage in the village had been completed but many were temporary fixes due to lack of money. Two weeks later, Broussac came to life as the harvest was organised. There were too many hands missing for the jovial activity of pre-war years to be revived but the normal rhythm of work took over from a temporary paralysis after the capture of the three young men and the damaging storm. The familiar rumble of wooden carts pulled by worn-down mules and one team of oxen owned by Alain Favel, echoed through the lanes from dawn to dusk. Women harnessed the animals and guided the teams in the fields where stiff old men slowly picked up the regular routine of scything by hand. Wooden carts were filled with harvested corn and maize and children scurried around gleaning the seeds and ears. Joseph loaned his mechanical steam reaper to speed the process.

The local mill owner had died a year ago, so Alain Favel and Antoine spent several days clearing the mill race and oiling the machinery to enable the old wooden wheel to rotate in the flow of the Aveyron River, powering the great round stones to grind the wheat.

As the fields were harvested of their crop, large brown hares and small grey rabbits with white scuts leapt out of their hiding places with children chasing them, hoping to catch meat for the stew pot. Once or twice, a young deer jumped agilely down the tall lines of maize to be trapped against the thick hedges bordering the fields. Pheasant and partridge flew with squawks and croaks into the air and were shot by village men.

Children were sent to the fields at mid-day with clay jars of cold well water and baskets of bread, homemade cheese and fruit. The harvesters sat in the shade of oak and chestnut trees edging the fields, wiping sweaty brows with dirty shirttails. By sunset, the workers were exhausted but there was a feeling of satisfaction as the fields became stubble and carts filled to the top rumbled back to barns and sheds. Children ran alongside laughing when the carts rolled from side to side down the ribbed tracks. Mules and oxen brayed their disapproval of the heavy loads and spat at the drivers. Clouds of invasive flies circled their eyes and rears, annoying the reapers. Each cartload meant farm animals could be fed through the bitter winter months and slaughtered when their owners needed meat to supplement their diet.

Young boys worked tirelessly alongside worn grey haired old men whose hands and limbs were stiff and gnarled with rheumatism and arthritis. Life in the countryside rotated around the seasons and certain jobs were critical regardless of weather conditions—sleet, snow, rain or storms. No one knew what the future held if the Germans invaded the *zone libre* and the Aveyron region.

It took two weeks for the crops to be harvested. Farmers grumbled loudly as they sorted the proscribed quotas the Germans would requisition. Luckily, the weather remained benign with just a few scattered showers to dampen the fields. Everyone was relieved when the crops were safely stored. Despite their exhaustion, families sat out on terraces and balconies celebrating, eating the evening meal, drinking wine and joking with neighbours.

The following Sunday, the church in Broussac held a service of thanksgiving for the successful completion of the harvest which was followed by a harvest *repas*. It was a muted celebration because of the absence of men who had not returned from the Great War. Their families had no grave to mourn over and were struggling to manage their property. Farm equipment had been abandoned in yards, silent and rusting for lack of hands to use it. By rural tradition, young men had the responsibilities of mending tractors and cartwheels, shoeing horses and mules, and carrying the crops on their strong shoulders. Many young families had moved to nearby towns for work in the 1920s and 1930s. This had resulted in one of the two village *épiceries* closing down and the café was usually empty after breakfast customers had left and before evening *aperitif* time. The local blacksmith had shut down and the water mill ceased operating.

By mid-October, ploughing started followed by sowing the seeds. This was a manual task for women and children who used straw markers to make straight lines. In the thin clear October mornings, the line of sowers moved across designated fields, the grain floating in the air before rustling down to the rich turned earth.

Trees and hedgerows were aglow with colourful leaves and berries. On sunny evenings, women walked the lanes picking red rose hips for their nourishing juice and blackberries for jam. From early morning, nimble children climbed fruit trees to shake down apples, plums and pears for collection by younger siblings.

"*Viens vite*, come quickly, Louis and Michel." Maria, Louisa and their friend Rose-Marie spread tarpaulins under the trees. Louis leapt up to the first branch of an apple tree, leaning over dangerously as he reached up to the next branch. He was laughing as he knocked the fruit on to his sister's head.

"I hope Maman will make *tarte tatin* for dinner tonight." Michel shouted as he nimbly scrambled up a pear tree. He collected the ripe pears in a large basket which he swung to the ground on a rope, then jumped down to pick up an empty pannier. He climbed another tree and swung agilely from branch to branch before handing the full basket to his sister perched on a lower branch. "We have 30 pears," she cried to Michel.

"How many apples have you got, Rose-Marie?" Louis shouted as he ran past her and leapt up to a branch of the next apple tree.

"Twenty big red ones and a few small green ones," his sister replied grinning and chomping on a large apple. "Here, catch. They're delicious."

Michel's friends Pierre and Luca came running into the orchard. "I'll help if we can take some home." He shouted at Michel. "Chantal's helping Maman to prepare the preserving jars."

It was a hot day and the children grew thirsty. They rested in the shade as they uncorked clay water bottles, pushing each other in fun. They carried on picking fruit until dusk fell and their mothers came. It took another hot day for the fruit picking to be finished as the children slowed down, losing interest. They wanted to jump in the river and cool down. Small children ran in groups up the wooded lanes to collect the prickly shells of sweet chestnuts from the earth. They scampered around, picking up nuts and putting them in straw baskets hanging on their arms. Louis, Luca and Michel climbed the old spreading trees with ease, pleased to be sheltered in the shady branches.

In previous years, fruit would be sold fresh at local markets but with wartime rationing, it was bottled and made into jam. In stone barns and wooden sheds, large aluminium pots were placed on gas rings or wood-burning stoves and glass preserving jars handed down from mother to daughter were filled with the steaming mixture, their spring tops pushed tight as airtight seals. They were labelled and placed on shelves in the *caves* with fresh fruit stored in wooden boxes.

Antoine took a group of children piled on his tractor trailer to collect walnuts from the trees lining the lanes. They were plentiful this year and would be sold for a decent price. He and his wife Claudine had sorted out surplus bottled fruit from last year's crop and planned to sell it at the *Fete de Chataigne* market with their walnuts. They'd eaten the last of their tame rabbits the week before and were keeping just a few hens for their eggs. "If only I could shoot game or even a few pigeons," he moaned.

"Set a few traps in the woods where it's hard to find them. I think we need to look after ourselves and not share with others. I pray that the Germans stay out of our area," replied Claudine. "Before this war started, I thought our *Maire* had more control over the area and the village. Now, it seems he must obey all the rules and restrictions of the Germans."

The last Sunday in October, the large village of St Martial, some five kilometres away, held its annual *Fete de Chataigne*—the Chestnut Fair. It was Liliane's favourite market as people travelled from around the Aveyron to bring local craftwork and produce for sale. This included the *vignerons* with that year's wine to taste—white, rose and *vin nouveau*.

Producers of oil made from local olives, maize, rapeseed (colza) and sunflowers (*tournesols*) had stalls offering small croutons of bread to dip in bowls for tasting. Cheesemakers brought a range of fresh goats and cow cheese, including the hard Cantal type. Butchers traded homemade sausages, pate and terrines as well as some game and poultry. This year due to rationing, the selection was very limited.

Liliane and her friends had a stall displaying their patchwork and knitted items for sale. Most of the stalls were set up in the undercover market—a large square of rough concrete with a tin roof. There were braziers with roasting chestnuts and hot snake-like doughnuts to savour. Liliane bought a bagful to share with family and friends in the café. She had arranged to meet with Josette, Paulette, Nicole and Marie-Francoise at midday.

Village cafes were overflowing with talking, smiling people and children running happily round the stalls. The *Fete de Chataigne* was a chance to share goodwill and good food with neighbours and relatives before they shut themselves inside to avoid the bitter cold and icy roads. The late autumn weather was mild and appetising smells of cooked food from stalls and cafés wafted around. Regis arrived at dusk with his accordion, wearing a brightly striped woollen hat, coloured waistcoat and white shirt.

Local men gathered under the leafless plane trees, wearing their Sunday shoes and dressed in clean trousers and shirt, many with a worn jacket and cotton cravat. They played competitive *boule* games or stood with hands in pockets, sharing the last few cigarettes, dark cloth caps placed on the back of their heads. When the market closed at dusk, a group of local musicians with accordions, guitars and a lone violin serenaded the café clients and several people got up to dance, including Liliane and her friends. The women wore dark dresses and coats with a cloche hat and black shoes buttoned with a strap across the instep and tapped their feet to the lively music.

The *Fete de Chataigne* was followed by *Toussaint* (All Saints Day), held on the first of November, when people gathered in family groups at village cemeteries to remember dead relatives. In the small cemetery of Broussac, bunches of bright chrysanthemums, bought at St Martial market, were reverently placed on elaborate stone tombs, decorated with carvings and icons of deceased family members. It was a sad and sombre occasion, as several older members of the Broussac community had died during the previous year. The event was followed by a mid-day meal held in the village *Salle de Fete* which lifted the mood of the villagers. Liliane brought baskets of fresh bread to put on the trestle tables amongst the pottery jugs of wine and plates of local cheese. The village echoed with the sounds of enjoyment by adults and children alike, and the lilting background of Regis's accordion.

These short periods of enjoyment were to be the last ones for Broussac inhabitants for many years. The dark threatening clouds of German rule soon overwhelmed the tranquillity of the farming community in the Aveyron and the Lot. News from Northern France was dire and everyday ragged, starving refugee families struggled down the country lanes, women lugging infants. Men dragged battered wooden carts stuffed to the brim with possessions, including an old mattress tied on top. They told tales of eviction, brutality, rape and destruction in the towns and villages. They hid their shame as fathers and mothers begged for water and food. Kindly farmers opened their barns so families could sleep amongst the animals. As they fed them, the women heard tales of the *maquis* who helped them through the desolate countryside of the Lot and Aveyron.

During the Christmas period, small groups of resistants (*maquis*) displayed their patriotism in front of war memorials in Alban, Gourdon and Martel. In Cahors, they placed tricolour wreaths on the statue of Leon Gambetta, a resistant from the 1870 Franco-Prussian War.

The town of Cahors and the *Departement* of the Lot became occupied territory in November 1942. Early in 1943, the first *maquis* units were set up in response to the Germans imposing the compulsory *Service du Travail Obligatoire* on 16–17 February 1943. This was followed on 30 March 1943 by a decree that stated young men were to be conscripted and sent to Germany.

Intrusion of War

In December, on a bright bitingly cold Sunday, Broussac held its Christmas market. The stalls were half-empty with few homemade items and garden produce on display but they were colourful with faded flags and paper decorations. The market livened up the malaise of winter as people gathered to gossip, dressed warmly in bright woollen scarves and hats, gloved hands holding wicker baskets or string bags.

The café was overflowing with locals sharing tables with family and friends, drinking coffee and mulled wine, children running excitedly among them. Regis played a selection of Christmas carols on his accordion, including the well-known, "*Il est nee le divin enfant.*" School children and adults sang along, requesting favourite songs when Regis had finished. In the *Salle de Fete,* trestle tables were covered with donations of food for the communal lunch. Some of the older folk had already taken their seats to share local gossip and news with neighbours.

At mid-day, when the sun was high in the pale wintry sky, the conviviality of the market was totally destroyed when a military jeep and two German trucks, one full of soldiers roared into the village. The *Maire*, horrified by the interruption to his mid-day lunch, hurriedly stepped out of the *Salle de Fete*, wiped his mouth and pulled away the napkin tucked into his neck. He glared at the military vehicles parked in his village, German flags attached to the bonnets fluttering in the cold breeze.

An officer leapt out of the jeep, stamped his booted feet together and adjusted his uniform. He made the 'Heil Hitler' salute then walked across to address the *Maire*. In heavily accented French, he announced that Hitler had ordered each country he conquered to provide manpower and materials for the war. "*Marechal Petain* has issued a proclamation called *Travail, Famille, Patrie*." The officer stumbled over the words—'Work, Family, Country'. He continued reading a notice held in his hand which clearly had a French translation. "Under the requirements of the *Service de Travail Obligatoire*, to be made law next February, all young men born between 1920 and 1922 must register at the *Mairie* for work in German factories." He finished reading the directive, handed it to the *Maire* with hand gestures indicating it must be attached to the wall outside the *Mairie*. He bounded back to the jeep with athletic ease, loosened his gun in his hip holster and shouted at the troops to search the village.

A group of soldiers, immaculately clothed in Nazi uniforms, their helmets set low on their heads to hide their faces, grimly marched round the houses, pushing open doors and stamping inside, guns at the ready to threaten young men who tried to escape. Other soldiers tramped through the market, heaving tables over and tipping produce to the ground, taking the wine.

Children cried out in terror as their older brothers were hauled out of their homes and *chasse* dogs filled the air with vicious barking and howling. Screaming women tried to stop their sons being captured but ten youths, with hands tied behind their backs, were shoved into the empty truck and the flaps tied down. In a cloud of exhaust fumes, the vehicles roared out of the village and hurtled down the lane to the next village to capture more young men.

The people of Broussac gathered round in stunned silence. The *Maire* was clearly shocked by the intrusion. He had received no notification of planned arrests. Women sobbed as they collected produce from the grass, much of the fruit and vegetables squashed by heavy soldiers' boots.

Men lifted overturned tables and tried to mend those that had been broken before loading them onto carts. There was a heavy silent anger to their actions, evident as they viciously unhitched the donkeys and tugged them into place in front of the carts. Dogs wildly running and barking in fear were kicked out of the way and mothers screamed at their children to stop their bawling. The *Maire* helped people to pack up their belongings and tried to comfort the women whose sons had been captured.

M'sieur Pascal, the priest, had not appeared to help his parishioners which seemed strange to those who attended his church, mostly old women these days. A few pointed remarks were made by the farmer's wives who didn't appreciate his pious remarks about God when their sons had died in the Great War. The old men gathered at the cafe to express their anger at the Germans capturing their grandsons, gesturing futilely with their fists and wildly suggesting reprisals for the Germans.

"I'll use my old hunting rifle to shoot the bastards if they come back," said old Michel, growling his anger.

"You'll do no such thing, you stupid old bastards," yelled Mme Pellier from her doorway. "Haven't you had enough fighting in wars?"

"We should set up a resistance group like they have in the north. Which of you is brave enough to take on the Germans?" Mme Ricard asked, shaking her head with its tightly plaited grey braids.

The villagers met in the *Salle de Fete* that evening. Small wooden barrels of local wine were set out and children sat on the floor sipping cups of milk. There was an atmosphere of despair and anger among the mothers whose sons had been captured and some were silently crying. The *Maire* tapped his wine glass for silence. "*Je suis desolee*. I am sorry for those of you who have lost sons today. I had no warning. You must believe that they will return when the Germans are beaten. They have been sent to work in factories, not to fight."

"*Vive la France,*" called an old soldier, Jean-Francois, grabbing the French flag from its socket on the wall and, through a mouthful of cheese, started to sing *La Marsellaise*.

Liliane spoke loudly, "*C'est une catastrophe*! Some youths have escaped to the hills but they have no food. My cousin fled to Cahors from northern France and told me there are *maquis* groups hiding around Brive and Cahors." She stood by the *Maire* holding the hands of her friends, Paulette whose son, Jean-Paul had been captured by the *gendarmes* at the village *Fete* and Josette, whose teenager, Gilles had managed to escape to the forest with his friend Michel, younger son of Paulette.

The villagers looked to the *Maire* for leadership and advice but sensed he was reluctant to get involved. He had no authority to help in regard to German food requisitions and was loathe to take action against the Germans at this stage. "Who could take food to the youths in hiding? Is there was a volunteer to take blankets to them?"

Joseph spoke up, "I'll go. I know the hidden tracks in the forests and hills through years of hunting game. I'll take my gun with me." He turned to the *Maire* and said, "You must talk to the *Prefecture* in Rodez. I won't say when I go but I'll let each mother know privately when the job has been done." Joseph continued, "I was a very young man when I fought in the Great War and survived with minor injuries. I want my revenge on those bastard Germans for what they have done to my country and the massacre of my family." He left, closing the meeting room door quietly and a concerted sign of relief passed round the room.

Walking back across the *Place*, Liliane discussed with Paulette and Josette how they could support their sons who had escaped. Josette was quiet, stunned by the tragedy of the day. Her youngest son, Gilles, was not strong due to a childhood illness and she was immensely worried how he would survive in hiding during the bitter winter months. Paulette appeared to listen but said she needed to talk with her husband. Marie-Francoise, who ran the café in *Villane-le-Foret*, sadly walked home, thinking about her empty house without any menfolk as her husband had died at the beginning of the war and her son was a prisoner of war.

The villagers had been caught unprepared and there was a tangible atmosphere of insecurity and fear. They drifted in a frightened stupor and there was no inclination to help neighbours. An element of suspicion circulated that the *gendarmes* had targeted some youths and ignored others. The village remained sunk in sullen silence punctuated only by the domestic sounds of animals-hens clucking, pigs grunting, donkeys braying and children crying. They asked M'sieur Pascal for comfort and prayers but his support seemed lacklustre and his patriotic fervour was lukewarm.

Liliane invited Paulette and Josette to her home the next day to discuss how they could help their sons. "We must be extremely careful. Joseph suggested he searches for them tomorrow night and takes some food. He knows the wild unused routes and is a decent man. I agreed that I will go with him in a week or so to take clothing and food. I'll ask Jean-Jacques to make a few extra baguettes," Liliane winked at Josette who had secretly offered some harvested corn from their fields.

"I'll give you some vegetables," replied Josette, "and you can use one of our donkeys. I know Joseph has his own, so you can load them both with supplies. They are surefooted when you climb up through the forested hills. Paulette, we don't expect help from you because your absence from the café will be noticed."

Paulette sighed in relief. "I'll knit hats, scarves and socks for them. It will be bitter cold on the *causse* in a month or so. The wind from the north in winter is biting and comes directly from Russia."

"Now, let's talk about different things whilst we do some patchwork," Liliane said with a smile. "We have to be brave, sensible and very cautious over this. I think there are some villagers who want to be friendly with the Germans so they can manipulate their farm quotas. I heard two neighbours whispering outside the *Boulangerie* last week."

Refuge on the Farm

Josette walked past the *Maire's* house with its grey painted wooden shutters and the large stone barns of her neighbours. The slanting light of the setting sun shone through the bare branches of oak trees lining the lanes. She had lived in Broussac for twenty years having met Alain at a *fete* in St Martial, and married him a year later. Alain's family had farmed in this area of the Aveyron for generations and she loved their ancient home which was a typical 'high-house'. It had three floors with an exterior stone stair leading to a covered porch over the main entrance. The *cave* or cellar was located at street level with a stone trough running the length of one side. It was used to house cattle in the cold winter months. The living room and large kitchen were on the first floor. The kitchen had an alcove on the north side with a vaulted ceiling called a *souillarde* or pantry. This was a cold place to store preserves, cheese and vegetables. Family bedrooms were on the second floor with access to a large attic. The farmhouse had a *pigeonnerie* (dovecot) on one side with a steep slate roof. Holes in the walls of the *pigeonnerie* allowed pigeons to fly in and out. They were kept for their meat and their droppings used to fertilise the vines. The roof tiles on both buildings were shaped like scallop shells which overlapped each other.

Josette walked up the twelve broad stone steps and unlocked the carved wooden front door with a large brass key. She hung it on a hook inside the pantry and put her patchwork bag down on the scrubbed wooden kitchen table. Although it was sunny outside, the two-foot-thick stone walls retained the cold and the wood burning stove glowed with logs. A blue patterned enamel coffee pot simmered on the hob and a vegetable *ragout* was cooking in an orange metal casserole inside. She washed her hands in the stone sink and dried them on a striped linen serviette. She poured a cup of coffee into a china bowl before sitting at the table to ponder the threat from the Germans. She must find somewhere safe for Martin to hide during the winter months. He was 17 and the right age for the *STO Releve*.

He had evaded capture for the *Releve* in the summer and was hidden in the cellar beneath their cow barn. Entrance to the cellar was at the top of a grassy ramp, protected by heavy wooden doors which had been locked since the war started to deter thieves and vagrants. The solid iron key to open the doors was big and heavy and usually hung on a hook in the pantry.

Alain was ploughing the storm-damaged *tournesols* (sunflowers) into the earth and would not return till dusk. He worked non-stop during daylight hours as he had little help, only two old men using hand scythes to cut down the *tournesols*. Thrashing the seeds from the flowerheads and collecting them was a task for his wife.

A few tears of despair rolled down her cheeks as she thought about her handsome son becoming either a refugee or transported to labour in a German factory. Alain was a taciturn man whose sole concern was to ensure the family farm survived through the war and to maintain a working relationship with the *Maire*. Alain had suggested that Martin hide in the cellar temporarily but wouldn't discuss other options. There were gaps in the thick stone walls of the cellar to let in air and light and when the milk cows returned from the fields in the evening, they generated warmth. Alain had cemented the floor of the cow barn several winters before, so there was no seepage from their droppings.

Liliane had suggested Martin could join Michel and Gilles in hiding but it was a risky solution as he must travel at night to their place of refuge. Josette couldn't decide whether to confide in Alain or find another place for Martin to hide. Winter in the Aveyron was long with thick frosts and heavy snowfalls in January and February. Village tracks would soon be impassable with ice and snow and the earth hardened, so no work was done in the fields.

After much deliberation, Josette decided the safest solution was for Martin to join Michel and Gilles in hiding. She started packing thick clothing and two wool blankets in a clean sack. She put fresh apples and cheese in a basket with dense loaves of bread that would keep for days and not turn mouldy. She decided to go to Liliane's house in the morning after her friend had finished her daily bread round. She could leave the items with Liliane and arrange a time when Martin could leave. She wouldn't tell Alain until the deed was done, so there was less risk of him forbidding her. Josette suspected that, deep down, Alain thought Martin should conform and enlist for the *STO Releve* in support of Vichy France requirements.

That night, the temperature dropped below zero and frost rimed the roofs of houses and barns, settling on stone walls. Josette had talked over her plan with Martin before dusk fell and Alain returned for his dinner. She gave her son a warm blanket, a metal dish of hot *ragout* and brought in extra hay for him to lie on and pull round him. She carried an armful of chopped logs from the *cave* in two loads and stacked them in the porch.

She added a few extra to the kitchen stove and went down a third time to get apples for a *tarte tatin* and a bottle of local red wine. Alain got his wine in bulk from the local vineyard in exchange for jars of honey and milk. He kept ten beehives which he moved regularly on a cart attached to his tractor, depending on which plants were flowering. In winter, the hives were covered and placed in a barn.

Darkness had blotted out the outlines of barns and forests when Josette heard Alain's tractor rattle into the yard. She lit a kerosene lamp and opened the kitchen door. Her youngest son, Luca rushed in laughing and placed cold hands on her bare forearms. He tugged off his woollen hat and scarf, his coat and boots, leaving them on the floor by the door and ran over to stand by the wood stove. Alain followed more slowly, removing his thick gloves and rubbing his hands together briskly. He sat down at the table and pulled off his mud-caked boots, placing them outside in the porch. A distinct odour of cow manure wafted through the kitchen. He pecked Josette on the cheek before taking off his heavy coat and hanging it on the back of the kitchen door. Luca sat at the table, chattering about the work he'd done and the birds he'd seen.

"*Maman, J'ai faim*. I'm starving. I saw a hawk pounce on a mouse as it ran out of the *tournesols*. It flew up to the big oak tree with the mouse hanging out of its beak. We saw a fox running across the lane as we drove into the farmyard.

Papa thinks it has stolen a chicken. I hope it's not one of ours. *Maman*, what's for dinner tonight?"

Normal life seemed to return to the village in the early weeks of winter although there had been no word from the young men in hiding. No news was heard from the captured youths either, only rumours that they were held in an internment camp whilst waiting to be transported to German factories. It was becoming evident that some villagers saw the Vichy regime and German rule as a means of improving their income. They were suspected of hoarding garden produce in cellars to avoid sharing with less fortunate neighbours and the legal obligation to register their food with the Germans. Others were poaching wild animals at night or stealing pigs from outlying farms. Villagers suspected that old M'sieur Compiegne had an arrangement with the local *gendarmes* to hide stolen game in the earth floor of his sheep hut.

Hardship

Winter hardened its iron grip with ice glazing house windows and steps, and frost lying thick in the lanes. Under a full moon, ice-coated plants in fields and hedgerows sparkled like sculptures in a gallery. Glistening frost-covered tree branches were etched against the black sky when Liliane and Joseph set out before dawn to search for the hidden youths. Josette and Paulette had given them food and knitted items that were smuggled out of the village in two panniers attached to one donkey. Two extra panniers slung on another donkey were crammed with fresh bread and cheese, and two earthenware pots of bean casserole. Liliane had dressed in her old clothes with a warm shawl round her shoulders for protection against the cold, serviceable boots and a scarf over her face to avoid recognition. Joseph wore thick cotton trousers and shirt and a heavy wool jacket. He tucked his hunting rifle in the bottom of a pannier. They left early to avoid nosy neighbours asking questions about their destination and had muffled the donkey hoofs with cloths.

Joseph led the way out of the village using a cart track that traversed the village from riverbank to forest. They rode in single file as they joined the steep cobbled Roman road between crumbling dry-stone walls overgrown with rampant vegetation. He guided them out of the thick forest onto a high wind-blown arid plateau, *la causse*. The silence and loneliness of the plateau was intimidating. It was an unpopulated area due to lack of fertile soil and continuous drying winds. In winter, it was bitterly cold with heavy frosts and regular snowfalls. No one had lived here for a generation and the few isolated buildings were abandoned. The youths could be hiding in these or in the forested hills.

Liliane and Joseph alighted from their donkeys in the shelter of a copse of ancient gnarled oaks. Joseph tethered the donkeys to a large oak tree and gave his hunter's call followed by an imitation of a bird of prey, the kite. Through the filtered light of the trees, they could see ruined farm buildings but no signs of habitation, carcasses of rabbits or shreds of cloth hanging on prickly blackberry bushes. Joseph gave another piercing call, then Liliane spied two heads peering over the yard wall. Joseph put his hand out to delay Liliane from rushing forward. "*Soyez prudent*. Careful. We must be sure they've not been discovered," he whispered cautiously. Joseph sidled between the trees and silently approached the farmhouse, gesturing to the youths to stay hidden. "*Soyez prudent. Tais-toi.* Careful. Be quiet. We could have been followed."

Joseph held out his hand to shake the dirty hands of Michel and Gilles and beckoned Liliane over to greet them. He left the donkeys hidden in the trees as they walked cautiously across the yard that was littered with broken farm equipment to the battered barn door which creaked as the youths heaved it ajar.

"We discovered this deserted farm a while ago when we were searching for shelter from a heavy thunderstorm that was crashing over the *causse*. The roof is badly damaged except in one corner, so we crouched out of the drenching rain and fierce wind. We didn't light a fire." Gilles paused for breath.

Michel continued, "We escaped capture in the village by running blindly up a track into the woods. We blundered on for hours over rough ground, desperately hoping that we weren't being chased by the *Milice*."

Gilles took over the story, "We're strong and young but the thick undergrowth and closely packed trees hindered us and drained our energy. We crossed a rocky stream trying to balance on stones and came to a fork but couldn't decide which track to take. Through the tree branches, we could see heavy dark clouds and daylight fading fast. We reached the edge of the forest and saw ahead the desolate empty space of the *causse* just as the sun disappeared."

Michel continued with the story of their escape. "We had to find a hiding place where the trees were thickest to keep off the rain. We'd no idea if the *causse* was inhabited."

Gilles nodded and said, "We walked back until we found a hollow filled with dead leaves under a large sweet chestnut tree. It had shed its leaves early because of the dry summer. We were desperately hungry and poked around, digging up chestnuts, peeling the spiky cases and ate them raw. We lay on the ground among dead crackly leaves and huddled together. We could hear the rustling of small animals in the bushes. We were scared that wild boar would sniff us or deer crash into our hiding place."

"We'd no idea what to do?" Michel whispered. "We had no food or water and couldn't go home in case the *Milice* were searching for us. Gilles huffed and puffed all night trying to sleep but I dozed a bit. When daylight came after a long cold night, we looked around but could see no evidence of being followed."

"We ate raw chestnuts for breakfast and needed a drink but couldn't find a pond or stream," Gilles said. "We had no idea where to go or how to contact our parents."

Michel said they had walked to the edge of the forest and spied the ruined farmhouse ahead on the *causse*. Looking carefully around, they had crept to the main entrance where a broken wooden door was swinging on rusty hinges. Gilles had peered inside and seen heaps of bricks, mangled remains of furniture, and broken kitchen China. The large stone fireplace had obviously not been used for a long time as there were crumbled birds' nests among the old ashes. They searched the house, keeping watch out of the broken windows for inhabitants.

"OK. Let's camp here," Gilles had suggested. "We need shelter from the weather and wild animals. I'll look for somewhere to sleep and you can search the yard. I don't think we should make a fire as the smoke will be seen." Michel had wandered outside and found an old well next to the barn. When he lifted the wooden lid, he saw a metal bucket hanging on a rusty chain and dipped it down to scoop up some brackish water.

Michel interrupted, "Looking over the *causse* I thought I knew where we were. I had a family picnic near here for my fifteenth birthday. I remember we had climbed up the Roman Road and used a donkey to carry the picnic basket and rug. We must have circled round in the forest. I hope my parents remember and wonder if we're hiding here."

Gilles said there had been a strong smell of rot and decay and dust clouded the air when they sat on the earth floor. "We used well water to wash face and hands but our clothes are thick with dirt and have large holes made by briars and branches as we clambered through the undergrowth. We slept on the dusty kitchen floor on mouldy straw mattresses I found in a bedroom."

That night they had heaved the warped door shut and heard scrabbling across the floorboards as mice and rats ran away from the intruders. During the long night in the dense silence, Gilles heard a vixen's harsh bark and flapping of a barn owl's wings. "I huddled closer to Michel, needing his warm body and the sound of his breathing. We crept out at dawn to search for berries to eat and found blackberry brambles and red rose hips growing wild in the hedges and stunted plum trees. In the garden of the farmhouse, we collected fallen apples and dug up wrinkled potatoes and carrots from an old *potager*. We found a broken chicken coop with three scraggy hens but no eggs."

Michel continued the tale. "We discussed what to do. Should we creep back to Broussac and hope the *Milice* had left or try to cross the *causse* and head east for Cahors? We could walk south to Rodez but the Germans are based there."

"We decided to stay here for a while and hope someone from the village found us. My father knows the hunting trails well," Gilles had decided. "Let's search for bits to make an animal trap. We could catch a rabbit and cook it at night. There's plenty of firewood." Gilles complained he was feeling griping pains in his stomach through lack of food. "My mother's a good cook and her meals are great despite wartime rationing."

"Heavy rain clouds had darkened the yard and forest as I returned from his trap-setting with wood for a small fire," Michel said. "We were glad to be together and safe. We stayed in the shelter of the farmhouse, scavenging for food in the forest but we were scared to roam the *causse*. Last week, we heard warplanes flying low overhead heading for Toulouse. We hid in the trees for the rest of the day."

Gilles continued, chewing his dry lips. "It's been hard and we're starving but safe. Then this morning, we heard footsteps outside the broken kitchen window and crawled across the floor to peer through the broken window. We could see dark shadows on the forest edge and a donkey."

"I think someone's found us," Michel had whispered to Gilles. "I don't think it's Germans or the *Milice* because they wouldn't use donkeys. I'll stand by the window. You hide in case I'm wrong and the donkey is a bait to capture us."

Michel had recognised the dark clothed figure as he walked cautiously from the forest. "It's Joseph. We're rescued." In his eagerness, Michel had climbed out of the broken kitchen window and waved to Joseph and the woman with him. "It's Tante Liliane and they've brought donkeys with paniers," Michel had shouted excitedly. "Come on, they've found us and we're saved." Gilles had climbed out of the window and ran across to the edge of the forest. Liliane pulled both youths to her and hugged them.

"*Mon Dieu*. Your maman was right! She remembered your birthday picnic, Michel, and thought this deserted farmhouse might be a good hiding place." Liliane let the youths pull out of her embrace and wiped her tears. "We must get the donkeys inside and unpack the food and blankets. We saw no sign of Germans or *the Milice* when we were riding here, so you should be safe for a while longer. We must return to the village by dusk."

"We don't want to arouse the suspicion of nosy neighbours." Joseph said briskly, not wanting to show his emotion.

Liliane unpacked the panniers, taking out two blankets, packets of cheese, fresh bread and a bag of vegetables. "I've brought two pots of vegetable stew. They're packed in straw, so I hope they're still warm. I don't think you should be lighting fires even though the farmhouse seems deserted. Stay indoors during the day and go out at night. It must be hard to be away from your family and camping here but it's safe for now."

Joseph agreed and said, "When I was searching for you, I met several youths from other villages hiding in the forest to the east of here. They said the Germans have trawled the whole area. They are young men like you escaping from the STO, the *Service de Travail Obligatoire*. I will try to find them on our next visit and ask if they can help you. I'll bring more food in a week and show you how to set traps for small animals. You must be careful as I suspect there are locals who want to be friendly with the Germans to get more food and may use you to trade for it."

They sat on the dusty straw bales and shared the food, the hungry youths eating voraciously, shovelling the bread soaked in juice into their mouths. Liliane and Joseph ate little recognising that the youths needed food to supplement their scavenging and conserve their strength. When they had finished eating, Liliane packed the remaining meal into bowls covered by cloths and placed them in a dusty wall cupboard. "Eat sparingly and this should last for a few days," she said.

Joseph and Liliane unhitched the donkeys' reins from the broken newel post of the rickety wooden stairs. Joseph shook the youths' hands and Liliane kissed their cheeks. "*A bientot. Soyez prudent*. Bye and take care," she said quietly trying not to cry because the lonely scared boys must spend more time in hiding. The youths went back inside the wrecked farmhouse kitchen feeling miserable and lonely. "I think we should save the cheese and bread and the rest of the stew for tomorrow." Gilles said between mouthfuls. "At least, our parents know where we are."

Michel nodded, "I don't feel scared but we must keep watch. We can take shifts. I'll stay awake for three hours, then you take over. Tante Liliane and Joseph were very cautious meeting us, so someone may be suspicious in our village." He felt inside the kitchen chimneybreast and shoved some of the bread and cheese into a space where a brick had been dislodged. "Better to hide the food in different places."

He peered out the broken window, noticed the yard was empty. "I'll fill the empty pots with water from the well bucket. At least, we won't be thirsty."

Gilles sat on the dusty stone floor and hugged his knees to his chest, resting his chin on them, staring vacantly across the kitchen. He wondered where his brother Martin was—still safely at home or captured by the Germans? His life had been pleasant and ordered in a comfortable home, plenty to eat and he loved working with the farm animals.

Michel came into the kitchen carrying two pots brimming with water. "I had a good look around and crawled up that hill over there to check we were alone. I wanted to be sure no one had followed Tante Liliane and Joseph. I think we should board up the broken kitchen window and heave the door shut. It's hanging from two hinges but gives some protection. Joseph left candles and matches for emergencies. It's getting dark, so let's get this kitchen secure in the last bit of light."

"Ok." Gilles got up to help with the repairs then lay curled up on a blanket on the stone floor, trying not to worry. Michel sat by the fireplace with his back against the wall, hugging his knees and peered through the chinks in the warped timber.

Liliane and Joseph rode back through the forest and down a muddy lane that was seldom used by the villagers. Bats were swooping around the rooftops mingling with chirping birds as they darted into nests built in the eaves. They led the donkeys to the rear entrance of Joseph's barn, tethered them securely then Joseph sauntered into the *Place de la Mairie*, nodded to Paulette and ordered a *pastis* for himself and old Michel.

Doors and windows of homes were open to the crisp country air and families were eating their dinner outside on stone terraces enjoying the last rays of the sinking sun. Climbing roses and wisteria that covered the stone walls had lost their leaves and pots of brilliant geraniums and begonias that filled the steps were brown. Laughter and light conversation filtered between the houses interrupted occasionally by a barking dog. Liliane popped into the *Boulangerie*, changed her thick coat and boots for her normal clothes and let Jean-Jacques, know she'd returned safely. "I'll go across to the café and sit with Josette and Paulette for a while."

She looked around at the café patrons and acknowledged the *Maire* and his wife, noticing that he seemed nervous and unsure. He had posted a notice on the board outside the *Mairie* that morning stating that the Germans were settling into the main towns of the Aveyron and the Lot, Rodez and Cahors.

They were checking train arrivals and departures at the stations and monitoring goods at weekly markets. The notice warned the villagers that the *Maire* was to inform the Germans in Rodez if he found locals selling or buying goods illegally or hoarding food and crops.

After half an hour, Liliane returned home to prepare the family's evening meal. She was quietly chopping vegetables in the kitchen and throwing them into a casserole pot when her daughter, Rose-Marie burst in. Her face was pale and her eyes flickered around the room nervously.

"What is it, *ma cherie*?" Liliane asked. "What's happened?"

"*Maman, Maman*, I was worried about you because you went out early. M'sieur Pascal brought two *gendarmes* to the school today who instructed us to tell them if we knew of anyone hoarding food. They threatened to search every barn and house for black market goods and for young men hiding from the *STO Releve*."

Liliane stopped chopping and tightly hugged her distraught daughter. She and Joseph had been extremely careful descending from the forest and hoped no one had seen them hiding the donkeys. Tomorrow morning, she would return Josette's animal to her. "Sshsh. *N'inquiete pas*. Don't worry, Rose-Marie. The boys are safe where the Germans won't find them but we had to take them food and blankets. I don't know if any of our customers would hoard food or sell crops illegally but it's wicked of the *gendarmes* to frighten children. Was one of the *gendarmes* Serge Pellier? His mother will be horrified to hear he's making threats. Now, go and wash your face and hands and bring a smile to the table for your papa and brother."

"*D'accord, Maman*. But my friends are frightened too. We don't understand why *Gendarme Pellier* and M'sieur Pascal are helping the Germans."

"War forces people to behave differently, so they can feed their families and keep them safe. You must tell me or your papa if you notice your friends are unhappy at school and your papa will talk to Madame Ziegler. Many older people in this village lived through the Great War and had bad experiences of the Germans, so they are worried for their family. Broussac is a friendly village where everyone knows everyone else. The Germans are based in large towns like Cahors and Rodez on the main railway line between Paris and Toulouse. They're not interested in country people except to provide their soldiers with food. Papa and I will keep you safe."

"*Merci, Maman*. What's for dinner? *Ragout?* Is it vegetable stew again?"

Liliane kissed her head and nodded before resuming her preparations for the stew. She was deeply concerned and decided to talk with Jean-Jacques in bed that night.

Oppression in Cahors

In late January, Jean-Jacques drove Liliane in his yellow 1930s Renault van to the nearest station, Lalbenque, where she waited for a train to Cahors. It was a cold frosty morning and she pulled her woollen coat tight around her body and secured her scarf more firmly. Outside the station, she noticed a few farmers wives sheltering from the cold wind and clutching straw baskets with linen covers tied tightly on top. She wondered whether they were going to the market in Cahors or visiting family. Two *gendarmes* were standing near the entrance, their gun holsters attached to a black leather belt. One of them looked bored and was smoking a cigarette. The other she recognised as *Gendarme* Pellier. He shrugged his shoulders and muttered some words to his fellow soldier. They stood to attention as the train whistled its approach into the station, hissing and spitting clouds of steam as it approached the platform. The metal framework of the station awning was blackened by soot, the smuts glinting in the rays of sunlight and sprinkling coats and hats.

Gendarme Pellier moved to the station exit and scrutinised people waiting to leave. Liliane looked up at the large metal clock and noticed the train was late. She joined the queue waiting to board, clutching her identity card and signed *Attestation* letter from the *Maire* with one hand and her suitcase with the other. She slowed her breathing as her papers were checked and she was ordered to board. She could see German flags hanging from the roof of the station. People waiting on the platform surged forward to embrace friends and relatives.

Passengers waiting to board picked up cases and cardboard boxes. Farmers' wives hung straw baskets on their arms and clutched the hands of small children as they herded them into dusty carriages.

She found a seat in a carriage at the back, squashed between an old lady wearing black, holding a straw basket, its contents covered by a cotton cloth, and an officious *gendarme* who peered at her closely. Paper and fruit stones were squashed on the floor under the slatted wooden seats and a strong odour of unwashed bodies and animal dung permeated the smoke-filled carriage.

The train set off after ten minutes, the carriages jerking as they realigned with the engine. They crossed icy lanes and roads on iron bridges, the whistle startling cattle browsing in ploughed fields. The train stopped at a small country station, the destination sign painted over, to allow passengers to alight and locals to board.

It speeded up for ten minutes before slowing to enter Cahors station emitting clouds of dark smoke which shrouded the carriages. Liliane stood up as the train stopped by the platform, clutched her case and held the bag with her identity documents close to her body as she manoeuvred past the old woman fumbling with her scarf and basket. Alighting on the platform, she noticed *Milice* were scrutinising each passenger as they walked towards the exit. Dirty grey smoke and steam from the engine obscured the end of the station adding to the air of gloom caused by the heavily clouded sky. Rain was splattering on the station roof and passengers hurriedly buttoned up their coats.

Liliane walked briskly to the exit and showed her identity papers to the *Milice.* As she looked for her cousin, she noticed the streets were empty. There were no cafes open with their bright metal tables and chairs on the pavement. A wintry wind blew damp brown leaves around her feet and bare trees swayed and tossed, rasping against the stone buildings.

A few wooden carts stood on the road outside the station and Liliane was relieved to see her cousin, Pierre, sitting at the front of a blue-painted cart; his strong calloused hands holding the reins harnessed to a brown horse. He was wearing a thick wool jacket and a flat black cap with a waterproof cape over his shoulders as protection against the heavy rain. He smoked a cigarette stub and stamped his booted feet on the wooden board to keep warm. He had a carpentry business on the north bank of the river which he'd inherited from his father. Logs were chopped in the forests surrounding the town, lashed together and floated down to his warehouse. He was skilful at constructing kitchen furniture and elegant salon pieces on demand.

Pierre looked up and raised his hand to Liliane. She slung her bag over one shoulder and tightly clutched her suitcase as she stepped up to the front seat. She kissed his cold cheeks and placed her suitcase behind the front bench. There were several items of carved wood lying in the back tray, partially covered by a ragged horse blanket.

"*Bonjour, ma cherie'. Tu va bien avec la famille et Jean-Jacques?*" Pierre said with a big smile and kissed her on either cheek as he wrapped the waterproof cape over both of them. "You and Jean-Jacques are well? It's a long time since we met for my daughter's wedding. What a beautiful summer's day that was." He lowered his voice and continued, "We'll talk about other matters at home. I'll drive through the quiet back roads. The *Milice* are scrutinising every train arrival and departure."

"I'm glad you wore dark clothes and a scarf on your head." Pierre shook the reins and clicked to the horse, "*Allez, allez. Vite, vite.* Go quickly," he shouted at the horse. He manoeuvred skilfully round other vehicles and passengers milling at the station entrance and headed for Boulevard Leon Gambetta. The main street was lined with beautiful nineteenth century stone buildings, among which were the *Hotel de Ville* and the *Palais de Justice*. There were spacious squares filled with cafes and restaurants. Cahors had been built on a Roman settlement and prospered in the Middle Ages. In 1308, the beautiful cathedral of St Etienne was built.

Pierre reached the end of the Boulevard and drove down towards a bridge spanning the width of the River Lot. He joined a queue of wooden carts and laden donkeys. Liliane could see a barricade at the entrance and *Milice* scrutinising travellers. As they reached the middle of the wide-spanned stone bridge, they saw an old man on a bike being stopped and his bike flung to the ground. He was hauled into a military jeep, shouting desperately, "*Au secours*, help." Nobody assisted him when his coat was pulled open and they could see the yellow star identifying him as a Jew fixed to his collar.

Pierre and Liliane kept their heads down as they passed a sentry box at the bridge exit manned by two *Milice*. Pierre guided his horse to the right and ascended a steep cobbled lane leading to a collection of houses built on the cliffs overlooking the river Lot. Liliane looked down at the town, noting the medieval bridge '*Le Pont du Valentre*' with its towers at either end and one in the middle.

"Liliane, you're brave to deliver my messages but I think it's getting too dangerous as I'm being followed. The *Milice* are growing increasingly aggressive and there have been denunciations by folk who suspect their neighbours are using the black market or are practising Jews. The *Milice* regularly inspect my workshop and new wood as it arrives to check for messages from the *maquis* secreted inside hollow logs." Pierre frowned and squeezed Liliane's hand. "*Sois prudent*, Liliane."

The River Lot, swollen by autumnal rains, rushed and splashed over the weir and against the low banks. Riverside cafes were boarded up and an air of gloom hung over the city, enhanced by dark rain clouds. It took five minutes up a steep winding track to reach Pierre's home. He was a school teacher and lived in the attached house with his family. It had a carved wooden door painted a faded blue with a brass ring knocker. The window shutters, also painted blue, were partly shut to keep out the cold.

The cart drew to a halt by the door, which promptly opened and a plump pretty woman came out of the front door wearing a worried frown.

"*Bonjour, Liliane. Comment allez vous?*" Simone smiled as she welcomed Liliane, kissing her on both cheeks. She reached out to take her case before ushering them inside to the kitchen heated by a round wood burning stove, a cast iron *Godin*. Her children, two pretty girls and a small boy sat waiting expectantly at the wooden table which had been laid for lunch with an embroidered cloth. They slid off their chairs and came to greet Liliane. "*Bonjour, Tante Liliane,*" the girls said politely.

"*B'jour, Tante,*" Hugo lisped and caught hold of her skirt asking to be lifted into Liliane's arms which she did, bestowing a light kiss on his soft hair. Paulette and Chantal stood waiting for welcoming kisses and an embrace.

"*Bonjour, mes petites. Vous etes belles, mes cousins.*"

"*Asseyez vous, Tante Liliane entre Paulette et moi.*" Chantal said excitedly. "Sit between my sister and me. *Maman* has made a special casserole for lunch. Would you like wine as papa will?"

Liliane complied as the children re-seated themselves, picking up spoons and taking a hunk of bread from the basket. Simone brought an orange metal casserole dish to the table, placed it on a metal grid. She used a copper ladle to spoon the steaming contents into china bowls. The children dipped their bread in and slurped the liquid in their spoons.

"*Bon appetit*," Simone said as she picked up her bread from the table cloth. "*Il y a beaucoup des legumes et quelques pieces de saucisson. C'est difficile a trouver du boeuf ou de l'agneau maintenant.* I hope you like sausage and vegetable stew. There's no meat available now."

It was quiet while the family savoured their food, serenaded by a clutch of chickens gathered outside the open kitchen door. When the family had finished eating, Simone told the children to play in their attic bedroom while she and Liliane cleared the table and washed up. The youngsters climbed noisily up the twisting wooden stairs, already arguing what game to play. Simone pulled a heavy brocade curtain across the bottom of the stairs and walked to the table to sit down.

"Have a coffee and tell us why you've come to Cahors to visit this nest of Germans?" Pierre asked. "Our house walls are thick and I have taken the precaution of barring the doors and closing the shutters."

"I don't think anyone will be climbing up to peer in the attic windows where the children are playing," he continued with a wry smile.

Liliane nodded and took a deep breath starting on a cautious note. "I wanted to check how you are. Our *Maire* receives official orders from the *Prefecture* but we get no news of the invasion and the location of the Germans. We're not permitted to use radio transmitters to hear what's happening in the rest of France and Europe. Our *Maire* seems to be indecisive because he needs to keep his job and his home. Food shortages and rationing make it difficult to feed the family at home." Liliane hesitated and took a sip of thick dark coffee to calm her nerves.

"Many young men living in the villages have been captured and transported to work in German factories, so it's the old men and the women who must work in the fields to satisfy German food and crop requisitions. We feel a deep sense of isolation and unease in our village." Liliane sighed heavily, wiping her mouth on a handkerchief tucked in her dress pocket. She bowed her head and whispered, "They've taken my Armand and his friends, Jean-Paul and Claude to work in their factories. Two sons of my friends have escaped capture by running to the hills. They are hiding in a deserted farmhouse on the *causse* but they cannot stay there during winter." Liliane wiped a few tears from her eyes and shrugged hopelessly.

Pierre put a comforting arm across her taut shoulders and looked to his wife who shook her head. "We feel an increasing sense of oppression as the Germans are approaching the town. Children are scared. We've seen people being dragged from their homes, beaten then thrown into trucks. This happened to our dear neighbours, Henri and Marie last week. We didn't know they were Jews even though we've known them for years. Their children played with ours." Pierre nodded sadly. He gritted his teeth as he continued. "We get no real news either and wonder if the Allies will invade and rescue us one day."

Simone nodded. "I still go to the market but the stalls are half empty and much of the produce is wrinkled. *Gendarmes* patrol constantly and help themselves to the best things. Everyone has to be very careful what they say to neighbours and friends because there is increasing suspicion of food hoarders and black marketeers."

Pierre continued, "Since December, there have been electricity shortages and shops must obey a 5 pm curfew. Food rations are always being cut and we need ration cards for everything."

"There is propaganda material everywhere. Petrol in towns north of the Lot has been requisitioned by the Germans and locals have to use charcoal gasoline for essential vehicles. Carts are pulled by donkey or horse. We feel constantly anxious and insecure as there are many denouncements and instant reprisals for people hiding guns, radio transmitters, Jews or hoarding food. We insist the children go to school with me."

Pierre sat with his head bowed on his arms for a few moments of despair then looked up and laid a hand on Liliane's arm. "You're welcome to stay for a few days but I think it would be safer if you left on the train tomorrow."

Liliane sat stiffly, twisting her hands in her lap. She had not known the situation had become so dire in Cahors as her last visit had been a year ago. She wished she'd brought a basket of farm produce like the old lady on the train but thought it would probably have been confiscated when she left the station. She lowered her voice and said, "I think you're right and I'll leave tomorrow but I have a favour to ask. Do you know of any young men joining the *maquis* in the Lot?"

"Well, I know there have been local acts of resistance and damage to statues by young men who arrive at night and disappear quickly into the forests. There is also an underground press. I can't tell you any more or write to you as letters sent through *La Poste* are intercepted. It's like being in prison!" Pierre shook his head angrily. "My classes at school are interrupted by official inspections and several of my pupils are too frightened to come. When will this end? I worry constantly about the safety of my kids and my pupils."

The children ran down from the attic, dressed for bed and kissed their aunt goodnight. Liliane hugged the warm little bodies tightly not knowing when they would see each other again. A few tears trickled down her cheeks which she hastily wiped away. The adults went to bed shortly after, Liliane sleeping on a makeshift bed in the kitchen. She had a restless night and rose early to get the first train out of Cahors. Pierre was alone waiting for her in the kitchen. "I must tell Madame Cantou I'm being watched and the Nazis are suspicious. She is a secret intermediary between the *maquis* group based in the Lot and those in the Aveyron." Pierre pressed small piece of paper into her hand. Liliane pushed it in her vest between her breasts. "*D'accord. N'inquiete pas.* Don't worry."

Pierre brought his cart to the front of his house and Liliane climbed up quickly and sat close to her cousin. She noticed in the early daylight that his face was thin and grey with worry, his wrists and hands holding the reins were skin and bone. He drove her to the station, pointing out the empty pavement cafes in the beautiful grand central square. He stopped in a side street behind the station, embraced her and said, "*Bon courage, ma cousine.*" Liliane kissed him on both cheeks and nodded to confirm she'd deliver the note to Madame Cantou.

She grabbed her suitcase and jumped down from the cart. She walked past elegant stone town houses with wrought iron balconies that were shuttered and unoccupied, their owners having fled south. She turned left into a narrow street and hurried to the station. She showed her identity papers to the *Milice* at the station entrance and ran to open a carriage door just as the train built up steam to hiss its way out of the station. The line ran over the many arched high railway bridge then headed southeast into the Aveyron.

Liliane alighted from the train and realised she'd had no chance to tell her husband of her early arrival at Lalbenque. She decided to get the rural bus which ran a service to the large village nearest to Broussac, St Martial. She walked to the village *Mairie* and asked the clerk to phone *the Maire* at Broussac to let Jean-Jacques know she was walking home from the station. It was a cold sunny day with a chill wind and the distance was three kilometres down a paved road. It gave Liliane time to think over what she had learned in Cahors.

She was deeply concerned over the whereabouts and condition of her son Armand and his friends Jean-Paul and Claude captured by the Germans several weeks ago. Liliane thought despairingly that was the last day when everything felt normal in Broussac and the future bright even though the Germans had invaded Northern France. She would speak with Paulette and Josette tomorrow and try to contact the local *maquis* who might give support to Michel and Gilles. The wintry weather compounded their vulnerability living on the *causse*. There were heavy snowfalls after Christmas and wild animals hibernated, so there would be nothing to eat.

Just after Liliane left Cahors, on 11 November 1942, German troops invaded the Free Zone (*zone libre*). Cahors was strategically important being located on the main Paris to Toulouse train line. It was declared a closed city and traffic in and out was banned with barricades erected at road bridges. Its inhabitants were only allowed to travel by foot and bicycle.

The Hotel Terminus became the headquarters of the Feld Gendarmerie (Army field command) and German railway workers. The Kommandantur lodged in the Hotel Europe on Rue Wilson, near *La Poste*, with Gestapo agents.

Liliane managed to contact her cousin Pierre by phone at *La Poste* in St Martial. He described the awful difference in the town of his birth. Large oppressive Nazi flags hung over every door and German official notices were affixed to walls bearing the swastika symbol of the Nazis. He said the citizens were short of everything, including electricity and shop-lighting was forbidden after 5 pm. Food rations were further reduced and ration cards were issued for everything.

"*Sois prudent. Je vous aime.*" Liliane replied. "*Bon courage.*"

Rescue by the Maquis

The weather turned colder, frosts hardening the edges of lanes and ploughed fields as bitter winds swept down from Russia. Heaps of firewood were stacked next to kitchen hearths and shutters barred against the weather. Few people visited the café and the *Epicerie*, but there was always a queue in the *Boulangerie* where it was warmed by the brick oven. Neighbours greeted each other politely but briefly, eager to get back indoors. There were few attendees at the local church which had no heating. Only the deeply religious sat shivering in thick coats and scarves. France had been declared a secular country at the beginning of the twentieth century, so regular church going was not expected.

Joseph made a lone trip to the *causse* hiding place with supplies for Michel, Martin and Gilles. He had taken Martin, Josette's son to join them as it was safer for him than living in the cellar of their cow barn. He reported that could see no evidence of Germans, so they could light a fire in the farmhouse for cooking and warmth. The youths were thin but managing.

Michel and Gilles had been cautiously pleased to see their friend Martin but anxious about their food supply. They had created mattresses for themselves using loose hay stuffed into the food sacks previously brought by Joseph. Martin used the blankets his mother had packed for him. Broken windows and doors were blocked with old boards torn up from the upstairs floor. Michel collected discarded bricks to build a small hearth for warmth and cooking inside the kitchen. They were surviving with Joseph's food parcels and trapping woodland animals but were fearful of discovery and survival during the bitter winter months.

Sitting round the tiny wood fire that evening, Martin told them about the increasing atmosphere of unease in Broussac with fierce bouts of anger between neighbours due to the shortage of food and suspected hoarding. "People are scared," he said. "The *Maire* has no information concerning the location of the Germans and the *gendarmes* are becoming more aggressive in their demands for supplies of grain, food and animals. Madame Pellier's chickens were raided and Madame Royal's pig stolen. My parents are herding their beef and dairy cattle into locked barns at night."

As the full moon rose over the countryside, the youths settled down to sleep in the warm kitchen after checking that the fire had been stifled and windows and doors were secured.

Several days later, Gilles woke suddenly and sat up. Something had disturbed him and he felt uneasy. Sharp rays of moonlight filtered through the broken shutters and striped the floorboards in the farm kitchen. It was completely silent and he crawled over to the door to peer through a split in the wood at knee level. In the bright moonlight, he could see four hooded figures standing beyond the farmyard wall holding weapons. He desperately hoped they weren't *gendarmes* or soldiers as he could see no tell-tale glints on metal buttons or buckles.

He woke Martin and Michel with a whispered instruction to hide in the pantry. Joseph had brought the old WW1 rifle and left it for them to use. Gilles checked it was loaded, quietly unbarred the door to crack it open. Torchlight blinded him and he felt a weapon poking him in the chest. He was skewered in the beam like a wild rabbit in a trap. He stepped to one side, careful to put his rifle on the ground and held his hands over his head. Two hooded men stepped into the room whilst two other men stood guard in the shadows outside.

Gilles bravely said, "*Dites-moi qui cherchez-vous? Je suis un paysan de Broussac et je cherche les noix pour ma maman.* Who do you want? I'm collecting chestnuts and walnuts for my mother."

"*Combien de personnes habitent ici? La maison est vide, n'est ce pas?*" The taller man removed his dark hood with one hand, the other holding the gun pointing in Gilles's chest. "We thought this farmhouse was empty. What are you doing here?" Without taking his eyes from Gilles, he shouted out the kitchen door to the other *maquis* and told them to search the house. They found Michel and Martin hiding in the pantry, dragged them into the kitchen and pushed them to lie face down on the floor.

"We escaped capture by the *gendarmes* who came to our village to take men for the *Releve*. We've been hiding here for a while. We want to join the *maquis.*" Michel lifted his head from the dusty floor, sneezed and spoke loudly and hopefully.

"*Nous sommes le maquis*. We are the *maquis*. Pick up your belongings, give us your guns, cover your faces and follow us. You'll be joining the *Maquis du Lot* and given false names. Jean Un, Jean Deux et Jean Trois. You will always refer to me as *Le Chef. D'accord*?" The youths nodded vigorously, bent to pick up their possessions and stuff them into sacks, slinging their coats and blankets over their arms. *Le Chef* kicked the fire ashes to ensure they weren't smoking and shouldered his gun.

He beckoned his men to follow as he marched out into the moonlit night and onto the *causse*. The men walked lightly and softly to the trees as the youths stumbled behind them. They marched for hours across the stony uneven ground of the *causse*, down a deep ravine clothed in thick forest, and along a river bed. As dawn lightened the sky, the *maquis* halted and told them to crawl through thick shrubs covering a steep rock face. Thorns scratched their faces and hands and tore at their clothes. Ahead in the moonlight, stood a dark figure pointing a gun at them. The *maquis* exchanged a code word and the youths were led inside a deep cave littered with blankets and straw beds on which sat several *maquis*. The cave was lit with a hanging oil lamps and a cassoulet pot hung over a fire.

"*Asseyez. Ces jeunes hommes ont habiter sur la causse. Ils se cachaient a la ferme et veulent joindre le maquis!*" These youths were hiding in an empty farmhouse. They want to join us but must be instructed in the dangers. They could have been followed by *gendarmes.*" *Le Chef* spoke forcefully to the group. "*Ils sont jeunes et negligent*! *Vous dormez ici. Le petit dejeuner est a six heures le matin.* Young people are careless. Sleep here. Breakfast is at 6 am."

The youths silently placed their scant possessions on the sandy floor and spread their blankets. They shuffled together for security in the dimly lit cave. They were unaware that rural resistance groups such as the *maquis* were ill-equipped with arms and relied on locals to provide weapons and food. The youths later discovered that this was not an organised group of *maquis* but merely a collection of young men, *refractaires,* who had escaped capture by the Germans for the *Releve*. They had made a camp on the uninhabited terrain of the *causse*, well away from towns like Cahors, Figeac and Rodez where Germans were now based.

The youths were roughly awakened before daybreak and given dry bread and water to drink. *Le Chef* informed them there would be no communication with external sources including family members. "We know the *Prefects* of the *Departements* of the Lot and Aveyron have been given the names of *refractaires* in order to arrest them. We expect you to obey without question any commands that are given. You will be tested tonight by taking guard duty at dusk. Until then, you stay inside the cave. Can any of you shoot?"

All three youths raised their hands. Michel said, "We were taught to hunt and shoot with rifles by our fathers. We gave you our guns," he continued.

"*De rien*. We'll provide weapons and you can practice at the far end of the cave where there's a straw dummy."

As darkness fell over the forest and *causse*, the youths stood at the entrance to the cave, guarding the *maquis* inside. Michel had been given an old service rifle with a few spare cartridges. Gilles and Martin were each given a pistol and a container of bullets to share. They were on guard duty for three hours. They heard strange noises everywhere—animal grunts and squeaks, the hoot of owls as they rose from treetops on large flapping wings. Grunts and snores from the *maquis* were amplified by the stone walls of the cave. Pale moonlight cast a weird aspect to ordinary objects, emphasising hollow trees and dips in the ground.

A cold gentle rain started falling after an hour, pattering on tree branches and dead brittle leaves piled on the ground. It steadily increased to a solid wall of water and the youths tried to edge further into the cave for shelter. Martin shuddered when he thought he saw a shadow move behind a tree. They could hear a military truck pass on a distant road, the engine loud in the still, damp air. The same thought entered their minds, *'Germans searching for them.'*

They were relieved after a few hours and allowed to sleep inside the cave until daybreak when they were given a sparse breakfast. *Le Chef* brusquely interrogated them, checking their background and schooling, and finally questioning their reasons for joining the *maquis*. Michel and Gilles had discussed this when they hid in the farmhouse so could give honest answers. "We can't work for the enemy, the Germans. We want to fight for our country, our honour, our freedom. Most of the crops and food are taken by the Germans or the *gendarmes* in league with them. There are many farms where the men are dead or prisoners of war and mothers and sisters must take their place in the fields and barns." Gilles stopped abruptly, out-of-breath with patriotic fervour. Michel nodded agreement.

Le Chef listened carefully, smiling sardonically at the innocent zeal of Gilles and Michel. "Why are you here?" He asked staring at young Martin. An awkward silence developed as Martin, the most timid of the youths, clasped his hands tightly and shivered. After a few seconds, he lifted his chin, adjusted his stance and stared directly at *Le Chef*, nervously licking dry lips with his tongue. Gilles and Michel looked aside not wanting to embarrass their school friend whom they had known all their lives.

Martin spoke aggressively covering his fear. "I won't desert my country to help in German factories and make guns to kill my countrymen. My uncles were killed in the Great War and my grandmother suffered terribly because of their death. I won't sit back while my family are starved or harmed by these brutes who think they can conquer Europe by massacring anyone opposed to them." Martin took a deep breath, wiping the spittle from his lips and standing defiantly, legs astride and hands on his hips in front of *Le Chef*.

"*Bravo, bravo mes petits soldats*. Now we understand each other. This is no time for complacency or *faux* patriotism. I know your village and my family is distantly related to Liliane Damour and your father, Alain Favel. *D'accord, allez, allez*. Let's go. We go to a secret training camp and travel by truck, so I must blindfold you. You'll learn how to handle guns."

"*Oui*." *Le Chef* lifted his hand in answer to the worried frowns on their faces. "Someone will let your families know you are safe but not your location. Collect your belongings and the guns you have been given and get into the back of the truck. Now, the adventure begins! Let's see if you have the stamina for fighting or are still puling youngsters." He finished his statement with a snarl and marched out of the cave into the pouring rain, splashing puddles aggressively.

Deprivation

The trees that surrounded Broussac shook their frosted branches as strong north easterly winds whipped around them. The winter sun sank low in the pale sky and no longer cast dappled shadows on buildings and lanes. The dense forests had an opaque impenetrable appearance and was home to boar and deer. The swallows had migrated south to warmer weather in North Africa. Locals rarely stopped to exchange news but scurried between shop, café and church. Market stall holders were wrapped in thick coats and wore knitted scarves and hats, and gloves with no fingers.

Inexorably, the power of the German war machine had impacted the lives of villagers and farmers in the *zone sud*. It felt like an uncontrollable tidal wave was forcing its way inland, destroying houses and barns, fields and forests, people and livestock. The ongoing shortage of basic food for humans and fodder for animals created a deep feeling of anxiety in the local population. There were arguments between women struggling to obtain a few vegetables to feed their families, pushing neighbours aside in their anxiety to buy the last knobbly carrots and potatoes. Housewives hid their provisions and shut kitchen doors so their cooking and the smell of fat wouldn't betray them to their neighbours. Fresh eggs were precious and used to barter for fuel or feed for livestock. The Germans had confiscated all petrol supplies and paid inadequately for the food and crops they regularly requisitioned.

In this atmosphere of misery and deprivation, old jealousies and betrayals that had simmered beneath village life since the Great War, now erupted in loud accusations between women and men. Children sensed the general uneasiness and behaved badly at home and at school. They fought and taunted each other about the importance of their fathers.

"My papa has the biggest farm and the most cows. Your father is just a village baker with no muscles," shouted Pierre to his friend Louis. "We eat meat and have a Citroen to drive in. Your father only has an ancient Renault van!"

"My father is an *artisan boulanger* and makes bread for all the village. Your papa tells secrets to the *Maire* and the *Milice*!" Louis replied angrily. The two boys had been friends, despite their age difference, because their mothers were friendly. Louis was grieving for his older brother Armand who had been captured by the *gendarmes*. His maman and papa seemed sad most of the time and his childhood friend's taunts hurt him deeply. He smacked the stone walls with a stick as he drifted home.

A deep-seated hatred between two local families came to a head the following day when Albert Larzac accused his neighbour, Jules Dufour of having an affair with his wife and demanded compensation. Their shouting match echoed round the village until Albert primed his hunting rifle and fired it at his neighbour's foot. Jumping in pain, Jules Dufour picked up the nearest large stone and flung it at Albert, hitting him on the head and drawing blood. "*Tu est mauvais*. You are evil. I'd like to murder you and your diseased wife!" Jules roared. He limped off as fast as he could down the lane to his house. The locals who had gathered round to watch the fight gradually drifted away and Albert marched off, muttering under his breath.

That evening, a strong smell of burning filled the chill evening air. Plumes of dark smoke erupted into the darkening sky followed by a dull boom. The *Maire* barged out of his office and headed in the direction of the explosion, accompanied by a crowd of interested locals. Within a few minutes, he returned and hurried inside his office to phone the *pompiers*, the fire brigade. Michel, the deputy *Maire* told the locals of the situation.

"Jules has set fire to his neighbour's barn where Albert stores his winter hay and hides munition for his rifle. The wall of the barn has been split apart and the old truck stored there is burnt to a heap of wood and metal. The *Maire* has contacted the *Prefect*ure and demanded a *gendarme* visits the village to investigate the fire and arrest Jules."

Within an hour, the sound of clanging bells disturbed the pigeons on the church tower and set *chasse* dogs barking. A fire engine belching diesel fumes roared up the lane to Albert's barn, followed closely by two *gendarmes* in a truck. By now, the news had circled the village and the locals gathered in the *Place de la Mairie* to follow the excitement. *Gendarme* Pellier appeared marching down the lane with an angry Jules attached to him by a set of handcuffs.

"*Il est stupide.*" Jules shouted, stamping his lame foot and wincing. "He's insane. I wouldn't touch his ugly fat old wife. He's storing illegal crops and firearms in his barn and I found out, so he's punishing me. He's too friendly with the local *gendarmes* and is hiding booze amongst the hay. He's been stealing my chickens and ducks to sell to the *gendarmes*. He's an evil criminal and so is his wife!" Jules' voice became quieter as he was pushed into the truck and the *gendarmes* drove him away.

The villagers stayed in the *Place* despite the bitter wind to discuss the unexpected events. The *Maire* remained inside his office and Michel briskly walked back to his house. "Jules is a decent man and has been lonely since his wife died last year. Poor man—now he'll go to jail." Joseph said, shaking his head. "Albert has hated him since they were children together and Jules won the school prize for the best footballer."

Next day, the *Maire* posted a notice on the wall of his office stating that all hunting rifles were to be handed to him and hunting (*la chasse*) was no longer a right for people living in the countryside. Many old men had kept their war issue rifles under floorboards and in attics for years. Hunting game was a centuries old right and tradition in rural France. The men were angry and determined not to cooperate. They had little meat on the table and hunting at night had been the only option to feed their families.

To add to their grievances, fuel for tractors and other farm equipment had been confiscated by the Vichy administration. Rusty bikes and wooden carts were dug out of barns to be used to transport men, crops and livestock between field and farmyard. It was no longer feasible to travel to other village markets to replenish food stocks or replace clothes that children had grown out of. Rural areas had been by tradition patriotic and loyal to Marshal Petain but his collaboration with the Germans was creating strong resistance in the countryside. The Vichy regime was viewed as a police state, forced to cooperate and monitored closely by the Germans. The *Milice* as representatives of the Vichy government, were the primary target of farmers' animosity.

As time passed and the Germans and the Vichy Government placed more stringent demands on the people, local *gendarmes* and *Maires* became less convinced of the benefits of collaboration and were inclined to quietly disregard German requirements. A mood of protest and hostility against wealthier landowners was developing amongst the poorer farmers due to severe shortages and deprivation. Farmers were reluctant to sell their produce at local markets because there was little to buy with their earnings. By 1943, the official food rations were 1,200 calories a day, too little to support the strength and health needed for farming.

In Broussac and local villages, women stood in long queues to buy essential food. Jean-Jacques resorted to making smaller loaves of bread and rationing one loaf per family. There was a queue outside the *epicerie* as soon as the shop opened and wives jostled for space. Often the dissatisfied queue dispersed early as the shop could not meet their needs even though they presented ration cards.

The *epicerie* owner stood in the doorway and looked at the sea of faces, feeling the heat of their animosity. He recognised most of the villagers and saw they were angry and troubled, even aggressive in their desperation to feed their families. He shrugged heavily and went inside the shop, locking the door and closing the shutters over the window.

Children were encouraged to glean the cropped corn and maize fields looking for leftover ears to thicken gruel. Stored chestnuts were peeled and crumbled to make flour, and acorns crushed for ersatz coffee. Barns had been broken into as homeless people searched desperately for hoarded food. The *Maire* seemed helpless when told of the break-ins. There was a sharp intake of breath by the group who reported the thefts, followed by an expectant silence until the *Maire* shrugged, lifted his hands helplessly and shouted.

"*Raprochez les Allemands. Je n'ai pas du pouvoir.* Blame the Germans. I have no power. They control everything and everyone. My job is a travesty. The *gendarmes* and *Milice* have more power than I do because they report directly to the invaders!"

"You must do something to stop them, *M'sieur*." A local farmer spoke loudly, confident he had the villagers supporting him. "We have never had thieves in Broussac. We always left doors unlocked. It's not right. It should not have been allowed to happen."

"So, why is it occurring?" A voice jeered from the back of the group.

"I will not discuss this." The *Maire* turned and walked into his office, slamming the door shut behind him. The angry crowd surged forward and up the steps to bang on the door of the *Mairie*.

"Our families are starving and our crops taken by the Germans. Do you expect us to suffer in silence? Our sons have been captured and taken to another country. Our wives and grandfathers are working desperately hard to plough the fields for spring and summer crops." The local farmers, Alain Favel, Armand Laron and Jean-Francois Pellier shouted angrily at the *Maire* as he pulled open his office door again. "Whose side are you on—the enemy or your neighbours?"

There was a swell of muttering, stamping feet and furious looks. It seemed the sky had darkened above them and the men's aggressive voices rumbled round the houses like a distant growl of thunder.

The *Maire* stood in his doorway, wringing his hands, unable to respond. He was scared of their enmity as he had no answers to give them. "*Allez chez nous, s'il vous plait.* Go home, please. I understand your hostility but in northern France, the situation is worse with the bombing. Families are taking to the roads as their homes are in ruins and are scavenging as they go. Refugees are overwhelming small villages and in Villefranche, they are sleeping in the streets, robbing people as they leave their homes to go shopping. I advise you to stay in your homes and try to manage. I will go to Rodez and meet with the *Prefect*, and try to help you." Aware of his distress, some of the crowd dispersed leaving a few old men to grumble angrily.

"Why did we fight in the Great War if we are starving now?" Their hostility re-ignited mass indignation in the group of locals still in the *Place*. "Where is *Marechal* Petain? What is he doing?" The men's voices grew louder and louder and fists were raised to bang on the *Mairie* door again. Slowly, their anger dissipated when the *Maire* stayed inside and their wives tugged their husband home for dinner.

The next Sunday morning, there was another commotion in the village. The village church had been broken into and silver altar candlesticks stolen. The priest was distraught, "*Mon Dieu. C'est un catastrophe.* How can I take morning mass with no candlesticks? They were old and have been in the church since the last century."

Alain Favel spoke up, "This is a terrible desecration. The church is to be respected and should be a haven of peace in these troubled times."

The *Maire* came out of his house and the priest ran up the steps to tell him about the stolen candlesticks. "*Il faut chercher tout les batiments.* We must search every house and barn to find them," the priest shouted wildly. "They are sacred and blessed and cannot be replaced."

The *Maire* shook his head and patted the priest sympathetically on the shoulder. "*Peut-etre, ils sont perdu.* Perhaps you have mislaid them," he asked gently. "Let's search the church before we start intruding on people's homes." However, a careful search of the church, its grounds and the graveyard was unproductive.

The *Maire* posted a notice outside his office requesting the thief to return church property to him. He personally visited every house in the community to request them to look round their homes and gardens. Nothing was found. M'sieur

Pascal made several searing sermons on the deadly sins, quoting the Bible and glaring at those present.

Spring arrived for a few days, the pale blue sky and warm sunshine a blessing after the long miserable winter. Broussac locals carried out their planting and repairs without enthusiasm or energy. They seemed locked in a disillusioned apathy, their minds and bodies affected by the privations of war, rationing and the thefts. Many of the fields were neither ploughed nor sown due to lack of manpower as their sons had been captured. Nettles, dock and other weeds proliferated as the earth warmed, brambles invading untrimmed hedgerows. The villagers felt their world was disintegrating beneath the formidable requirements of the Germans. Hard winter frosts had cracked paved roads, and heavy rains had washed away the surfaces, filling holes and ditches with muddy water, so travelling was difficult between villages and each place seemed locked in wretched isolation.

To add to their misery, there was a continuing stream of refugees crawling down the roads, ragged and starved, pushing old folk in wheelbarrows and snivelling babies in makeshift carts. Children cried as they stumbled along, tears making channels in dirty cheeks, many without shoes, their limbs like sticks. Old people with gaunt faces held bulging sacks of family possessions draped across their insubstantial shoulders. They begged hopelessly for food or shelter and the villagers gave what they could and offered temporary shelter in empty barns. They told stories of German brutality and massacres in the towns and communities they stumbled through. Entire villages had been burnt to the ground leaving the horror of scorched stone and heaps of ashes, and charred bodies lying in twisted shapes. Inhabitants, including women and children were lined up and shot.

The *Maire* and M'sieur Pascal helped where they could, providing shelter in church and school. Jean-Jacques made extra bread when he could obtain the flour and resorted to grinding discarded wheat ears donated by the locals.

A few farmers, including the *Maire* had radios and tuned into the BBC when they had reception. The transmitters were covered and hidden in cellars or barns in case the *Milice* decided to inspect houses for illegally held guns and radios. The news communiques were disheartening and the pathetic excuses of the politicians were vacillating and despairing. Up till now, the French had placed their hope and trust in Marshal Petain, then it was broadcast that the veteran soldier had surrendered.

Vichy France Spring and Summer 1943

Suspicion

The bedroom shutters were firmly closed when Liliane and Jean-Jacques quietly discussed the problem of local *Milice* and the priest collaborating with the Germans. "I've noticed many of our customers are nervous and don't stay to chat with their neighbours. They are suspicious of neighbours ordering extra bread, claiming they have family staying so they need extra rations," Jean-Jacques said thoughtfully. "I thought at first they were uneasy because of the rationing and pressure to meet crop and food quotas ordered by the Germans." He turned onto his back, his body sliding into the usual dip in the mattress.

"Rose-Marie came home from school very upset this afternoon because *Gendarme Pellier* had visited and warned the children to inform the *Maire* if they knew of families hoarding food and crops. I told her to let us know if he came again." Liliane responded sadly with a deep sigh.

"Have you noticed anything odd or suspicious with our neighbours' attitude when you're delivering their bread? I desperately hope that jealous or fearful neighbours don't accuse or betray each other to the *Milice or gendarmes* as happened in the Great War."

"*Non*, but I don't usually see my customers because the men have left early to go to work and the women are inside cleaning and washing. *Bon nuit. Je t'adore*." Liliane undressed, put on her nightgown and snuggled under the feather quilt. Her husband leant over and kissed her.

They were woken in the middle of the night by a loud argument emanating from the house at the back of them. They could hear the wife of Pierre Dalmain angrily berating her husband and the clang of a metal saucepan hitting the stone wall. Liliane quietly pulled the shutters open a little and leant out of the window. Pierre Dalmaine stood by a wooden cart laden with sacks of corn and maize. He was dropping them through a trap door into the cellar of his house. He had the carcass of a deer hanging from the front board of the cart, dripping blood. He'd not heard Liliane opening the shutters and was angrily muttering to himself. "*Stupide. Ma femme est stupide*."

Liliane gently pulled the bedroom shutters together but didn't latch them for fear of disturbing M Dalmain in his illegal activities. She whispered what she had seen to her husband. "*Tais-toi*. Keep quiet and don't get involved," advised Jean-Jacques and turned over in bed.

Liliane observed the behaviour of her customers more closely as she cycled round the village delivering bread the next morning. She left home as the sun rose over the forested hills and passed a tractor and several men on bikes hurrying to the fields to continue ploughing. They nodded at her or said *Bonjour* as usual as did the women who collected bread from their doorsteps. She decided to go to the café after taking her bike back to the *Boulangerie* and change her dress. Joseph and old Michel sat at their normal table, sipping ersatz coffee and eating pieces of bread. Joseph waved at her and old Michel said, "*Bonjour*." The early morning rush was over and Paulette was washing up behind the bar when Liliane walked over and whispered into her ear. They walked into the living area.

"Last night, Pierre Dalmain and his wife had a loud argument in the back lane outside our bedroom window. I think he's hoarding or smuggling food as well as poaching deer," Liliane said quietly. "Jean-Jacques told me to ignore them. Have you seen anything suspicious?"

"I heard a heavy donkey cart rumbling through the *Place* before dawn, but it could have been carrying crops to their barn. I couldn't see who it was but I think the donkey's hooves were muffled because there was no tapping noise on the cobblestones," Paulette replied. "I miss Michel because he always got up to serve the early customers. I have to wake Louisa and Maria because they sleep so heavily and Jean Luc is usually in his shed working before breakfast."

"Rose-Marie came home very upset yesterday because *Gendarme Pellier* had instructed them to spy on their friends and neighbours. Did Louisa or Maria mention anything to you? Did they seem scared or worried?"

"*Oui*. They didn't want to talk about school but went straight to their bedroom and shut the door. I thought it was probably some silly prank they had been involved in at school. I'll ask them over dinner tonight, so Jean-Luc can talk to them. Josette is very worried about Michel, Martin and Gilles. They can't survive in a deserted farmhouse with no food and no fire. How can we help them? Jean-Luc can't ride a donkey or walk easily up hills with his wooden leg. I can't leave the café because it would be noticed."

"I heard that the *Releve* deserters have set up groups called the *maquis* and may be hiding in the Aveyron and the Lot." Paulette anxiously bit her lips and pushed her hair back.

After dinner that evening, Liliane told her husband about her conversation with Paulette. "I will ask M'sieur Cantou at *La Poste* if he has any information about the current location of Germans."

"*Sois prudent*. Please be very careful who you involve. Most of our neighbours know that Michel, Martin and Gilles are missing and may suspect that they are avoiding the *STO*. People in the village whose sons have been captured are resentful that some youths escaped while theirs were sent to work in Germany. I've noticed the odd nasty remark amongst farmers' wives waiting in the *Boulangerie*."

"*D'accord, ma cheri*," Liliane replied.

Victor, the village handyman came into the Boulangerie the next morning. He had wild curly hair, a dirty face and rarely changed his clothes. He was usually annoyed about someone and often aggressive. This time, he was incensed that his neighbour had accused him of stealing firewood stacked in his house yard. "*Homme stupide*. I chop my own wood. He owns a big house and thinks he's a landowner but his family lost their land during the Revolution. People think the *Revolution* helped the poor peasants." Jean-Jacques served him two baguettes then ignored him.

It was Victor's usual rant, so no one took any notice until he backed his ancient tractor into the stone wall surrounding the *Boulangerie*. Jean-Jacques stopped pounding bread and stormed outside waving his fist angrily. "*Merde. Allez, allez,*" he yelled. "Go away before you do more damage!" Jean-Jacques's customers smiled to themselves.

Madame Pellier was talking with Pierrette about her neighbour, Pierre Dalmain. "I'm sure he's hoarding food," she said loudly as she always did because she was deaf.

"Sshsh," Pierrette whispered a reply. "The school children were told to inform on food hoarders. We don't want German interference here."

Farmers were finding it more difficult to meet German demands and supply local communities with food. Produce at weekly markets was noticeably decreasing and there were more tables with household items or clothes to sell or barter. Most people had already eaten the rabbits kept in backyard hutches and there were rarely fresh eggs for sale.

The Maire's Opposition

Bertrand Danton had been elected *Maire* of Broussac five years ago. He was popular for his kindness and dedication to the village. He was known as a 'man of the land, *un paysan*', whose family had farmed in the area for generations. He spoke with a strong *Occitane* accent. When he was not involved with Mayoral duties, Bertrand worked tirelessly on his land, sharing his experience and farm equipment with other farmers. He was an intensely loyal man and enjoyed going to church services and village events. He used to hold regular meetings to talk about agricultural improvements and local news.

Bertrand found his role to be particularly onerous since the Germans had divided France into the *zone nord and the zone libre or zone sud*—the latter area administered by the Vichy regime. When the *gendarmes* had visited Broussac in late 1942 and told him of the requirements of the Vichy Government, he was polite and smiled agreeably but was unsure of fully collaborating with them. The *gendarmes* expected him to provide information on the location of *maquis*, the hiding places of *refractaires* and which villagers hoarded food or dealt on the black market.

Rural communities in several *departements* were hostile to collaboration with the Vichy regime. Bertrand knew the *Prefect* of the Tarn *Departement*, neighbour to the Aveyron, had warmly supported the Vichy regime and its regionalism policy in December 1941. In the *Departement* of the Lot, a village *Maire* had sent a letter in 1942 to the local *Prefect* listing what *les paysans* expected from Vichy, their economic demands and frustrations. The *Prefect* had dismissed these, stating that 'the peasantry was basically uninterested in politics'.

By the end of 1942, civil disobedience began to take hold in rural areas. This included isolated incidents of obstruction to Vichy authority and widespread hoarding of foods which were subject to requisitioning by the Germans. There was escalating resistance to the STO *Releve* when German garrisons were established in the *zone sud* by January 1943 and the *Milice* was set up. Bertrand listened secretly to BBC Radio, so knew the British were encouraging workers not to respond to the *Releve* and *Maires* to protect village men of enlistment age. The *Prefects* had ordered all *Maires* to designate one villager, preferably the local agricultural and grain merchant, to collect crops and goods requisitioned by Vichy from local farmers and transport them to the nearest train station.

Alphonse Germain owned the agricultural business in Broussac as his father and grandfather had before him. Bertrand trusted him to be honest, so had allocated the collection of crops to him. The villagers put out sacks of maize, wheat and corn on the side of the road on a regular basis so Alphonse could take them. Vichy inspectors visited each farm checking the amounts of produce and livestock. Farmers were bitterly resistant of this requirement and many decided to sell direct rather than submit to Vichy and abide by the regulated prices for crops and food. They started moving their animals out of the fields and temporarily hiding them in the forests but it was difficult to hide crops.

Bertrand took a brisk walk at dusk every day to check the condition of his crops—maize, wheat and hay. He found the tranquillity of the land and the clear crisp winter air invigorating. It helped to dissipate the contamination of the *gendarmes'* demands. On his ancestral lands, he was at peace and could decide how best to administer and protect the hamlets and farms that were his legal responsibility. In February 1943, an expanded set of demands and commands had been dictated from the Germans, relayed by local *gendarmes*.

Early in 1943 on his daily walk, he considered his options—to fully comply and be subservient, to blindly ignore the demands or to tread a wary path between the two extremes. By the end of his walk, he had decided to maintain a subtle policy of obstruction and to feign ignorance of hoarding and black marketing by his friends and neighbours. He would not share this decision with his wife or anyone in the village except for his long-term friend Joseph who had no family or wife to worry about. He met with Joseph the next evening for his regular *pastis* at the cafe, ostensibly to discuss a proposed game of *petanque* with *Villane-le-Foret*. Maire Danton nodded to his villagers and shook their hands, then sat with Joseph at a table inside in the rear of the café.

The friendship between Joseph and Bertrand had developed over two decades founded on their experiences in the Great War, their love for rural life and a lively interest in French politics. They enjoyed convivial but heated discussions on Napoleonic Law, the war strategies of Generals Petain, Laval and de Gaulle. As old soldiers of the Great War, they had experienced first-hand the useless destruction and disaster of trench and tank warfare, bombing raids and the displacement of thousands of people. Now, the countryside was again affected by the desperation of ragged starving bands of refugees stumbling down the lanes, begging for scraps of food and clothing.

Sipping his *pastis* and speaking quietly, Bertrand briefly outlined his recent decision. "Our neighbours have already experienced accusations of theft and food hoarding, a needless house fire as well as much unpleasantness. This war is destroying village life and I'm informed that the Germans will continue using the *Milice* to impose more restrictions and demands on us. I must take a stand to protect my villagers even though this may have repercussions."

Joseph was surprised by the dramatic change in the *Maire's* attitude but his expression didn't reflect this. He listened quietly while Bertrand outlined his plan to mitigate German influence and *Milice* demands in the environs of Broussac. "I will do everything I can to support you, Bertrand. Our village is poor and locals are living at subsistence level. The *Milice* strut around and terrorise people with their newfound power, especially *Gendarme* Pellier, who is a spy for the Germans. I don't trust the priest as I suspect he is giving information about the villagers to the Germans in Rodez. I think we should be wary of supporting the *maquis* for fear of reprisals. We need to involve Liliane and Britt Ziegler who both hate the Germans for family reasons. I think Madame Cantou at *La Poste* would be prepared to take messages."

"*Tres bien*. Keep me informed. My wife must not be involved." Bertrand finished his glass of *pastis*, shook his friend's hand and hurried back to the

Mairie for his evening meal. Joseph strolled across the *Place* to *La Poste* where Mme Cantou was locking the front door. "*Bonsoir Paulette. Comment va tu?* How are you? Can I talk with you inside for a few minutes?"

"*Oui, bien sur.*" Paulette Cantou unlocked the door to her house and turned on the lamp in the kitchen. "*Assieds-toi,* Joseph."

Joseph sat down and briefly explained how the *Maire's* attitude had changed in response to the overwhelming demands by Germans and *Milice* on Broussac villagers. "I agreed we must cooperate and help each other in order to survive this war, even if there is danger. Will you support us? I told him my concerns regarding the loyalty of our priest."

"*D'accord*, but what can I do, Joseph?"

"I understand many official directives are despatched via *La Poste*. When they arrive, would you ask Britt Ziegler to translate the German into French and let Bertrand know, so he is forewarned of additional demands and commands?"

"*Bien sur*. Will you talk to Brit?"

"*Oui*, and I will discuss this with Liliane. She is a natural leader in the village and has contacts in Cahors through her family, so may hear useful information about Resistance in the Lot."

"Liliane hears news about other villages in the area and what locals are saying when she does her bread delivery. I warned her to be careful and not share anything with her sewing friends who tend to gossip," Madame Cantou said thoughtfully. "Josette and Paulette are naturally concerned about repercussions on their captured sons in hiding."

"*Mon Dieu*. What a terrible state of affairs! When the Great War ended, I hoped there would be peace in Europe for decades. A chance to rebuild towns destroyed in the north and starvation to be eradicated as farmers concentrated on feeding the population of France." Joseph shook his head sorrowfully as Madame Cantou handed him a glass of *vin rouge*.

"*Merci et sante*. At least, the vignerons are allowed to continue growing grapes and making wine! I'll go to Liliane's and tell her what's planned and how she can help. I'll pretend I've run out of bread!" Joseph said with a wry smile as he left *La Poste* by the back door, kissing Madame Cantou on the cheeks. He walked down the lane and into the backyard of the *Boulangerie* where he knew Jean-Jacques would be preparing his dough for the next morning. As he knocked on the door, he wondered whether he should talk with him and Liliane. He knew they had an exceptionally loving and close relationship and would share any useful gossip heard in the *Boulangerie* and on the delivery round.

"*Bonsoir*, Jean-Jacques. Can I talk with you and Liliane for a few minutes please? I've been discussing the impact of the latest German demands with Bertrand and he has told me his change of plans."

"*Entrée*, Joseph. I'll ask Liliane to come down. She's reading a bedtime story with Rose-Marie. *Assieds-toi. Du vin?*"

"*Non, merci. Pas du vin, merci.*" Joseph sat on the three-legged wooden stool placed in front of the bread oven which had been damped down for the night and pondered his approach to involving these old friends in the *Maire's* plan to mitigate German power in Broussac. He suspected there would be repercussions but hoped they could be avoided by a united village and cautious opposition.

"*Bonsoir Joseph. Ca va bien?*" Liliane's cheerful voice made him jump and he stood to kiss her cheeks. "How can we help you?"

Joseph briefly described his recent conversation with Bertrand and the *Maire's* request to form an opposition group in the village, comprising Paulette Cantou, Britt Ziegler, himself and Liliane, and maybe Jean-Jacques but definitely not the priest.

"Bertrand emphasised that secrecy is crucial to avoid German repercussions. He suggested each person in the group meet with him one evening next week to talk about ways to help him protect Broussac villagers and local farm folk. I said I would support him. Bertrand is concerned that recent thefts, unrest and aggression in the village indicate a growing loss of cooperation and friendliness. It's crucial to keep villagers safe from belligerent *gendarmes* and German demands. Think about this. Bertrand insists there be no coercion only a willingness to support him." Joseph put on his black cap, kissed Liliane's cheek and shook Jean-Jacques's hand before leaving via the backyard.

"We should lock up and think about it. I've noticed some customers are ruder than normal to their neighbours and I hear them gossiping about ways to upset them. One woman said she opened the yard to let her neighbour's *chasse* dogs roam free because she was fed up with their nighttime barking. She threatened to poison them! You know who I refer to!" Jean-Jacques held open the door and locked it before following Liliane into their kitchen. She brewed two bowls of *ersatz* coffee and they sat at the table by the warm stove. Liliane blew gently on her liquid, shrugged then sighed, unsure how to react to Joseph's astonishing request. They ate their meal in silence thinking how they could help and what impact it could have on their family.

Child Evacuees

On a warm summer's evening in July, Britt Zeigler sat in her favourite cane chair on the front porch of the schoolhouse enjoying the soft light of the setting sun and the melodious birdsong. Climbing roses and purple wisteria scented the air. She heard the neighbour's *chasse* dogs barking and the doves cooing on the church spire.

She switched off the radio that was playing quietly in the kitchen behind her when she recognised the priest walking from the *Place de la Mairie* towards her. She had befriended him at the Paris *Lycee*. He wore dark priestly robes and carried a leather briefcase under his arm. "*Bonsoir, Madame Zeigler. Comment allez vous? J'ai visiter M'sieur Danton et M'sieur Pascal parce que j'ai une probleme.* I have talked with the *Maire* and the priest about helping refugee children from the suburbs of Paris?"

"*Bonsoir, M'sieur Quillan. Entrée, j'ai du vin rouge,*" Madame Zeigler replied ushering the priest into her kitchen. She locked the door, filled a glass with wine and sat down. "What's the problem. *Raconte-moi ce qui c'est passe?*"

"There are dozens of orphaned children left in Paris because their parents have been captured, imprisoned or killed. In some cases, the father joined the French Army in 1939 and is now a prisoner of war. The mother has to work and has no one to care for her small children during the long hours at the factory. I want to establish a safe corridor between Paris and the south of France, so these children can be brought to safety by train and placed with foster families. Since Renault's Boulogne-Billancourt factories were bombed on 4 April this year, many families living in the suburbs are desperate to evacuate their children. The *Creuse Departement* was a refuge for the children of the civilian exodus of 1940. There are many child refugees whose parents have died on the roads because of bombing or disease. I am undertaking a mission to set up safe houses *en route* from Paris to the south. Two primary school teachers have volunteered to accompany small groups of children and ensure they are taken in by foster parents. You may have met them. Could you provide a safe house for a small group of children for a few days?"

Britt was stunned. She had intended to shut down all contact with Paris and her life as a school teacher. She sat very still, hands clasped in her lap, thinking about the difficulties of housing a stream of city children in a small rural village like Broussac where everyone knew each other. She was touched that M'sieur Quillan trusted her to help.

The silence lengthened as the priest slowly sipped his wine, understanding that his request would cause complications to her sheltered life and probably danger.

"I need to know more about *les petits refugees* and the evacuation process. Broussac is a small close-knit community which has experienced difficulties and trauma caused by the requirements of the Germans during the last few years."

"*D'accord*. The children live in my parish or their relatives do. Some older ones have already been evacuated to North Africa, leaving their younger siblings with their mothers in Paris. Others have been living on the streets because their homes and family were destroyed by Allied bombing. Some were taken in the mass civilian exodus in 1940 to stay temporarily with relatives living in other *departements*."

"Must you have an answer tonight?" Britt asked. "Do you have a place to stay tonight?"

"*Oui*. The Maire said I can sleep in the *Salle de Fete*. I will come in the morning for your decision." The priest got up, kissed Britt on both cheeks and followed her out of the back door. It was almost dark, so it was unlikely the locals would see him leaving.

Britt sat for a long time at the kitchen table. She vividly remembered the various children she had taught and the feeling of fulfilment she'd experienced. It had taken considerable courage to leave Paris on her own and settle in a new place. Despite the impact of war on Broussac, her time here had been safe and serene. She knew what atrocities the Germans had committed in Paris on innocent people and felt unsure about the consequences of bringing defenceless children into the village. She went to bed later than normal, carrying an oil lamp to light the stairs to her attic bedroom. She slept little, her mind brimming with options.

She was still undecided what answer to give when the priest arrived next morning. "M'sieur Quillan, I need more time to look for safe hiding places for a group of lively kids. The local *gendarmes* are vigilant and regularly visit the village checking on conformance with German requirements. We've had several young men captured for work in Germany."

"*D'accord.* I must return to Paris on the morning train. Can I contact you again?" M'sieur Quillan obviously understood her dilemma but needed a plan to save these unfortunate children. "*Au revoir, Madame Zeigler. A bientot.*"

"*Au revoir.* Contact me through Madame Cantou at *La Poste.*"

The priest left by the schoolhouse back door, jumped on his bike which he'd left in a nearby hedge and rode briskly to the train station at Lalbenque. It was a long ride over bumpy lanes and he felt a strong sense of having failed in his mission to protect the orphans of his parish.

Britt Zeigler walked across to the *Boulangerie*, hoping to meet Liliane and confide in her. There was a lengthy queue of villagers waiting patiently outside to receive their bread quota. Britt noticed that the women were gossiping amongst themselves and there was no obvious animosity. She went back to the school and opened it, gently chiding the boisterous children as they charged into the schoolroom. The school was separated into two sections in the same hall— one for the youngest children and the other for older kids. Chantal, wife of the Deputy Maire taught the small children reading and writing. Britt focussed on giving lessons in maths, history and geography with the others. There were about ten kids in each section and their playtimes in the school yard were timed separately. Britt found the work satisfying and enjoyed the intimacy of knowing the children's siblings and family.

It was a lively and interesting day as Chantal was teaching the young ones some clapping songs and Britt decided to take the older children to visit the ruined chateau for a history lesson. After the children had left to go home, she and Chantal sat down for their usual bowl of coffee on the schoolhouse porch. Chantal was very concerned about her son, Claude. She had received no information from the authorities after his capture by the *gendarmes* one year ago. Michel and Bertrand contacted the *Prefecture* in Rodez on a weekly basis but they had no information from the Vichy Government about the location or condition of the youths.

"I feel I am just existing minute by minute in the protective cocoon of the village but I know atrocities are committed elsewhere in France." Britt placed her arm around her friend's shoulders. "*Bonjour, Liliane.* We were just saying that it feels like we are safe in Broussac but the Germans are slowly and insidiously taking over our lives."

Liliane sat down on the porch and sipped her coffee. "*C'est vrai*. I feel I can no longer control everyday life nor think of a future for my family," she said sadly, wiping tears from her eyes.

Britt agreed and continued, "*Mes cheres amis. J'ai une grande probleme.* My friend, the priest, who supported the *Lycee* where I worked in Paris, arrived unexpectedly by train yesterday. Let's go inside and I'll tell you."

Liliane and Chantal followed Britt into her kitchen. The door was locked and the blue shutters partially closed on the latch. "*M'sieur Quillan* wants to set up a safe corridor to enable orphaned Parisien children to leave the city and travel south. His mission is to find foster parents for them for the remainder of the war. He assured me he knows the kids and their families and that many are living on the streets or are children of single mothers whose menfolk have been captured or killed. I respect him and I think it's a compassionate mission but I'm anxious about involving people in Broussac. He has returned to Paris now and I told him I couldn't give him an answer immediately. I haven't spoken with Bertrand yet."

Chantal and Liliane looked at each other, both understanding the risk of reprisals in Broussac and surrounding villages. Liliane spoke after a few minutes of heavy silence. "Everyone in the village is struggling to feed their families. Where would the children stay and for how long? I assume these are lively kids who'll need exercise and occupying? Many houses in the village are lived in by old widows like Madame Ricard and Madame Royal who cannot care for children. I think we have enough problems supporting the *maquis* who are hiding our young men."

"I agree with Liliane. Has *M'sieur Quillan* suggested how we feed them and how long these unfortunate children need to be housed for?" Chantal said.

"*Non*. Thank you for discussing this. I don't know what to do," Britt shook her head and smiled at her friends. She understood their caution as both had sons in captivity and were notable people in the village.

That night she sat up late in the kitchen, sipping a glass of wine and pondering her responsibility as a humane school teacher. When school was finished the next day, she decided to walk to the local chateau which had been destroyed during the French Revolution. She remembered seeing a large stone cellar with a vaulted brick ceiling. The entrance was shielded by overgrown bushes and steep stone steps led down to an iron-studded wooden door. The aristocratic owners had reputably hidden there when revolutionaries had burnt down their chateau during the French Revolution. Over the years since then, locals had taken stones from the ruined walls to repair their barns. She pondered whether the cellar could be a temporary hiding place for orphaned Parisien children.

She trudged uphill through thick oak and chestnut woods that were alive with chattering birds and small animals. The air smelt of moist earth and vegetation. She saw clumps of tiny bright violets nestling in the roots of trees, yellow cowslips in the grass and wild bramble bushes. She was startled by a small dun-coloured deer leaping lithely through the trees.

The ruined chateau had been built on a rocky escarpment overlooking the valley of the river Aveyron. She sat down on a flat rock to scan the stunning panorama and savour the aromatic country air. She could see a trail of smoke from a train moving along the valley bottom. There was no other habitation nearby, so the chateau must have been built in the early Middle Ages for defence against the English. It could also have been a Cathar stronghold against the Catholic clergy.

Britt brushed the vegetation aside and walked down the stone steps to the cellar door which had been wedged open by stones. She disturbed a tiny grey mouse sitting on the steps in the sun. The cellar had an irregular paved stone floor, a brick vaulted ceiling that was black with smoke and an arched stone fireplace singed by fire. There were piles of leaves and scattered mouse and rabbit dung on the floor. Along two sides were wooden racks that would have housed bottles of wine and shelves for preserves. The floor was dry but the stone walls were flaking and cold. She thought this space could be used as an emergency hideout for evacuated children but it would be dark and lonely at night. She walked back up the steps lit by the rays of the setting sun and climbed down the hill to the village acknowledging neighbours with a wave and *'Bonsoir'*.

Within a week of the Parisian priest's visit, Britt received notification through Madame Cantou at *La Poste* that a small convoy of orphaned children travelling in a covered truck had set out from Paris, heading south to safety. They were accompanied by two teachers and were expected to arrive in a village outside of Cahors within two days.

Britt took the message to the *Maire* the next afternoon when school had finished. She had to wait whilst Bertrand talked with Madame Ricard who was complaining that children had stolen vegetables from her *potager*. Her house was opposite the school and when the children were particularly boisterous and noisy in the playground she moaned to Britt, demanding she control the kids better. "*J'ai une grande probleme*. Children are stealing my vegetables," she complained. "I have enough problems as a widow doing the garden and keeping my house clean and I need vegetables to keep me healthy. My legs pain with arthritis and my back hurts when I do the gardening. I have told Madame Zeigler."

"She should tell the children that stealing is a sin!" Madame Ricard had risen from her chair when she saw Britt entering the room. She glowered at her, clutched her handbag under her arm and marched out the door. Bertrand shook his head in despair. "Madame Ricard thinks everyone in the village should support her because she lives alone and has no children to care for her. *Mon Dieu*, that woman is in my office every few days complaining about something!" Bertrand shrugged and sat down heavily behind his desk. "How can I help you?" He smiled at Britt. He admired her courage in starting a new life in Broussac as a widow and the villagers spoke well of her teaching.

"*Bonjour, Bertrand. Je pense que Madame Ricard n'aime pas les enfants*. She grumbles to me often about the children. I received a message today through *la Poste* from M'sieur Quillan, the priest from Paris. He is sending a group of orphaned kids from Paris by truck and they should arrive at a village outside Cahors within a few days. Two teachers are with them and the truck driver. I hope they encounter no German roadblocks but I suspect the driver will keep to small country roads for safety. M'sieur Quillan requests Broussac to house the kids for a day or two until the driver finds a safe route to go south. I inspected the chateau cellar and the orphans could live there temporarily but we need to provide bedding and food. Maybe good clean clothes. We must help these deprived kids but it will be impossible to keep their visit a secret. What do you think?"

"I agree and told M'sieur Quillan when he visited that I would help. I think the chateau cellar provides good shelter for the children. I will arrange for a fence to be erected round the ruins with a danger notice stating there are broken walls and ditches. I've been intending to do this and it will prevent nosy neighbours and naughty kids from going there."

Britt left with a smile and a cheerful *Bonsoir*. She walked across the *Place* to the *Boulangerie* to talk with Liliane.

Bertrand stayed in his office, rubbing his chin thoughtfully and frowning. He knew there was a risk in harbouring child evacuees but rationalised that they were of no importance to the *Prefecture* or to the *gendarmes*. He decided not to inform the authorities. He hoped Pierrette, his wife, Liliane and Britt could provide them with food and bedding.

Two nights later, Britt met in Bertrand's office with Pierrette, ostensibly for an *aperitif* and a chat about the progress of the school children. He had invited the village priest, Jean-Marie Pascal.

The windows of the *Mairie* were closed but the shutters left open, so they were in full view of villagers enjoying their aperitifs.

"*Bonsoir. Bien.* The orphans arrive at midnight. Joseph will meet them at the bottom of the Roman road and guide the truck up a nearby lane to the chateau."

"*Une moment, s'il vous plait.*" Joseph held up his hand. "I think there is a secret tunnel from the church crypt to the cellar of the *chateau*. It was used by the *chateau* owners to escape the savage massacres during the Religious Wars and the Revolution. Then I'll investigate to check if it is safe as an escape route for the children. The walls and ceiling may have collapsed or the entrance barred from the church."

"*D'accord.* I have left food, drink and blankets for the children in the *chateau* cellar and candles. Let me know when all is well. *Bonsoir.*" Bertrand stood up and opened the office door.

Joseph found Liliane in her garden and quietly told her that the secret tunnel seemed be clear of water and rock falls. "I've agreed to meet Britt just before midnight at the bottom of the Roman Road." Liliane nodded and let Joseph out into the lane by the back gate. She filled a basket with bread and fruit and packed a knapsack with cast-off children's clothes donated by Josette and Paulette. She nervously carried out her daily tasks running over possible problems in her head. At dinner, her family noticed her silence and shaky hands as she served the meal. Jean-Jacques tried to ask her the problem but she avoided his gaze, answering the children's questions with a distracted air.

"*Nous parlons demain matin*, Jean-Jacques," she whispered as they got into bed. He nodded, kissed her lingeringly on the mouth, pulled up the blanket and turned over to sleep. She was awake for an hour or two pondering over her role in helping evacuee children. She consoled herself by assuming there was a low risk that other villagers would find out.

Liliane slid out of bed and hastily donned her work dress and cardigan. She kissed her husband's closed eyelids and quietly crept down the wooden stairs avoiding where they creaked. She opened the kitchen door which she had not bolted after dinner, slid on her clogs and walked out into the back yard. Luckily, there was only a sliver of moon but the sky was brilliantly lit with thousands of bright pinpricks light outlining the constellations and the Milky Way. She met Britt at the back of the schoolyard and gave her the baskets.

"*Merci*," Britt whispered, took a few deep breaths and set out up the narrow lane at the back of row of village houses their shutters firmly barred showing no glimmers of lamplight.

The church clock rang the hour of midnight as she hurried out of the village and up through a wooded lane, lined with oak and walnut trees. She arrived at the base of the Roman Road as a dark truck with no lights pulled into a farm gate. Joseph slid out from behind a dense oak tree, nodded to Britt and briskly walked across to the truck. The driver, who was unrecognisable as he wore a dark hood, stood at the tailgate of the truck and pulled aside a tarpaulin hanging across the back tray. Muffled voices and squeaks were the only indication of children crouched in the back. They jumped down as instructed and gathered in a small tight group around two taller figures. The children and adults wore cloth masks and hoods to hide their faces and hair.

"*Bonsoir mes enfants*," Britt whispered. "*Suivre-moi.*" She held out her hand to two small children cowering beside the truck wheels. They were shivering, maybe from fear or the chill night wind. Joseph took the hands of two other children and pointed with his arm in the direction the group would walk. The only light was from the sickle of moon and the stars. Trees were shadowy outlines, wavering in the night wind, their ragged tops shivering slightly. The still air felt moist as the group trudged up the uneven muddy lane, shuffling through broken twigs and acorns. Shallow puddles smelt of damp mud and vegetation, wayside flowers closed and scentless. Two barn owls flitted above them, light feathers looking ghostly in the starlight, their calls like whispers.

After ten minutes, the group reached the summit of the wooded hill and stopped briefly to look down on the shadowy outline of the village, its houses huddled together for protection. The ruined chateau lay ahead, the broken walls appearing crenelated against the dark sky with the single remaining tower stark like a pointing finger. The children had been lagging for a while as they were exhausted after the long unnerving drive south from Paris. Joseph relinquished the cold hands of the two children he had been helping and walked up the grassy slope to the chateau. He carefully descended the stone steps, feeling his way in the dark and heaved open the cellar door which he had taken the precaution to oil and unbolt earlier. The door creaked gently as it swung outwards on rusting hinges. He pulled out a small kerosene lamp, lit it and placed it midway down the steps to highlight them as the children descended into the black pit of the cellar.

The furry shape of a rat darted across the entrance making the children jump with fear. "*Tout va bien, mes enfants,*" Joseph reassured them. Britt followed them and closed the door slightly to shade the light. Metal camp beds had been set in two rows on the damp flag stone floor. Each had a small cushion and a woollen blanket.

On a folding table nearby were some pieces of bread, cheese and fruit. "*Bon appetit, mes petits,*" Britt whispered as the grubby children's hands reached out to the table. They huddled together on the beds clutching the food as if it would be stolen before they could take a bite. In the light of the kerosene lamp, they looked angular and bony, their wrists and legs devoid of flesh, just loose skin. The food was greedily eaten and Britt helped the two smaller children to lie down. "Joseph will stay with you tonight," she said with a smile. "*Bon nuit.*" She got up from the floor and touched Joseph's arm, muttering, "*Merci mon ami.*"

Britt climbed the steps out from the cellar, slid through the gap by the door and trudged thoughtfully back down the hill to the village. She knocked on Liliane's back door, whispering, "*Tout va bien, les pauvres.*"

Britt unlocked her yard door in the dark, climbed the stairs to her bedroom and slithered under the bed clothes. She was awake for a while but then felt her body slowly relax in the warmth and security.

She hoped no one knew about the refugees hiding in the *chateau*. The cellar was cold and damp even in the height of summer and the children cowed. She had noticed that several older children were supporting the little ones who stumbled with exhaustion and fear.

Support for the Maquis

The *maquis* chose a night of impenetrable darkness to visit Broussac, shooting randomly to warn the villagers. Old men and boys clutching ancient hunting rifles rushed out to defend their homes. Tethered dogs howled in fear and children's cries echoed from the houses. A group of shadowy figures moved from hidden corners to gather in the *Place de la Mairie*. It was impossible in the inky blackness to identify how many there were. A disembodied voice called, "We need help. The Germans are seeking reprisal for an attack by us two days ago on a tank convoy near Rodez. We're starving and injured and need medical supplies. Hide them in the church crypt." The voice was of a desperate young man trying to be brave. His *Occitane* accent identified him as a local.

Liliane moved to stand in the light at the *Boulangerie* entrance and put up her hands to show she had no weapons. "We'll help. Return to your hiding place now," she quietly addressed the indistinct figures who then melted away into the deep shadows between the buildings. A large pale barn owl, disturbed by the voices, flapped lazily into the air from its perch in a hay barn and perched on a tree branch, its round glaring eyes reflecting the light from the *Boulangerie*. The villagers drifted away to their homes, relieved they had a choice to help the *maquis* if they wanted to.

"Our son could be with them, so we must help," Liliane whispered to Jean-Jacques as they shut and barred the front door. She knew that not all villagers supported the *maquis*. She'd heard a local farmer living in the Segala had denounced them to the *gendarmes* saying, "I am a loyal Frenchman who fought in the Great War. There is a *maquis* unit hiding in the woods opposite my farm."

The next morning, Liliane went to the *Mairie* and asked Bertrand to support the local *maquis*. "*Bonjour,* Bertrand. The *maquis* are hiding our sons and should be helped. They're not criminals but *refractaires*, young men refusing to fight and work for the Germans."

Bertrand sat at his desk drumming his fingers as he ran through different options in his mind. He wanted to help but was aware of the possible repercussions on innocent villagers, old people and children. He'd heard about the nameless atrocities committed in the north of France and refugees travelling along the roads escaping German cruelty and betrayal.

"I'll donate food and raid the *Mairie's* medical supply."

"*Merci.*" Liliane opened the *Mairie* door and walked down the steps, waving to café customers as she walked to the *Boulangerie*. She nodded to her husband who was serving the queue of customers waiting for their bread quota. "I'll have a coffee with Josette, then come home to make lunch." Jean-Jacques lifted his head and smiled at her, mouthing the words, "*Tout va bien*? All well?"

Liliane said '*Bonjour*' to the customers and took a fresh baguette from the shelf, wrapped it in a serviette and walked across to Josette's farmhouse where she pushed open the kitchen door. "*Bonjour, Josette.*" Her friend was washing up at the sink and dried her hands before kissing Liliane on her cheeks. "*Merci pour du pain. Assieds-toi, mon ami. Je suis tous seul. Alain travail au champs.*

Thanks for the bread. Sit down, I'm alone," she lowered her voice and whispered, "*C'est le maquis qui visite?*"

"*Oui. Ils ont besoin du nourriture et des vetements. Je crois il y a trois ou quatre jeunes hommes.* They need our support. I think there were three or four youths from the *maquis*. They sounded scared. Bertrand will help. *Quelle catastrophe.*" Liliane put her face in her hands, worried about their sons.

Josette patted her shoulder and said, "I'll give you food and an old pair of trousers and two shirts of Alain's. He's working in the fields. I wish we knew where our sons are." She put a coffee pot on the wood stove to boil, placed two bowls on the kitchen table and sat down. "Bertrand has to be careful and not antagonise the local *gendarmes* and the *Prefecture* in Rodez. We don't know who to trust these days." They sat in silence sipping coffee, thinking what other tragedies could happen to the village.

Liliane rose after an hour and kissed Josette. "I must cook lunch though it won't be much. We shared a two-egg omelette last night because we have one old hen left which is too tough to eat. I'm making lots of vegetable and weed soups these days," she said sadly.

"We killed our last pig yesterday. I'll give you a small piece of pork to put in the soup in exchange for the *baguette*," Josette sighed.

"Everyone is getting thinner. I've noticed the old ladies, Madame Royal, Madame Pellier and Madame Ricard are not taking their afternoon walks these days. I think they're scared to leave the safety of the village."

As Liliane returned home Jean-Jacques was serving the last customers. He ran out of bread at midday because of flour quotas. He winked at her. "Have you come home to cook me a nice roast?"

"*Non, c'est encore la soupe,*" Liliane replied and blew him a kiss.

He walked in the kitchen door ten minutes later and washed his hands in the sink. Rose-Marie came rushing in, "*J'ai faim, maman.* I'm hungry."

"Sit down and I'll serve soup with your papa's best bread." Liliane gave her daughter a kiss and placed a china bowl on the table with bread croutons floating on top. Rose-Marie chattered about the maths lesson she'd had and how she'd got all the sums correct and earned a red star from Madame Ziegler. "*Maman.* Who came to the village last night?"

"I think it was refugees," Liliane replied.

"I'm going to play with my friends at the river now."

"*D'accord.* Don't fall in." Liliane replied with a smile. Her lively daughter seemed unaffected so far by events in the village. She was an intelligent child, curious about everything and enjoyed school.

Rose-Marie shut the kitchen door and Liliane took the soup dishes to the sink, then sat down to tell her husband about talking with the *Maire*. "He will support the *maquis* but we must be careful not to bring disaster on the village. I spoke with Josette, and when school is finished, this afternoon, I'll talk with Madame Ziegler, then find Joseph." Liliane heaved a sigh as she turned to wash up the lunch crockery.

Jean-Jacques hugged her, then went back to the *Boulangerie* to clean up. He was finding it hard to be cheerful each day with his customers. He had trained as a *Boulanger artisan* and intensely disliked making substandard bread using poorly milled flour, often mixed with crushed acorns or sweet chestnuts. He was very concerned about Armand his eldest son as there had been no news about where or how he was living. He felt despair about the future for his family. The requirements of the Vichy Government were increasing, affecting everyone in the village and surrounding farms. His customers looked shabbier and thinner, young children wearing clothes too small for them were grizzling with hunger. Old people seemed more infirm, leaning heavily on their sticks. The weekly village market had shut down due to lack of produce for sale and the spring fete was cancelled this year. No one wanted to leave the safety of the village. He was concerned about his wife helping the *maquis*.

For a few days, life was peaceful in Broussac. Liliane collected clothes and food for the *maquis* from her friends. Joseph filled sacks with the items and put them in the crypt behind a wooden statue of Jesus. The *maquis* slid quietly into the village to pick up supplies that night.

Liliane checked the crypt next morning and found a scribbled note saying their sons were safe and thanking them. She tucked the note into her apron pocket, wiping a tear of relief from her cheek. The following Friday after the breakfast rush in the village café, she met with Josette and Britt Zeigler. Paulette brought four coffees to the table at the back of the café and the friends quietly exchanged news.

"Our last chicken has stopped laying, so we have no eggs. Luckily, it's spring and there are plenty of vegetables in the garden, so I feed my family on soup and bread." Liliane complained. "I would give a hundred francs to buy some pork or beef."

Britt nodded, then changed the subject. She placed some tiny homemade macaroons on the table to share with her friends. "The children seem to be managing at school. There have been no nasty arguments or boys fighting in the playground. I think it's because they're hungry as their diet is less than it should be for growing kids. Mothers come to meet their children when school finishes rather than let them wander home alone."

"No one knows when the *gendarmes* or Germans will make an unexpected visit to the village. I received a letter yesterday from my friend, Claudine who is still teaching at a *Lycee* in Paris. She wrote that there have evolved two types of community in the city—those who are collaborating with the Germans and flaunting the benefits—silk stockings, designer clothes, expensive meals and wine, like Coco Chanel. The majority are workers who hurry with bowed heads through the streets, manage on reduced food rations and try to stay out of sight. She mentioned seeing more Jewish families being thrown out of their homes, their belongings confiscated or burnt. All must wear the hateful yellow star. Claudine wrote she will go to her family home in the Limousin soon for safety. I wrote back and asked if she'd heard news about the young men taken for the *Releve*. She thinks they've been transported to German factories. I suspect all personal mail is opened and scrutinised, so I must be circumspect when writing to Claudine. She said there were several German children attending her school who are family of German officers or diplomatic staff." Britt sighed heavily. "I miss the life in Paris, the entertainment and art galleries, but I'm so glad to be safe here in Broussac."

The four friends parted soon, greeting neighbours as they walked home. They agreed to meet at the café in a few days to exchange news. There seemed to be an ominous threat hanging over the village. The *Prefecture* in Rodez regularly gave instructions to the *gendarmes* to monitor any villagers hoarding food and crops, and listening to BBC radio.

Germans in Cahors

In April, Paulette Cantou came into the *Boulangerie* to collect her bread. She gently pulled Jean-Jacques aside and whispered, "I've received an urgent message from my friend who runs *la Poste* in Cahors. It's about Liliane's cousin, Pierre. Can I speak with her?"

"*Mais oui*, but she's out delivering bread. I'll give her the message."

Madame Cantou nodded, bought her customary baguette and walked back to *la Poste*. She told her husband, "Liliane will be upset as her cousin has been taken by the Germans. His wife sent a message."

Liliane finished the early deliveries and returned home to collect fresh bread for *Villane-le-Foret*. Jean-Jacques asked her to go into the kitchen, shutting the door behind him. He hugged his wife and told her to sit down. Liliane frowned and looked anxious.

"Paulette Cantou came to the *Boulangerie* whilst you were on the delivery round to tell me she'd received an urgent message from *la Poste* in Cahors about your cousin Pierre."

Liliane opened the sealed paper and quickly skimmed the contents. Her face blanched and her hand shook as she passed it to her husband. "*Mon Dieu*," she said bowing her head, tears dropping from her eyes. "*Pierre est un prisonnier des Allemandes. Simone ecrit le message hier matin.*" She looked anxiously at Jean-Jacques. "The Germans have taken Pierre. Simone will be distraught. Her parents were taken from the family home in Strasbourg in 1917. They were never seen again and Simone lived with an aunt till she married Pierre."

Jean-Jacques hugged her, then went back into the Boulangerie to serve the queue of customers waiting patiently. Liliane sat at the scrubbed kitchen table, tears streaming down her face. She and Pierre had spent many childhood holidays in Cahors. She took a cotton napkin from her pocket and scrubbed her cheeks, lifted her head and stared through the kitchen window, thinking how could she help Simone and the children. There was only one answer. She must take the train to Cahors and find out where Pierre was held. She desperately hoped he wasn't with the Gestapo. He had said on her last visit that he helped the local *maquis* so someone must have told the Germans.

Decision made, Liliane walked into the *Boulangerie*, kissed her husband and squeezed his arm before picking up two paniers of bread for *Villane-le Foret*. She loaded the yellow van and drove down the lane deep in thought. She daren't risk her husband and children being involved, especially as Armand was now a German captive. She'd discuss it with Jean-Jacques that night. He was a calm, practical man and would support any sensible solution to help Liliane and her family.

It was a long anxious day and Jean-Jacques decided to close the *Boulangerie* early. Rose-Marie would be home from school soon and they didn't want to tell her that *Maman* would visit Cahors again. They agreed Liliane would bike to the farm where Louis worked to tell him she would be going to Cahors for a few days. She pedalled furiously down the lanes, nearly bumping into a tractor slowly turning out from a field. She managed to slide into a ditch to avoid him, covering her feet and legs in mud. When she reached the farm, she could see her son washing under the pump and called out to him. She pulled him over behind a stone wall and quietly explained the problem with Pierre and her decision to go to Cahors to help Simone.

"*Mais, Maman, c'est dangereux. Les Allemandes sont dans la ville.* The Germans invaded Cahors before Christmas. The farmer listens to radio broadcasts at night in his barn and tells the news to me and his family."

"*Je sais, mais Pierre est ma cousin et Simone n'a pas de famille.* I know, but they're family." Liliane pulled her son close to hug and kiss him before cycling back home, anxious to make the journey before dark as there were no lights on the lanes and her bike had no lamp.

A week later, Jean-Jacques drove Liliane to the nearest station in the yellow van. The lane was badly potholed from winter storms and he drove carefully. It was early and there were many *artisans* and office people queuing to show their ID documents and work permits to the uniformed *gendarmes*. They pulled a few people out of line and locked them in the station waiting room but Liliane was waved onto the platform. The train steamed in with clouds of smoke and crunching wheels. Armed *gendarmes* marched on to the platform to scrutinise the embarking passengers. Liliane recognised *Gendarme Pellier* dressed in his formal uniform amongst them. He nodded acknowledgement and ordered her to get in the carriage. She found a seat, placed her small case between her feet and kept her head down for the journey.

The train hissed into Cahors station; the engine almost hidden in clouds of grey steam. There was a strong odour of coal and tiny black smuts coated the platform. Liliane disembarked and queued to get her documents inspected at the exit. She walked into Cahors town centre, noticing the alien presence of German soldiers and Nazi flags hanging over the doors and windows of the Hotel Terminus. The streets were silent with no rattling carts and stuttering old cars, no shouts to horses and people. The cafes and shops were shuttered. A spiteful wind tossed rubbish piled in the gutters and rattled the flagpoles with their threatening banners of Nazi crooked black symbols and poorly latched windows. Rain lashed the buildings and swept down the Boulevard carrying the debris of discarded vegetables and wrapping paper from the market. It pooled in doorways and lapped around vacant café tables and chairs. The rising wind gusted down chimneys, billowing smoke from wood fires. It moaned around corners and untended balconies, tearing out plants and flinging them into the street.

Liliane was pushed around the corner by gusts of wind onto the main street, *Boulevard Leon Gambetta*. She heard an ominous rumbling of heavy engines and motorbike exhausts. She saw a procession of military vehicles and small tanks moving down the centre of the Boulevard ignoring pedestrians and bikes. People huddled on side pavements, trapped against the walls and shuttered banks and shops. Official notices in black gothic type were fixed to their doors. They sullenly watched German soldiers marching behind the vehicles in tight formation, helmets shining and guns held ready. Barricades had been erected at both ends of the Boulevard. A soldier lifted the butt of his rifle and smashed an open café window and a baby began to scream. Soldiers continued breaking doors and windows, barging inside buildings, stuffing items of value into their pockets and heaving furniture onto the pavement before setting it on fire. People started running wildly down side streets, trying to escape the overwhelming force of the Germans.

Liliane dodged down a narrow, cobbled street that led to the medieval cathedral. She intended to shelter inside, hoping that the ancient right of safe refuge in a Catholic church was still recognised by the enemy. Thunder rolled overhead as she reached the cathedral. Hundreds of people of all ages, some carrying cases and bags, others clutching babies and toddlers were pushing against the partly opened carved wooden doors. Priests were ushering them into pews and handing out water. The dim light of candles and the comforting smell of incense had a calming effect on the crowds.

Liliane sat on a stone bench against the wall with a mother and three small children who were rubbing their wet eyes and mouths. The mother told them to hold hands as her eyes pleaded with Liliane to help her. Liliane took out a few bonbons and gave the two older children one each to suck. "We are safe for now," she whispered and smiled at the smallest child who held out her hand to Liliane. Feeling strangely comforted by the closeness of people and the tranquillity of the ancient cathedral, Liliane drew a deep breath and thought how she could get to Simone's house.

Finally, the rumbling of military vehicles lessened outside and the crashes and screams decreased. Liliane nodded to the mother and edged her way to the main door, left ajar to allow sunlight to brighten the aisles. She elbowed her way through people sheltering in the cathedral porch and crowding in the square outside.

Priests were mingling and handing out water. There was a chill wind and rain was pelting down. People were dressed in coats and scarves, many looking worn or ragged, others were more smartly dressed. Liliane worked her way to the back of the crowd and slid down a narrow lane that led to the river which she must cross to reach Pierre's home.

She decided to walk across the main bridge, identity documents in hand, hiding in the crowds evacuating the city. The bridge parapets were slick with water as she bowed her head to her chest, her hair covered by a thick scarf. The crowd inched along and Liliane shuffled with them, attaching herself to a family where the father was tugging his children and an old lady sat in a rickety wooden cart. The children were crying in fright and the mother tried to quieten them and keep the old woman from falling off the cart. Liliane smiled at the mother and held out her hand to assist the old woman. German soldiers and uniformed *gendarmes* lined the roadside, scrutinising people, pulling some aside.

The icy rain sprayed her face and dampened her shoulders, and made the road slippery. It took a long time for Liliane to reach the far end of the bridge, her thin woollen mittens were soaked and her hands frozen trying to hold the old woman in the cart. The number of uniformed *gendarmes* and German soldiers lessened as the family passed onto the unpaved road that climbed steeply up the hill to a cluster of houses where Pierre and Simone lived. Liliane kissed the children and their parents and wished them, "*Bon courage.*" They gave her wan smiles as they continued trudging up the hill and out into the countryside.

Simone was peering through the lace-curtains at the window and quickly came to the door when Liliane knocked. "*Bienvenue ma cousine.* Welcome," Simone whispered as she pulled Liliane inside before kissing and hugging her. She looked pale and anxious, her children clinging to her dress. They looked unkempt and the kitchen was barely warm, the wood stove glowing with a few small logs.

"*Tu viens, Liliane. C'est un catastrophe. Pierre est un prisonnier depuis deux semaines et nous n'avons pas du nourriture ou du bois.* I can't go out to get food and wood because it's not safe to leave the children alone. The Germans may come and search the house. It's two weeks since Pierre was taken." Simone sobbed, hiding her head in her hands.

Liliane hugged the distraught mother. She told the children to sit down as she had come to help and brought fresh bread and eggs. "*J'ai porter du pain, des oeufs. Asseyez-vous et nous mangeons ensemble.*" Liliane hugged the children, pushing them onto a bench and helping Simone sit down. "Let's eat before I look for your papa. *N'inquiete pas*. Don't worry."

The children wiped their tears and silently ate the food. Simone made a pot of coffee with ground acorns and poured glasses of water for her children, kissing their cheeks. "*J'ai beaucoup de peur.* I'm alone and scared. Are the Germans hurting Pierre? Is he being fed?" Tears fell down her face. Liliane washed the plates in the stone sink, pouring herself and Simone a cup of black coffee before she answered. "You stay here and I'll go out to buy food and firewood."

Liliane opened the front door, stepping carefully on the slippery stone steps. She looked up into the heavy sleet falling from a leaden sky, licking the icy drops from her lips. There was a chill wind that went through her mittens and coat. Neighbours were brushing sleet from their front doorsteps. They looked up sharply as Liliane shut the door, then carried on, heads bowed, not acknowledging her which was unusual as she knew many of them. Liliane briskly walked to the *epicerie* where she showed her ration card and bought a loaf of bread, a few eggs and a slice of cheese. She picked up a small bundle of firewood and placed a few francs on the counter. No one spoke to her.

A slick coating of ice on the road was treacherous underfoot as Liliane hurried back to Simone's house with her supplies. "*Voila*," she said cheerily as she opened the front door. The girls were sitting on the floor by the fire, reading to each other. Hugo was playing with a wooden train set under the kitchen table. Simone sat frowning, clenching her hands.

She looked very relieved when she saw Liliane. "*Je suis tres inquiete. C'est dangereux.* I was anxious. Is it dangerous?"

"*Non*," replied Liliane with a smile. "*Tous les voisins sont dedans. J'ai acheter du pain, du fromage et du bois.* Everyone is inside as it's cold and wet. I bought bread, cheese and wood."

The family spent a pleasant evening together, enjoying the food and warmth. The children went to bed early, so Simone and Liliane could discuss how to help Pierre and organise basic necessities for him. Liliane shared Simone's bed and hugged her before drifting into a disturbed sleep. Simone tossed and turned but eventually fell into a deep sleep.

"Je doit visiter la Mairie et demande les nouvelles de Pierre," Liliane said at breakfast. "I must go to the *Maire* and ask about Pierre. Don't worry, I'll be careful." She shrugged on her coat and gloves, tied on a scarf and walked carefully down to the Boulevard Leon Gambetta and the Mairie but the windows were shuttered and the door barred. She walked to the Hotel Terminus next to the railway station where the German army field command headquarters were based. Large flags with the Nazi symbol flew from every window and entrance. Military vehicles were parked outside and soldiers stationed at the main entrance. Liliane hesitated at the bottom of the steps, took a deep breath then walked up to the soldiers. She pulled off her scarf and smiled in a friendly way but they ignored her, just stamped their booted feet, guns held across their chests, helmets covering their eyes.

Liliane hesitated, wondering what language to use for her request. "*Je pense que mon cousin, Pierre Lasalle est dedans. Il y a un probleme*? I think you have my cousin. Is he in trouble?" The soldiers continued to ignore her, staring across at the train station. Liliane had turned to go when the entrance doors were pushed open and a uniformed man, his chest covered in medals stepped out, loosening his gun holster. The soldiers stood to attention, raising their arms in the 'Heil Hitler' salute. The officer returned the salute, then saw Liliane descending the steps. He barked a command and two soldiers grabbed hold of her arms and hustled her in through the open door into a large hall filled with military personnel. Liliane tried to resist and explain her reason for being there. She was forcibly hauled down stone stairs to a dark evil-smelling corridor and pushed inside a barred door which was slammed shut and locked.

The gloomy cell had no lighting and was empty of furniture. A small metal grille was inserted high up that provided little light and air. She stood absolutely still on the filthy concrete floor, terrified she had been captured and would be tortured or sent to an internment camp. She was shaking with fear and cold due to the clamminess of the damp stone walls. She heard faint rustlings of cockroaches and the scurrying of rats. A uniformed soldier unlocked the metal door, walked straight to her and stared into her eyes. He shook his head and walked out slamming and locking the door behind him.

Liliane collapsed onto the dirty cold floor, sobbing with terror. Daylight slowly faded from the open grille and the room grew bitterly cold. She huddled in a corner, thirsty, hungry and desperate. She remained there all night until the dawn light filtered through the window grille. The door was opened and a tin cup of water put inside, then slammed shut and locked again. Liliane crept across to the cup and gulped down the murky water. She moved to the furthest corner near the grille where she could feel a slight breeze. She stood on tiptoes and peered out of the grille which was at street level. She could see booted feet march past and stumbling people in wooden clogs. She slumped back on the floor, pulled her coat tight and retied the scarf over her hair.

By mid-day, when the cathedral clanged the ancient bells, the feeble sunlight had disappeared and she could see sleet whirling past the grille. Her stomach growled and ached with hunger, her tongue and mouth were dry and rough. She tried to be positive, knowing she had taken no illegal action. She had no idea why Pierre had been captured. It was pitch black now in the room as night had fallen. Liliane was lying huddled in her corner, trying not to cry but shivering with cold and hunger when the metal door was unlocked and a torch shone in her face, blinding her.

"*Raus, raus.*" A uniformed soldier marched across the cell, pulled her up and dragged her to the open door, pushing her down a long dark corridor and up the stone stairs. He pulled her to the entrance and shoved her outside onto the icy steps, then shut and locked the heavy door. Liliane's shoulder felt bruised where she fell down and her hair tingled with being tugged. The empty street was dimly lit by two street lamps near the train station. She hauled herself upright, slid down the rest of the steps and crept across to the shelter of the station waiting room. It was dark but dry and a little warmer. She perched on the wooden bench and tried to work out how she could return to her cousin's house.

It was a long, dark uphill walk and she had no energy left. She knew it was dangerous to remain at the station. She sidled out of the station exit and leant shivering against the cold wall while she scanned the area. It was dark but a slender line of light on the horizon forewarned of dawn. The streets leading from the station were empty but she waited in the shadow until she saw the wooden shutters of the café swing back and a glimmer of light from a window.

A *Boulangerie* van appeared on the street, pulled by a bony brown horse, the baker sitting on the board at the front. He guided the horse to the kerb edge by the café, jumped down and knocked on the window. "*Bonjour. C'est Jean avec du pain.*" The café door opened with a tinkling bell and the café owner appeared in the lamplight. Liliane saw a way out of her predicament and hurried across the street, calling, "*Bonjour, un moment s'il vous plait.*" The *Boulanger* stopped handing over his baskets of bread and looked at Liliane with a frown. "*Qu' est ce passe?* What's the problem?" he asked cautiously.

"*Bonjour. Je suis perdu. Je suis la femme du Boulanger a Broussac. Vous connaisez mon mari, Jean-Jacques Damour?*" Liliane stood hesitantly in front of him, aware that her clothes were rumpled and her shoes dirty.

"*Entrée, entrée. Il fait froid dehors.*" The café owner, a smartly dressed middle-aged woman stood at the doorway. She scrutinised the streets then firmly shut the café door, pulling down an indoor blind. "*Asseyez-vous et j'arrive avec du café.* Come in and sit down, it's cold outside." Liliane pulled out a metal chair at a table near the back and sat down, tidying her headscarf and tugging her coat across her chest.

"*Alors*. Who are you and why are you in the city so early?" Liliane bowed her head, wondering how much she should tell the café owner and the *Boulanger*. "My name is Liliane Damour and I live in Broussac, a village in the Aveyron. I am visiting my cousin Pierre Lasalle and his family. I got lost trying to avoid the German soldiers and tanks when I went to buy food. I hid in the station waiting room because of the bad weather. I must get back to my cousins as they'll be worried." Liliane spoke defiantly, her chin raised and her shoulders tensed.

"Are you honest or were you captured by the Germans for some crime?" The *Boulanger* questioned her brusquely. "The Germans are everywhere and suspicious of everyone."

"*Oui*. I'm speaking the truth. Can I ride with you over the river and up the hill please? I'm so cold and scared."

The café owner stared at Liliane for a few moments, then said, "*La pauvre*. Poor thing. Do you know her husband, Pierre?"

He nodded, handed over his baskets of bread, drank his expresso then ushered Liliane out the door and told her to hide in the back of his van. He shook the reins and the horse ambled over the bridge and jogged slowly up the hill.

As she crouched uncomfortably in the back of the van surrounded by empty crates, Liliane tried to think over her options. Simone needed help to find Pierre but had no idea where he had been taken to or why the Germans had captured him. Liliane realised that staying with her sister-in-law wasn't practical as she was drawing attention by her presence and nosy neighbours could notify the *gendarmes*. Besides, she couldn't continue to sleep on the kitchen floor because the house only had two bedrooms and Simone said that access to food and fuel was difficult.

When the *Boulanger* reached the top of the hill, he halted the cart and told Liliane to get out and walk the rest of the way. Liliane trudged the few metres to her cousin's house and rapped on the door. Simone opened it a little and gasped at seeing Liliane. She pulled her inside then slammed the door shut. Liliane noticed that the *Boulanger* had stopped a few metres further on and watched her before driving on.

"*Qu'est que ce passe?*" Simone asked anxiously as she pulled out a chair for Liliane. "What's happening? Did you find Pierre?" Simone slumped in the chair, her hands shaking as she poured a glass of water from a china pitcher and gave it to Liliane. The wood fire gave out a warm glow and made the simple kitchen feel cosy to Liliane whose hands and feet were frozen. She leant forward and touched Simone's shoulder as she told her what had happened at the Hotel Terminus. "I didn't see Pierre and I couldn't ask about him as I feared I would be imprisoned. I don't know how to help you more at this time because your neighbours could report a stranger and you have no spare bed or food. I'll get my bag and get the morning train back home if I run fast. The rain is not falling so heavily now. *Bon courage et bonne chance.*"

"Please don't leave me and the children as we have no one else to help us." Simone gathered her children to her and tried to control her fright. "Pierre left a letter for you." Simone handed over a small sealed package.

"*Je suis desolee.*" Liliane washed her hands and face in the sink and picked up her bags, folding the letter between some sheets of newspaper lying on the table and tucking it about her chest. "This will keep me warm."

"I'll try to discover more about Pierre and send you a message through *La Poste*." Liliane hugged her cousin and the children, unlocked the door and ran out to the wet muddy lane. She had thirty minutes before the train left for Montauban and Toulouse, stopping briefly at Lalbenque.

The narrow-paved street was empty except for a people brushing their front steps. A scraggy cat followed her as she trudged down the hill, avoiding gutters piled with rubbish and coated with ice. Liliane heard the train steam into the station, wheels clanging and brakes squealing. She hurried as fast as she could, breathing heavily when she reached the station just as the train stopped at the platform. She pulled out her identity documents and showed them to the *gendarmes* at the entrance. There was a crowd of people exiting from the train, so the *gendarme* waved her in and she hurried to open the train door and slid inside, breathing a sigh of relief. Her shoes were damp and dirty and her scarf was flapping loose.

The carriage was half-empty with only two shabbily dressed farmers' wives clutching straw baskets on their laps. Liliane saw the scraggy cat that had followed her sitting on the platform, enveloped by the steam from the engine. She crossed her fingers inside her gloves and prayed the train would leave soon. She alighted safely at Lalbenque station and decided to leave a message at *La Poste* in Lalbenque to ask Paulette Cantou to tell Jean-Jacques. A few small birds fluttered between the houses their feathers fluffed up for protection from the rain. Liliane pulled her coat tighter and crossed the slippery road to *La Poste*. Few people were around and many house shutters were closed for warmth. She opened the door to *La Poste* and greeted Madame Mercier and two women. She waited until they were served and, with a smile, asked Madame Mercier to send a message to *La Poste* in Broussac.

The lane to Broussac was muddy lit by a pale sun rising above the skyline. Liliane felt safer and warmer; now she was walking along the familiar road to her home village. The oak trees lining the road raised green frothy limbs to the cloudy sky and a few crows sat on the branches, croaking to each other. The country air was fresh and brisk, smelling of damp earth and leaf mould. A handful of bright hips were still attached to the thorny twigs of wild rose bushes and a faint smell of woodsmoke from wood stoves wafted on the light breeze. After an hour's walking, she could hear the bells of Broussac chiming.

A smell of fuel and the mechanical sound of an old engine warned her of a vehicle approaching. She looked up, then shouted with happiness as the yellow van chugged along the road. It was Jean-Jacques coming to meet her. He pushed the rusty door open, leapt out and ran to greet his wife. He had a few tears sliding down his face.

"*Ma chere femme. Tu es sain et sauf. J'etais tres inquiete.* I was so worried. Madame Cantou gave me your message, so I shut the *Boulangerie* and drove here as fast as I could. *Mon Dieu, je suis heureux.*" Jean-Jacques hugged his wife fiercely. "We missed you, *ma cherie.*"

Liliane laid her head on her husband's chest, listened to the comforting steady beat of his heart, and felt his arms clasped tightly around her, giving warmth and safety. She looked around at the soggy fields, the bare hedges and up at the dark heavy clouds and realised again she was fortunate to have a loving family and a nice home. She knew she had a duty to help her cousins even if it was dangerous.

Liliane unpacked her case whilst Jean-Jacques returned to the *Boulangerie* for the evening customers. She collected some old vegetables stored in the cellar and prepared a casserole, adding a few pieces of dried meat she had bought in Cahors when shopping for Simone. She placed the pot on the wood stove, glad of the warmth after her cold journey then sat at the kitchen table waiting for Jean-Jacques to come. She felt shaken by her temporary imprisonment and the raw brutality of the Gestapo. It was obvious that they'd decided she was guilty of some crime, but why had she been released from incarceration so quickly? Liliane fervently thanked God that she was safe at home. The dense silence of her cell and lack of basic necessities had been terrifying for a woman who had only known kindness in her life from a loving family. She worried what fearful treatment her cousin, Pierre was subject to and what crime he had committed. She despaired of being able to help him although she knew that Simone needed support and food for her children. She realised that tomorrow she must report the situation in Cahors to the *Maire*.

The light shining in the kitchen window faded as the sun sank lower in the grey cloudy sky. Small colourful birds were gathering on rooftops and trees singing their evening chorus, unaware of the treachery and violence being committed by an invading military force. Their songs were soft and brightly tuneful and soothed Liliane a little.

She opened the kitchen door and placed some crusts on the windowsill. There was little to eat in fields and hedgerows at this time of year, especially as the recent heavy rain had drenched the vegetation. She hung two tiny chunks of fat on a string from the shutter latch to attract blue tits and green finches. Rose-Marie came running down the lane from school, yelling to her mother, arms stretched wide in happiness. "*Maman, tu est revenu. Je suis tres heureux.* Maman, I'm so happy you've returned. Madame Ziegler asked where you were and said would you meet her for lunch tomorrow?"

"*Ma chere fille. Je t'aime beaucoup, beaucoup. Tout va bien.*" Liliane followed her daughter into the kitchen and kissed her cold cheeks before hugging her tight. "*J'ai visiter ma cousine a Cahors. J'ai acheter une petite tranche de tarte de miel pour vous.* I visited my cousin in Cahors and bought a small slice of pie as a treat."

Rose-Marie hung her coat on the hook and placed her schoolbag on the table. Jean-Jacques opened the kitchen door with a big grin. He rubbed his hands briskly and took off his coat. "*C'est froid ce soir*. It's cold this evening." He kissed his daughter and sat down by the wood stove. "*Hmmm. Il y a un odeur de casserole. Impeccable.*"

Rose-Marie put the soup spoons on the table and smiled as her mother placed a terracotta bowl of steaming casserole in front on her. With sighs of enjoyment, the small family ate their simple *repas* and talked about the small happenings of the day, content to be warm and safe.

When Rose-Marie had gone to bed, Liliane and Jean-Jacques sat by the kitchen stove with a half-empty bottle of red wine as Liliane recounted her experience in Cahors. "*Jean-Jacques, j'ai beaucoup de peur.* I was so cold and scared locked in a dark cell. I didn't know what they would do to me if the Gestapo thought I had helped Pierre." Liliane was fraught, the words tumbling out of her mouth and tears draining down her face. Jean-Jacques moved his chair closer and placed a comforting arm around her shoulders. "Simone didn't know why they arrested her husband but the neighbours ignored me as I walked to the shops for food. I thought I might never come home. It's too frightening. I'm not a brave person just a country wife and mother."

Jean-Jacques brushed away the tears and kissed her cheek and thoughtfully replied, "You must stay away from Cahors and we'll try to help Simone another way. Does she have friends nearby?"

"Simone gave me a small package from Pierre. I wrapped it in newspaper and tucked it inside my coat. I will look at it tomorrow. *Simone est tout seul, pas de famille.*" Liliane shivered despite the warmth of the wood stove. "I must tell Bertrand what I saw in Cahors, German soldiers everywhere, shops and banks shuttered. They were breaking into houses and stealing. There was a heap of furniture burning in the main *Place*, dragged out from the houses. Soldiers were sitting at café tables, drinking coffee, watching and clapping, their officers strutting around giving orders. There was hardly any food in the shops."

"Cahors is an important town for the Germans as it's on the main train line between Paris and Toulouse and the south of France. They can transport trucks, tanks and soldiers easily and quickly to Narbonne and Perpignan. Yes, you must tell Bertrand tomorrow. Now, it's time for bed. Drink your wine as it will help you sleep." Jean Jacques squeezed Liliane's shoulder, shut down the wood stove and went ahead to light the stairs. "*Bonne nuit, ma cherie,*" he said softly as they lay in bed.

Sabotage

Jean-Jacques rose early the next morning as usual and left for the *Boulangerie* leaving the shutters partly closed. He kissed Liliane as she ran downstairs. Liliane heard the kitchen door shut and pulled out her clothes from the armoire. She dressed and sat in the cane chair beside the bed to open the package from Simone. It was sealed and wrapped in brown paper. A thin piece of paper slid out with tiny ink marks. She peered more closely and identified a rough map with faint train lines and roads crisscrossing the paper. On the back were coded words in faded ink. She took the paper to the window and identified a date and a single scrambled word.

She scurried back to the chair and folded the map into tiny squares to tuck inside her vest. Apart from official communication links between *La Poste* in the villages and towns of the Aveyron and Lot, she'd heard that messages for the resistance were disguised in articles, drawings and poetry in underground newspapers. Her cousin, Pierre must have felt betrayed and terrified of being taken by the Gestapo to leave a personal message for her. It was obvious that Simone had no knowledge of his resistance role in the Lot.

Liliane went downstairs and across to the *Boulangerie* to collect bread for the day and loaded the yellow van. She must carry out her deliveries as fast as possible to avoid the risk that *Gendarme Pellier* would trap her for interrogation. She was brusque with *Boulangerie* customers, merely nodding to them instead of exchanging pleasantries. Fortunately, there was a long queue and her husband was fully occupied. She backed the van out of the backyard and squeezed down narrow lanes between houses to put bread in baskets set on doorsteps and windowsills. She took a rarely used back lane to reach *Villane-le-Foret* and placed a straw basket of bread inside, waving to her friend the owner of the cafe.

Liliane stopped at the ruined chateau on the way home and put Pierre's message in an agreed hiding place that she'd told Joseph when delivering his bread. He needed to set up a *rendezvous* with the *maquis* that day. Liliane and Joseph had been recognised as the only members from Broussac who were permitted to interact with the local *maquis*. The Resistance had established a safeguard against infiltration and betrayal by organising members in a pyramid structure. This ensured only two members of any group interacted or carried out operations together. They had designated code names and were instructed to keep no records of messages only to convey them by word-of-mouth.

Liliane suspected Pierre's paper message was a desperate attempt to inform the *maquis* of a planned assault on the local railway line intended to prevent resupply of German units in the Aveyron. It was common knowledge that main rail arteries like the Paris-Toulouse line were repeatedly repaired after being damaged by Resistance groups. The Germans had resorted to using truck convoys to transport fuel, food and arms, but these were often attacked as Resistance groups became more organised, trained and better equipped. Sabotage was one of the crucial methods of fighting German forces in Vichy France. Postal and railway workers cut electric lines and cables and tampered with telephone lines.

Liliane worried day after day that the sons of her friends, Martin, Gilles and Michel were forced to become involved in these terrorist activities by the *maquis* group who had rescued them. The three women, Josette, Paulette and Liliane regularly met to share titbits of information and console each other. Their parting words were no longer a cheery, "*A bientot*-see you soon—but the sombre words, *Bon courage*."

A few days later, Joseph met Liliane in the cellar of the ruined chateau and told her that high-tension cables and lines between Montauban and Brive had been cut by the *maquis* with the help of electric engineers. This was a crucial contribution to sabotage carried out by railway workers who had cut the railway tracks in 27 places and wrecked 38 locomotives.

"Tell your friends their sons were not involved in this attack and are still being trained. The *maquis* hiding place has changed several times since we took supplies to the youths six months ago. They work in guerrilla units carrying out quick hit and run raids. This latest sabotage action is unusual as it's a joint effort. Several *maquisards* were killed. Have you heard from your cousin or his wife?"

"*Non*. I'm worried how his wife and three children are managing in Cahors trying to find food." Liliane frowned. "I pray each night that the Allies will invade soon and we survive until them."

"I heard on BBC radio that the British are sending explosives to *maquis* to sabotage factories and power stations. Allied soldiers and airmen are being trained to handle top-secret communications between Britain and the French Resistance. They have trained specialist teams to sabotage lines, supply arms and improve command of partisan groups." Joseph responded quietly. *"Croisez les doights et sois prudent, mon amie."*

He kissed Liliane and slid quietly out behind the ruined walls.

Liliane used the old underground tunnel between the chateau and the church and crept silently up the damp steps. She sat with closed eyes in a pew in front of the altar. She knelt on a cushion, placed her hands together and raised them to the shadowy statue of Jesus behind the altar, whispering a prayer to him for the safety of her sons.

She heard a rustling behind her as the priest slid into the pew. "*Tout va bien, Liliane?*" He whispered. Liliane nodded and stayed seated for a few more minutes before walking briskly home. She didn't trust him as he was friendly with local *gendarmes*.

Jean-Jacques walked into the kitchen a few minutes later and sat at the table fiddling with his pipe and tobacco. Liliane saw that his hands were unsteady and a deep frown creased his forehead between his heavy eyebrows. He drew on his pipe then gestured to Liliane to sit down at the table. "*Gendarme* Pellier marched into the *Boulangerie* this morning and walked to the head of the queue of waiting customers, pushing Madame Ricard and Madame Royal to one side."

"*Je demande deux grande baguettes maintenant et j'ai deux questions. Ou est votre femme? Je doit parler chez nous.* Where is your wife? At home? I must speak with her." *Gendarme* Pellier rudely interrupted the two old ladies. "The Gestapo in Cahors interrogated her yesterday and ordered me to find out why she was in Cahors."

"*Bonjour, Gendarme* Pellier. Can I have coupons for two loaves of bread please?" Jean-Jacques requested politely and calmly. A few of his customers had backed out the door and others looked aghast at the threatening behaviour of a *gendarme*.

"*Non, non, non*! I'm permitted to receive extra bread because I'm working on an important investigation into a suspected plot to attack the Paris-Toulouse railway line by the Resistance. The Gestapo believe your wife is involved." *Gendarme* Pellier aggressively stood with his hands on his hips and his chin thrust out. His uniform cap was pushed onto his head to hide his face and his message was violently delivered.

Michel Duroux, deputy Maire moved to the front of the queue and placed a firm hand on the *gendarme's* shoulder. "*Albert. Qu'est qui se passe? Liliane est une vrai Francaise.* Liliane is true patriotic Frenchwoman."

Gendarme Pellier snatched his baguettes off the counter and marched out the door, banging it shut behind him. There was a collective sigh of relief before the customers continued chattering nervously.

Summer Hunting

Liliane walked down to the river early one June morning. The balmy air smelled fresh and perfumed after the night's rain. Along the banks, cow parsley grew to knee height and tiny white daisies sprinkled the grass. The hedgerows were full of buttery yellow cowslips and scarlet pimpernel. After the long harsh winter and the wet spring, it was a joy to be walking through leafy lanes with birds hopping between tree branches or flying to perch on the top. A blackbird sang from a grey tiled roof and swallows were swirling and chirping and skimming the water. She heard a moorhen piping and saw the heron land neatly on the opposite bank.

After the trauma of her journey back from Cahors and the continuing anxiety in the village, she needed the peace of the river to think over her options. Should she continue to help the *maquis* risking the safety of her family or withdraw from liaising with the Resistance? She felt completely alone as she couldn't discuss her predicament with her husband or friends without endangering them. Her hometown had been taken over by the Germans, her cousin captured by the Gestapo and her refuge in Broussac threatened. She had an obligation to protect Louis and Rose-Marie and ensure no blame was placed on Jean-Jacques.

She'd received no news of her son Armand or recent news of the youths hiding with the *maquis*. She thought Martin, Gilles and Michel were safer out of the village. Yet she couldn't stay at home as a country housewife without feeling that she'd let her cousin and son down by not supporting the fight of the *maquis* against the Germans. She'd heard that an increased number of *gendarmes* and *Milice* were carrying out regular searches in the countryside. They were hunting for *refractaires* hiding in abandoned barns and dense forests, acting on reports given by local informants. Liliane suspected the village priest and her neighbour Pierre Dalmain had passed on news to the *gendarmes*. These hunts were intended to reassure the Vichy Government and the Germans that everything was being done to capture youths nominated for the STO who went into hiding and were secretly supported by local people. She felt nothing but revulsion for the treachery of the priest and her neighbour. By doing nothing, she indirectly condoned their actions and the Vichy Government using the brutality of *Gendarme Pellier* and the Gestapo.

The church bells chimed the noon hour and Liliane was reminded that her family expected their mid-day meal. She lingered to watch two brown ducks take off from the river, briskly fluttering their wings and heard the hollow tapping of a woodpecker searching for insects in the chestnut wood. These were the soothing sights and sounds of the countryside that had cocooned her during her married life to a good man. She couldn't risk his life and livelihood or their children's future so she must get a last message to the *maquis rendezvous* that afternoon. Joseph had told her the *maquis* had received a consignment of arms and explosives from a parachute drop on the *causse*. The thought of personally being involved in violence made her shudder and conflicted with her deep Christian beliefs.

Decision made, Liliane walked briskly back home, waving to her neighbour Madame Ponthier watering her pot plants on the windowsill and avoided stepping on her terrier which was yapping at her heels. "*Allez, allez,*" she told him. She ran up the steps to her house, removed her muddy clogs, slipped on a pair of knitted slippers and walked into the kitchen to prepare lunch. It was the usual bland vegetable soup enlivened with sprinkled pieces of goat's cheese and croutons. Her daughter and son rushed into the kitchen, pausing for a kiss before fighting over a place at the stone sink to wash their hands. Liliane hugged them both, feeling relieved about the recent decision she'd made. Jean-Jacques arrived within minutes and could see a lightening of spirit by the expression on his wife's face. "*Bon courage, ma cherie. Sois prudent.* Take care, my beloved wife," he whispered and kissed her on both cheeks.

Joseph visited later that evening with the latest news. In June, a list of approximately 1,300 *refractaires* was sent from Limoges *Prefecture* to Toulouse and *gendarmes* were hunting them across *Departement* borders. They were supported by undercover surveillance police.

"We must be very careful. *Gendarme Pellier* is on the prowl day and night. I'll take your message to the *maquis rendezvous* tonight. *Gendarme Pellier,* in his arrogance and pleasure in newfound power, sees me as a bumbling senile old man. Which is exactly how I act with him!" Joseph smiled and winked. "Now, for some good news. More local youths have escaped STO conscription and are hiding in caves in the gorges of the Aveyron closer to Villefranche and have set up a new *maquis* group. They're secretly supported by tradesmen in Villefranche and local railway workers. Now, I must slip out of your back door, avoiding Madame Ponthier's terrier who is as watchful and mean as *Gendarme Pellier*!"

Joseph had memorised Liliane's message in his head as he knew paper notes were too dangerous to carry. He knew the *Milice* had thoroughly searched the *Mairie* files for information about *maquis* actions.

"Joseph is a very brave man. He should be dozing by his fire-side at this time of night at his age." Jean-Jacques sighed and re-lit his pipe with saved shreds of old tobacco and crumbled oak leaves. It gave him time to formulate an important question for Liliane. He breathed in the tobacco mix and laid his pipe on the corner of the wood stove. He leaned forward in his chair, looking closely at his wife. He noticed how she had aged in the past two years with anxiety for her family and fear for the future. He could see new lines fanning out from her eyes and mouth and a several threads of white in her dark hair. He felt an emotional tightening of his stomach and his eyes watered as he imagined the danger for Liliane.

"*Ma cherie*. Have you decided to continue with your liaison with the *maquis*? Are the risks important to you? I know it's because of your cousin's involvement and capture, but please be extra careful because of our children. No, don't tell me anything." Jean-Jacques held up his hand. "I'm trying to understand and view your activities as patriotism but it's so dangerous." He put an arm round his wife's shoulders and bade her sit down. "You must reconsider. We've lost our eldest son to the Germans and I couldn't bear it if you were captured and interrogated. *Tu es ma raison d'etre*. My reason for living."

Liliane looked up from her clasped hands and steadily regarded her husband. "How did you know I had made a decision?"

"You went early to the river bank and that's your quiet place to think over crucial decisions and actions." Jean-Jacques reached across to tuck a few curls behind her ear and briefly kissed her on the lips.

Liliane felt tears gather in her eyes at the perception and understanding of her husband. She breathed in then told him her final decision. "*Mon cher epoux*. Joseph will deliver my resignation tonight. Let's go to bed now. It's been a traumatic day and we need peace in each other's arms." She rose and turned down the lamp, slipped her arm through her husband's and kissed him firmly.

Vichy France Autumn and Winter 1943-44

Disintegration of the Village

Throughout the cooler darker autumn days, there had been a noticeable increase of *gendarmes* and *Milice* snooping round Broussac. They conducted weekly inspections of barns, cellars and outhouses, searching for illegal hoarding of crops and food. They peered in empty chicken and rabbit coops and frightened old ladies by climbing up ladders to look around attics. They questioned everyone regarding hiding places for *maquisards* and members of the Resistance. Jean-Jacques was hauled away from the *Boulangerie* by *Gendarme Pellier* and interrogated about his wife's activities.

"He dragged me down to his cellar, pushing his mother away, so she fell to the floor. He handcuffed me to a metal pole and spat questions at me, challenging me to expose you." Jean-Jacques was by nature a calm and reasonable man. Now, he was shaking with fury as he told Liliane that evening after the *Boulangerie* closed. "My customers were horrified. Michel and Victor tried to stop him dragging me down the steps. Madame Ricard fainted with shock and was helped to a chair to sit down."

They ate a subdued dinner with the children. Liliane gazed round her warm homely kitchen and gently stroked the arms of Louis and Rose-Marie. They paused briefly from spooning their soup and smiled at her. Her heart felt almost at breaking point. She was torn by her patriotic duty to her country and care for her beloved family. She felt a tense coil of anger throb in her mind and a flood of acrid bitterness fill her stomach. The Germans had captured her eldest son and given no details of his condition or location. They were terrorising harmless villagers and had tortured her cousin and members of the *maquis* in Cahors.

Liliane heard a commotion outside and rose to pull back the shutters. Bertrand Danton was being dragged out of his home and down the steps. An oil lamp fastened to the wall of the *Mairie* cast a blurry light on his face, emphasising the shadowed lines of sheer terror.

Gendarme Pellier looked elated and victorious. He held a radio under his arm and a gun in his hand. He had locked handcuffs to his and Bertrand's hands. His police vehicle was parked in the *Place* and the *Maire* was shoved inside. M'sieur Pascal, the village priest, stood outside the church and acknowledged the *gendarme* with a 'Heil Hitler' salute. The villagers had long suspected that he was a spy and an informant for the *Milice*. Only a few elderly people attended Mass now, the remainder staying home. Everyone was extremely cautious talking to him.

After a few days, the *Maire* was brought home by the *Milice*. Bertrand was limping and stumbling, his hands dripped blood and his mouth had only empty gums as his teeth had been knocked out. Madame Danton opened her door and shrieked with horror when she saw the condition of her husband. He had been a virile healthy, smartly dressed man who had been interrogated so badly he was almost unrecognisable. His wife helped him inside, waving away help from the villagers who had gathered in the Place. "*Bon courage, Bertrand*," some shouted.

It seemed an evil wind was blowing through Broussac when the *Maire*'s elderly parents collapsed with shock and died the next day. They were found by Michel the Deputy *Maire* when he visited them to tell them about the disaster that had befallen their son. He walked to the *Mairie* and whispered the bad news to Madame Danton. She nodded and quickly shut the door. Michel informed the priest and arranged a day for the funeral. All the villagers would attend as the elderly couple were part of the fabric of the village and liked by all. Three days later, the church bell rang sonorously at 1030 and 1100 am. There was a hushed crowd of people standing by the church porch, signing the formal funeral book. They acknowledged each other with stiff nods but no kisses were given or *Bonjour* spoken. Pierrette Latour played sombre music on the old wooden piano and the brief service was delivered by the priest. Many tears were shed by the elderly, long-time friends of old M'sieur and Madame Danton. The villagers respectfully moved towards the porch door and walked to the village cemetery for the burial. In a break with tradition, Michel read the service at the family grave.

A few days later, *La Poste* failed to open at its normal time. A handwritten note was pinned to the door stating that it would be closed until further notice. M'sieur Cantou visited Michel, and informed him that his wife had been taken by the *Milice*. He was distraught and angry. "What has she done?" He asked, shaking his head in fear.

Later that day, *Gendarme Pellier* delivered Madam Cantou to *La Poste*. She was unharmed but terrified and unable to speak. The villagers were shocked and horribly afraid of talking with or meeting their neighbours. The *Boulangerie* was open only in the morning but there was no lively chatter as women queued for their rations. The *Epicerie* displayed a few items on shelves erected outside but customers were not allowed inside.

The *Maire* slowly recovered and limped to the café on occasions. When he drank his coffee, the liquid dribbled down his chin as he had no teeth. He became thin and gaunt as he was unable to chew food or sip from a spoon as his mouth was raw and painful. He had aged twenty years.

Liliane no longer met with her friends to chat and sew and rarely spoke to Britt or any villagers when she delivered bread. The café at *Villane-le-Foret* was closed and Marie-Francoise left to stay with cousins in the *Montagne Noire*.

Winter Suffering

Autumn slipped in with gusty winds shaking dead leaves from trees. The vibrant colours of red, gold, yellow and ochre brightened the days as they tumbled and fluttered into rutted lanes and ditches. Red squirrels leapt between tree branches intent on filling their bellies to last the cold winter months and to store the remainder. Their bushy tails waved as they balanced on hedgerow and posts. Swallows flocked together in the sky or perched on rooftops, chirping and chattering ceaselessly from dawn to dusk until they left in swarms to hibernate in Africa. Mild days with pale sunlight soon merged into cold nights and the first frosts coated the ploughed fields, shining with an iridescent glow.

Heavy mists cloaked the Aveyron River as it flowed through deep rocky gorges. The mist thinned on the high ground in mid-afternoon as the weak sun provided a tepid warmth. The thick forests were permanently damp as trees dripped with moisture from heavy rains. It seemed as if a dense colourless blanket hung low in the sky, seeping moisture onto the fields. Late-harvested crops like maize were stacked damp in tall wire containers with little chance of drying out. Old canal tiled roofs leaked into bedrooms and many homes had buckets strategically placed under ceiling drips. The villagers moved around the village huddled in wool coats or rainproof jackets.

The weekly market had shut down after the harvest as German requisitions took a larger share of the crops. There was no travelling between villages due to lack of fuel for transport, which had been requisitioned by the Germans and there was little spare feed for horses and mules to pull carts. Some houses in Broussac were falling into disrepair due to lack of money and the availability of materials. Broussac had lost many artisan skills as their menfolk had either deceased or were working for the German *STO, Service Travail Obligatoire.*

Throughout the year, Broussac and other local villages had cancelled traditional fetes and celebrations except for holding an Easter Mass. The Harvest Supper and *Fete de Chataigne,* normally the highlight of October was cancelled and only *Toussaint* on 1 November, the Day of the Dead was observed. Many villagers had lost family members due to starvation and weakness, especially among the elderly.

The villagers collected walnuts, acorns, chestnuts, wild plums and blackberries from the woods and hedgerows, storing them in secret places so rapacious *gendarmes* couldn't purloin them. At night in outhouses, women boiled fruit for jam and preserving using shaded lamps and candles for dim light. Apples were stored in wooden boxes and many a village man constructed a false wooden wall in his cellar to hide the food.

Obtaining firewood was also a secret process, each farmer stealthily cutting down trees on his land at night and villagers collecting dead branches from their inherited tiny wooded areas. Each family picked and collected only for themselves not sharing and exchanging as they did before the war started. It was necessary for personal survival. Women slipped out before dawn their heads covered by a dark shawl, carrying an empty sack to fill with anything edible or useable.

Jean-Jacques struggled to get enough supplies of flour to make bread for the villagers. He extinguished the wood fire in the brick bread oven at dusk to conserve fuel and rose before dawn to relight it for his early clients. He opened the *Boulangerie* for a few hours each morning as his customers waited silently on the stone steps, wrapped in woollen coats and hats, shuffling their booted feet to keep warm. The steps were often slippery with hoar frost and the elderly had to be helped to prevent them slipping.

Liliane stopped her delivery rounds because of the lack of flour and her fear that *Gendarme Pellier* would interrogate her and take her to the Gestapo. He made no secret of his suspicions that she was still receiving and delivering messages for the *maquis*. M'sieur Cantou opened *La Poste* for one hour twice a week while his wife remained alone indoors.

Paulette closed the village café as she could no longer reliably obtain basic foodstuffs such as coffee, milk, bread and meat. Her husband Jean-Luc filled his days making wooden objects with no intention of selling them. There were few children in the village now as their families had departed to stay with relatives down south or in isolated regions. Mornings were not announced by the raucous crow of the cockerels as they had been eaten; chickens and rabbits had disappeared in the stew pot months ago.

As winter tightened its grip and bitter winds blew in from Russia, the first flurry of snowflakes swirled round the village laying a thin coating on roofs and laneways. The last dead leaves were torn off the plane trees in the *Place de la Mairie* and fruit trees in back gardens.

Shutters remained barred all day and the village closed down. A dense grey blanket of cloud pressed down on the rooftops and birds sheltered under eaves for warmth. There were no women gossiping on front steps while they brushed away the dirt or swept the leaves. No children ran through the lanes shrieking with laughter kicking a ball or chasing each other. The fields had been ploughed in autumn and lay fallow and tractors were housed with cattle and other farm animals in the great stone barns.

Before dawn on a bitter cold day after Christmas, Josette heard a hard knock on her front door. She was placing more logs in the kitchen stove and brewing a pot of coffee. Alain was working in his shed attempting to mend his old plough. Josette felt terrified to expose herself at the open door. A male voice hissed a few words and she heard a thud as something was deposited on her doorstep. She counted to ten, then carefully pulled the heavy wooden door ajar. A wrapped body lay across the stone steps, the shroud still leaking blood. A few tufts of brown hair stuck out the top. She screamed then collapsed back into her doorway, hitting her head on the flagstone floor.

A tall shadow appeared in the doorway blocking out the faint daylight. Josette sat up and continuously screamed in terror. Alain bent and picked up the dead body of one of his sons, gently placing it on the flagstone floor beside his wife. He pulled back the dirty bloody shroud and saw the bone-white features of his youngest son Gilles, frozen in death. He leant against the kitchen wall and slowly slid down until he was crouching at the same height as his son. His expression was of stark horror and his broad strong shoulders started to shake. Josette pulled herself off the floor and laid her head on his arm, tears flooding down her face. The youth's parents sat together for a long time until the stove had consumed the wood to a bed of ashes and the spiteful wind chilled every inch of their bodies. Alain had pulled the body of his son across their prone legs, so they could fully mourn his premature tragic death.

His parents carefully lifted his precious body between them and laid it on the kitchen table. They unwrapped it and in the smoky dim light of the kerosene light spied the entry of the bullet wound that had stopped his beating heart. Gilles's face seemed peaceful with his eyes closed but his mouth was twisted with the pain he had suffered in his last hours. Josette and Alain took a chair either side of the table and gazed at their beloved son, remembering his simple jokes and easy manner, his constant energy and curiosity in everything was tragically extinguished for good. Alain reached out his hand and held his wife's over the bright tablecloth.

As the kitchen darkened with the dusk, Alain rose and picked up a few logs from a straw basket and a match to re-light the stove to heat the coffee. He placed a fresh baguette on the cloth and searched for a piece of cheese which he cut in two and laid alongside the bread. *"Mange, ma cherie. Il faut manger."* He brushed aside a few tears and sat down again, pouring the hot coffee into two china bowls, tore off a piece of bread and dipped it into the drink. He and Josette sat for a while longer until Josette found a blanket. Alain lifted his son, so it could be tucked around his thin corpse, leaving the face uncovered so he and his mother could press a few last kisses on the chill unlined forehead. Then he opened the door to their cellar and carefully walked down the steps to place the body in the cold cellar overnight.

When he walked back to the kitchen, he found Josette weeping over a scrap of dirty paper. She looked up at him and whispered, "Gilles was shot by the *Milice* while standing on guard duty last evening. *Mon fils est mort pour la Patrie.* My son died for his country." She bowed her head to her arms laid on the table and sobbed as her heart broke at the brutality and futility of war and the needless death of her beautiful son.

Malignant Forces

The impact of German cruelty stalked the lanes of Broussac and fear of the future haunted villagers and farmers. Farming families were leaving the land and travelling to relatives in the south in carts and old vehicles using fuel saved in tin cans in the farthest corners of barns and empty outhouses. Madame Ricard's daughter, Claudette came to fetch her and take her to the comparative safety of a small village in the Corbieres, the foothills of the Pyrenees. The *Milice* were based in Foix and rarely visited due to transport restrictions. Claudette's husband was a rural priest and they had three small children. His parish extended from Foix to the mountains. Due to poor roads, few travellers passed through the area and they had seen no German forces. Winter commenced early in the Pyrenees and snowfalls had coated the highest peaks with a sparkling cover of heavy frost and light snow.

A friend of the *Maire,* Armand Dubosc drove his wife and family to relatives living in the *Montagne Noire* where he was informed active *maquis* bands prevented German forces from carrying out raids on settlements in the thick forests. Madame Dalmain left to live with her widowed sister in *Ceret*, a small town near the Spanish border. She declared to all who would listen in the *Boulangerie* queue that she was fed up with the aggressiveness and irrational behaviour of her husband. "He can wash his own clothes, though I doubt he can be bothered, and cook his own meals!" she stated emphatically, stamping her foot and raising a small cloud of flour from the floor of the *Boulangerie*. Her neighbours sighed in sympathy, wishing they could leave and stay with relatives.

Professional people from Paris moved into their summer houses. Norbert Legrand, a respected *notaire* in Paris settled into his *maison de maitre* in the hills above Broussac with his wife and teenage son, Albert. She had worked as a nurse in the *Faculte de Medecine* in Cochin. Britt Zeigler had used his services when she had to sell her apartment in Paris. A renowned doctor had shut down his practice in Bourg-la-Reine and moved into his holiday house in *Villane-le-Foret*.

Starving ragged refugees crowded the main roads from Parisien suburbs, tugging and carrying listless children and pushing the elderly and infirm in improvised wooden carts. Locals provided food but were suffering from a shortage of food staples such as meat and the strict rationing of bread. They ate only what they could grow in their *potagers* so meals were vegetarian casserole thickened with stale breadcrumbs and corn.

Many of the villagers, including the *Maire* and Madame Cantou of *La Poste,* had until recently listened in secret to BBC radio broadcasts hoping for positive news of the Allied advance. They heard that confrontation between the *maquis* and the Vichy Government had become more ferocious as German forces imposed crippling restrictions over food and fuel. The villagers realised this war would be long and devastating but French morale was boosted by news that the Germans were losing soldiers, arms and vehicles on the Russian front at an unprecedented rate. The villagers no longer believed that Marshall Petain would protect them, as with every concession he made to the Nazis he showed his weakness to resist them.

Early in 1942, Britt had become involved in resistance with local schoolteachers in the Aveyron and the Lot, and market towns in the *Lozere*. She was passionately patriotic to France and desperate to support any underground activities actively sabotaging German forces and protecting defenceless farms and villages. She had a secret radio transmitter to receive and send coded messages for the Resistance. She heard about life in the occupied zone, the deprivation and poverty, the destruction of villages.

She had barely slept since the start of this war and the torture and death of her German husband. She knew the *maquis* sheltered in isolated farms with their numbers enhanced by *refractaires (STO* deserters). The *maquis* used guerrilla tactics to be ready for immediate mobilisation and moved continually. They were loyally supported by the rural population.

She liaised with well-respected school teachers, Raymond Fournier and Renee Salvignol who were based in the town of *Saint-Affrique*. They were supported by Leon Freycinet, one of the directors of the Roquefort cheese manufacturer located near Millau. Renee was captured and tortured by the special anti-maquis police known as the infamous Marty Brigade, but survived. Britt had also been in contact with a group of *maquis* based in the sheep-rearing *causses* whose leader, Alfred Marle, was arrested on 6 February 1944 and died in Rodez of torture by the Gestapo.

The Resistance and the *maquis* had taken on the responsibility to organise the supply of provisions to local villages, forcing farmers and butchers to control food prices and use leniency with food rationing. In agreement with farmers, milk destined for the black market was re-distributed by the *maquis* to children of poor families.

The *maquis* expected local villages and towns to support and shelter them and to supply information on German movements. From mid-summer 1943, the rural population were more involved in certain areas. Under orders from Laval and German leader Fritz Sauckel, French authorities were forced to search more diligently for *refractaires*, and to use threats of fines or imprisonment for parents supporting them. The escalating risk of *denouement* for concealing these individuals by farmers and villagers forced the *maquis* and *refractaires* to increase the security of their camps and hiding places by moving them to dense forests, hillside caves and isolated farmhouses and sheep huts. The Massif Central region, north of the Aveyron was ideal for this situation.

In April 1944, Britt was secretly warned that *the Regional Intendant of Police, Marty*, based in the Montpellier region was ordered to investigate *maquis* bands in the Aveyron *Departement*. He was notoriously fanatical in his investigations of small villages, isolated farms and locals suspected of hiding the *maquis*. His reports identified that the *maquisard* were disciplined and well armed with hand and machine guns because of effective parachute drops organised by British agents. He demanded the Regional *Prefecture* and the Vichy Government station a detachment of German forces at Rodez. His investigations specified that the Aveyron Police were failing to provide information of local *maquis* members and actions to the German authorities.

By the summer of 1944, confrontations between the *maquis* and German forces in the Aveyron and Lot *Departements* intensified. The Vichy Government had failed abysmally to curb the desperation and subversive power of the *maquis* particularly in the remote Aveyron. The *Departement* was bordered by the Massif Central to the north and protected by high rugged plateaux in the east and north-west, and the dense forests of the south. Travelling was difficult as the region was bisected by steep rocky gorges and fast flowing rivers. It was almost impossible for German forces to effectively search the region.

In March and April 1944, the regional *Intendant of Police,* Marty reported that camps of *refractaires* and *maquis* bands were increasing exponentially and that local police were 'negligent in rooting them out'. He was convinced they posed an escalating threat to German control and activities with their rapid raids and assaults. Their information was provided by local people.

Marty's zealous investigations uncovered effective sabotage of electrical power supply which caused 2,500 workers to stop work in Decazeville, an important administrative centre in the Aveyron. Marty recommended a war of terror and destruction to annihilate *maquis* camps and houses of local Resistance sympathisers.

Vichy France Summer 1944

Maquis Attack

The setting sun spread a warm orange and red glow over the countryside and the new moon hung like a thin slice of lemon in the pale blue sky. It was a humid Sunday evening with mosquitoes and midges collecting in swarms around water troughs and wells. Despite the increasing shortage of food, the villagers sat on their stone terraces and wooden balconies to enjoy the warmth. Their children were listless and scrawny in makeshift clothes, the parents gaunt with hunger but needed the company of neighbours to share their distress at the brutality of German reprisals.

Before dawn the next day, the local *maquis* quietly moved twenty men into pre-determined defence positions around *Villane-le-Foret*. They had given no advance warning of the ambush to the *Maire* or other villagers. They settled at various vantage points bordering the road to St Martial and hid on wooded bends, assumed firing positions on the dusty ground, propped on their elbows. They were waiting to ambush a German convoy due to pass within the hour. Their leader had learned of the convoy the previous night through Britt and had quickly mobilised *maquis* forces. Britt rose early as usual, and knowing about the *maquis* raid, closed the school and encouraged parents to keep their children close to home because there had been whispered reports of increased German forces.

As the sun rose, spreading summer heat on the prone bodies, the *maquis* heard the mechanical rumble and grating noise of heavy trucks about a kilometre away as they climbed the hill. They had been informed the convoy comprised three covered trucks and two military jeep escorts and was coming from Rodez. The *maquis chef* ordered them to hold fire until the vehicles were fully in sight as they descended the road to the banks of the Aveyron River. They speeded up down the incline, bumping over the rutted track, gears grinding to control the speed.

Without warning, the *maquis* heaved a huge log down the wooded slope to block the road. The German vehicles were just rounding the bend and the first jeep had to brake rapidly, slewing across the track and tipping on its side by the river bank. The following trucks had no indication of this disaster and trundled round the corner with too much momentum to slow down, thudding into the jeep and piling into each other. The *maquis* forces leapt out of the woods firing rapidly into the vehicles and at the soldiers jumping out onto the road. Bullets rained down on the convoy and a few soldiers returned fire but the *maquis* were a moving target, sprinting between trees and trucks.

A lucky shot hit the engine of the first truck, entered the fuel tank and the vehicle burst into flames, its occupants unable to escape through the tied down canvas flap at the back. The *maquis* kept shooting until they could see no movement. Soldiers lay dead and dying, their bodies twisted into impossible positions, their eyes staring sightlessly at the deep blue sky. Their uniforms were black with blood and flies greedily sucking the moisture. Smoke wafted on the breeze and the acrid tang of cordite overpowered the earthy smell of the woods.

The *maquis* hastily searched the trucks, throwing supplies and weapons onto the road. They shot anyone still in the vehicles, avoiding the engine on fire. Within minutes of the ambush, the trucks had been pushed down the incline into the river where they lay on their sides, spewing smoke and fuel and the *maquis* had disappeared into the forests, carrying the captured food and weapons in canvas backpacks. They had lost one man and were helping two who were injured. They moved silently through the forest, disturbed only by the harsh sound of crows enjoying the road kill and the shrill cry of a red kite high in the sky. They had used the cellar of Broussac chateau as temporary hideout the previous night but needed to travel through the dark to reach safety on the *causse*.

The villagers in Broussac and *Villane-le-Foret* heard the shooting and hastily locked house doors and windows, dragging cats and dogs into the cellars. There had been much furtive exchanging of news, heard on the BBC radio or through the rural grapevine.

The *maquis* had left Michel and Martin at the hideout as a precaution against the youths being tempted to warn their families in Broussac of the ambush. They had been involved as lookouts in several local raids in the area but were not considered mature and ruthless enough to kill. The *chef* of the *maquis* force had fought in the Great War and was a hard bitter man who hated the Germans after experiencing their brutality in the trenches. The youths had never been told his name or those of his group and only permitted to take on lookout duties and foraging for food and fuel. For the past year, they had matured rapidly, learning to track through the forests without leaving a trace and to control emotions and needs. Their bodies and minds had hardened through sheer necessity of survival. The sheltered life with their families had been almost forgotten and their loyalty was only to the *maquis* group who had sheltered them.

The *maquis* had a stolen radio in their hideout which kept them informed of the progress of the war, German troop movements and attacks on villages and towns. For important raids, they joined with other groups defending against attack by convoys of German soldiers and had prevented massacres in two remote villages.

The Das Reich Division based in Caylus took its revenge in August 1944 on the innocent people of Broussac. It was a reprisal operation following the attack by the *maquis*. During the mid-day lunch, when the villagers were at home sharing a meal with their families, a convoy of jeeps and trucks filled with German soldiers roared into the *Place de la Mairie*. The commanding officer leapt from the lead jeep, his face a mask of fury, holding his gun which he pointed at the *Maire* standing at his front door. The officer gestured to his troops to get out of the trucks and ordered them to force the villagers from their homes. Soldiers kicked down doors and smashed windows, searching inside the houses, tipping everything from cupboards, upending tables and chairs, ripping apart beds and curtains, smashing crockery.

Their brutality was not random—they were clearly searching for the *maquis*. Someone local had betrayed them. Old Madame Ricard stumbled out of her house and tripped over, unable to get up. Liliane tried to help her but was stopped by a rifle butt thrust in her face. The villagers were told to lie on the ground whilst their possessions were flung outside in a heap which the soldiers lit with flaming torches. Old people were panting and coughing with the smoke and children were sobbing in fear, mothers placing arms around them to protect them.

After an hour, the soldiers gathered around the jeeps and held a discussion with their commanding officer. Clearly, they had not found who they were searching for. Two soldiers grabbed the men nearest to them, Pierre Dalmain and Serge Lefevre, handcuffed them and pushed them into the back of a jeep. The soldiers got back in the vehicles and drove off raising clouds of dust that spread over the prostrate figures.

When the roar of engines was a distant murmur, the villagers shakily got to their feet, brushed down their clothes and helped the old folk to rise, several had grazes and cuts which needed attention. Liliane and Paulette collected bandages and ointment from their homes and Josette brought an ewer of clean water. She bathed and bandaged cuts and bruises and brought cups of water for the injured.

Madame Ricard had a broken arm which dangled through the sleeve of her overall. Liliane helped her into the *Boulangerie* and put a splint on the arm using a thin piece of firewood before taking her home. The shocked frightened villagers drifted back to their houses, women crying and the men talking angrily, unhappy at their inability to protect their family. The village remained silent and locked the next day but the Germans did not return and nor did Pierre Dalmain and Serge Lefevre. Once again, the Maire felt powerless to protect his villagers.

Many towns suffered savage reprisals in May because of *maquis* attacks and SS divisions infiltrated more than twenty towns and villages in the Lot killing the locals or deporting them to transit camps, including women, and destroying houses. In June and July, attacks and ambush by the *maquis* increased, including paralysing an important railway depot and destroying German lorries. Many *maquis* were killed or captured and taken to transit camps and prisons in the cities of Montauban, Gaillac and Toulouse. Captured women from Gaillac internment camp were taken to Ravensbruck and other concentration camps. In one town, all the exits were blocked, the men rounded up, houses set on fire, villagers hanged or thrown into a fire, women locked up in a church and men shot.

In the *Departement* of the Lot, *maquis* forces occupied the town of Cajarc and ambushed German vehicles travelling from Cahors to occupy the town of Gramat. A convoy of 'Das Reich Division', which operated around Montauban, Figeac and Caylus, had been ambushed. In the *Departement* of the Lot, postal and railway workers had cut electric cables lines and circuits. Railway lines had been sabotaged in 27 places resulting in the wreck of 38 locomotives. In Capdenac and Figeac, the *maquis* had occupied the train station, wrecked the railway line and equipment to cut the main Paris-Brive-Toulouse line.

There were reprisals and raids in the *departements* of the Aveyron, the Limousin and the Tarn et Garonne. The SS burnt, killed and mutilated *maquis* forces in the town of Villefranche de Rouergue. However, against all odds, limited weapons and fighters, the *maquis* efforts appeared to be turning the tide in rural areas against the German invaders.

Escape Route

The day after the *maquis* attack, Britt met with Joseph in the *Mairie* behind closed shutters. Another group of child evacuees had arrived two nights ago and were presently housed in the cellar of the chateau.

"There will certainly be more revenge by the Germans for the *maquis* attack. We must move the children out of the village tonight. I can use my old truck to ferry them to the next safe house in the *Montagne Noire*," Joseph urged. "They'll be frightened because they'll have heard the bombing and shooting yesterday. I have a route planned which diverts round the main roads and towns. During the afternoon siesta, I'll pack their belongings and some food and meet you at the chateau tonight at midnight."

"I'll warn the local *maquis* of your arrival as their group headquarters may be compromised and in danger. I intend to accompany you with the children, so they are better protected. Yes, I can shoot and have a pistol which I have used before," Britt responded to the raised eyebrows and questions that were expressed on Joseph's face. "I believe I am in danger too because of my liaison with the Resistance in Paris conveying messages. My friend in Paris warned me yesterday. I've never explained but my husband was executed in Paris for treason as he was part of a secret group of German officers trying to assassinate Hitler.

I was tortured by the SS in the early days of the war after my husband was captured and shot for unproven treachery to his country. The SS used violence to compel me to betray the secrets they thought my husband had regarding the

German invasion of France. My hair turned white then and I have a limp because my leg was broken by repeated blows. They smashed my fingers too. The SS threw me out onto the street and my friends protected me while I recovered then helped me to escape and move to Broussac. My friends believe the SS are still searching for me so I could endanger this village." Britt sat calmly on the wooden chair, unashamed of her support for her husband or the French Resistance.

Her confession was met with a fraught silence until Joseph smiled and admitted he would be glad of her support. "Dress warmly and please don't bring too much luggage!" Joseph winked at Britt and patted her arm.

"Michel can explain your absence to the parents and close the school to protect the children in the event of another reprisal attack on the village."

Britt gave Joseph a warm hug. She brushed away a tear and walked quickly across the *Place de la Mairie* to the schoolhouse. She'd already packed a small leather briefcase with essential documents and a small cardboard case with a few clothes. She walked down to the river to help ease the sadness she felt at leaving her home and friends yet again. She had felt safe in this isolated village and protected by the kindness of the villagers. She breathed in the moist air, perfumed by recently cut grass and nearby flower gardens. There was a familiar continuity here as the families of ducks swam upstream, the grey heron stood on the gravel mound in the river and swallows dived to scoop up water.

She suspected the uneasiness of the children in the school today was due to their awareness of the tense village atmosphere. Everyone expected a second reprisal attack and a few families were leaving in whatever transport they could use—carts drawn by men and animals, piled high with furniture and small children, including cats. Household dogs were tethered to the cartwheels to run alongside. There were tearful embraces as neighbours kissed each other on the cheeks and self-consciously patted the children's heads.

Britt walked to Liliane's house as dusk blurred the trees and barns across the river. She opened the kitchen door and stepped inside.

"Is it time for you to leave?" Liliane asked quietly and rose to embrace her friend. Jean-Jacques sat by the stove, smoking his usual pipe and looked up from his newspaper to greet Britt.

"*Oui. Je doit partir cet nuit. Merci beaucoup pour ton amitie.* I must go tonight for the safety of the village." Britt kissed Jean-Jacques on his cheeks and gave Liliane a final hug. "Please explain to Rose-Marie and Louis. I've enjoyed teaching them. *Soyez prudent.* Take care."

Late that night, Britt picked up her small cases and left home, closing the door very quietly. She had been sitting in her bedroom since dusk, nervously twisting her hands, unable to settle. She had gazed out of the open window onto the sparsely lit *Place de la Mairie*, saddened by her secret exit from a village that had welcomed and protected her for several years. She slipped silently down the back lane, past the shuttered houses and out of the village up the ancient Roman road leading to the ruined chateau.

Britt hurried, listening for human disturbance but comforted by the normal night sounds of owls flying to trees, hooting softly, a vixen screaming as she devoured her prey and the heavy bodies of cows shifting their position in the fields nearby. She reached the chateau and spied a small truck partly hidden in a copse of trees. She tapped on the truck window and Joseph got out and embraced her. They silently approached the wooden door to the chateau cellar and gently lifted the metal bar locking the door. Joseph lit the lantern hanging inside the door and shone it inside, placing a finger on his lips. Several small children sat on the stone floor, huddled together in the dark. They wore an assortment of dark ragged clothes that partially covered emaciated bodies. Their eyes were full of fear and the smallest child whimpered. "*Il a faim,*" an older child said. "He is hungry."

"*C'est dommage mais on se depecher maintenant*," whispered Joseph. "We must hurry. Get in the truck, we leave now." He ushered the children out of the cellar and helped them climb into the rear of his truck. "*Doucement.* Quietly." Britt climbed into the passenger seat as Joseph started the muffled engine. He drove across a fallow field and turned onto a deep lane, bordered by dense forest. He and Britt heaved a sigh of relief that they had disturbed no one in the village. The truck bounced down the rutted lane then Joseph turned right to join a narrow forest track threading through a dense forest of oak and sweet chestnut trees.

As he drove south, Joseph's intention was to bypass the Germans based in Rodez, then drive across unpopulated countryside past the small town of *Requista* to *Lacaune*, over the *Monts de Lacaune* and due south to the *Montagne Noire*. The *rendezvous* with the *maquis* was by a small lake where they could hide in a wooden hut. Driving at night was safer as long his truck lights were covered with thin gauze. He prayed the children would sleep most of the way as the journey would take many hours. Hopefully by daybreak, they would be travelling down isolated lanes through the *Monts de Lacaune.* He had attached a spare truck wheel underneath in case of a puncture.

After a few hours, Britt took over the driving to allow Joseph to rest. They had no maps and there were few road signs so Joseph had made a rough sketch on a piece of brown paper. Britt stopped once to check using her torch and let the children out. At daybreak, Joseph took over and increased the speed, so they would reach the *rendezvous* at midday.

He intended to leave the children with the *maquis* in the capable hands of Britt, then drive back to Broussac that night using the same route. Joseph reached the *rendezvous* just after mid-day. They had not seen any army convoys or German troops marching the lanes. He parked his truck under a thick canopy of oak trees, untied the tarpaulin flap covering the back of the truck and helped the children out. They were sleepy, frightened and hungry. Britt laid out a picnic on a grassy patch in the trees. The group waited nervously for an hour before they spied two shadows flitting between the trees. Joseph stood up, checking around the truck then waved his cap whilst slowly approaching them. "*Bon voyage*," he whispered the agreed password. The shadows detached themselves, shook Joseph's hand then walked towards the wide-eyed children huddled together on the ground.

"*Bon voyage*," Britt said, repeating the password and stood up. "*Tout va bien,*" she said helping the children to get up. The *maquis chef* looked over the children and shook Britt's hand. "*Ils sont petits*," he stated doubtfully. "They're small and thin. I hope they're strong enough to cope with the arduous journey for the next two days. We'll be walking across rough terrain to get them to a safe village."

"*Bonjour. Je m'appelle, Britt.* I am Britt their schoolteacher. I'm here to help and can carry the little ones if necessary. They're orphan refugees from Paris and I've arranged for them to be adopted by a family living in Mazamet. They've been living on the streets in Paris, existing on scraps of food thrown in bins or gutters. Their parents have been killed and they need somewhere to live in safety." Britt smiled at the children aware of their frightened stares and ragged clothing.

"*D'accord. Allez.*" The *maquis chef* shouldered his rifle and backpack. His assistant did the same and the two men tramped out of the forest clearing. "*Suivre-moi,*" he said, waving to them to follow him.

Britt gave Joseph a hug and thanks for the safe drive. "*Mes enfants, on va au Mazamet et ton nouvelle famille. Ils sont gentil.* Children, we go to Mazamet and your new family. They're kind people." She placed the remains of the picnic in her knapsack and waited while the children grouped together before following the *maquis*. They walked for two nights and two days over rough terrain, through dense forests, down muddy cart tracks, running over roads when told to. They seldom halted for food and rest and the children staggered at times, falling to the ground in their exhaustion but they were hardy little souls, toughened by a life on the streets of Paris.

They reached an isolated farmhouse outside Mazamet and knocked on the kitchen door. An old woman pulled the door slightly ajar and listened carefully to the password before ushering the group inside, locking and barring the solid wood door. The battered children sank to the floor, nodding with exhaustion. The woman gave each of them a mug of water and a crust of bread. She took them through a peeling painted door and down stone steps into the cellar. Blankets had been placed on the floor and the children collapsed onto them. Britt whispered, "*Merci,*" and found a corner to sit. She leant her head against the stone wall and closed her eyes in relief at their safe arrival. The children would rest for a night here before being taken to the foster families living in the surrounding countryside.

Reprisal

Two days later, in the faint light of a mid-summer dawn, Joseph was stalking through a hay field ready to shoot a rabbit for the pot. He stood for a moment and listened to the melodic trill of the skylarks as they rose swiftly from their hidden nests in the reddish-brown soil and soared effortlessly into the deep blue sky. He heard the sweet song of a blackbird serenading the dawn, perched on a branch of a sapling oak tree. He could see brilliantly patterned butterflies land on flowering poppies, buttercups and white daisies, their heady perfume filling the soft warm air. He glimpsed a small rabbit with a white scut scamper through the hedge while he stood spellbound by the peaceful fields and forests. A lone woodpecker tapped on the bark of a tree searching for insects and a red kite floated high overhead, its forked tail feathers guiding its flight. He never tired of the peaceful country sounds and the slowness and steadfastness of rural life.

This tranquillity was abruptly disrupted by the grinding rumble of military trucks coming from *Villane-le-Foret*. 'The Germans,' he thought, '*I must warn the village.*' He sidled out of the field into the shelter of a deep ditch and was horrified to see how fast the convoy drove down the lane and into the village of Broussac, guns firing at unshuttered windows.

Joseph ran down a parallel lane that led to the church, its door permanently left unlocked during the day. He raced up the nave to the base of the bell tower. He heaved open the strong wooden door protecting the bells and reached up to get hold of the dangling ropes but they were too high. Joseph pulled a chair underneath and precariously climbed onto the seat to grab a rope which he swung wildly with as much strength as he could. After a few scary seconds, the thick plaited rope started to swing the heavy cast iron bell that hung from a thick wooden beam high in the tower. He moved the chair and grabbed another rope while the first bell was still swaying and clanging. He could smell burning wood and heard terrible screaming as he ran to the door and into the nave behind the altar where he bumped into the priest who was clutching his cloak around his bare chest. "The Germans are here. Grab your valuable relics and escape to the woods," Joseph yelled at him. M'sieur Pascal grabbed the last pair of silver candlesticks and a tarnished silver dish and dashed down to the crypt, hoping to escape using the hidden tunnel to the ruined chateau.

Jean-Jacques was making the first batch of dough for twenty baguettes and placing them in the bread oven when he heard truck engines filling the air and a strong smell of exhaust. He peered out the open door of the *Boulangerie* and gasped in horror as he saw the *Place de la Mairie* packed with military vehicles, Nazi flags waving on their bonnets and engines throbbing noisily. Liliane ran in the back door past the bread oven and joined him. The *Maire,* his hair uncombed and his clothes hastily pulled on, stumbled down the steps to confront another threat to his village.

Joseph circled the village, racing from house to house, keeping to the shadows as he rapped on doors and windows. "*Les Allemands invahirent le village. Fuyez au forets vite,*" Joseph shouted angrily. He crept nearer to the *Mairie* and joined M'sieur Danton on the steps to give him support. Alain had run out of his house to support the *Maire* and so had Antoine.

The priest had returned and stood at the door of his church waving vigorously to encourage his *paroissiers* to take refuge inside. *"Venez, venez mes amis et mes enfants. Dieu vous protégé."* He held a wooden bowl filled with pieces of bread that were intended for communion mass planned for 10 o'clock. An unruly group of panicking villagers were pushing and shoving to get inside the church to shelter from the gunshots and the flames of houses set alight.

A soldier ran by laughing as he shot a small child crawling across the cobblestones of the *Place* to reach his mother leaning in a doorway, blood pouring down her face because a soldier had punched her to gain entry to the house. He laughed again as he threw a hand grenade into the café, killing and injuring about a dozen people who were taking their first bowl of coffee for the day. Liliane tried to save the child but narrowly avoided being shot by diving into a nearby porch. She could see bloodied bodies sprawled on chairs and slumped on the café terrace. A howling dog who had lost its back leg raced haphazardly between the tables, desperate to flee but unable to on three legs. Café customers were screaming in pain holding stumps of limbs or putting hands over their blinded eyes. Liliane edged back to the *Boulangerie,* realising that she could not help any of her neighbours. The damage and injuries were too horrific to be treated by an amateur nurse.

The terrible smell of burning flesh contaminated the fresh country air mingling with the cordite tang of gunfire and grenade. The acrid smoke of burning metal clouded the air as tractors were set on fire by the soldiers and belched out black chemical fumes.

People were rushing out of their homes, clutching babies and children and precious objects and heading for the forests or the church, trying to shelter from flying debris and bullets. The café burned fiercely, consuming everything and everyone inside and on the terrace. The weakened walls crumbled onto the street and snakes of burning wood crept towards the *epicerie* where vegetables and fruit had been piled outside on wooden shelving. With a whoosh, the fire caught the shelves and flamed up the folded shutters and into the shop setting the sacks of dry produce alight.

Joseph could see soldiers shooting at random and throwing grenades through open doors and windows of houses. Several soldiers were carrying booty to stack in the military trucks parked behind the jeeps. A few brave village men resisted and tried to prevent their homes from being invaded so brutally but they were no match for heavily armed military men. Their screams as they were thrown to the ground and shot mingled with the cries of frightened children and the wailing of women trying to save their family.

The soldiers moved swiftly along the main street pursuing villagers who were fleeing through lanes and fields trying to escape the murderous onslaught. Partly clothed people fell to the ground outside their homes and the bloody bodies of dogs littered the lanes, unable to defend their owners.

A group of soldiers were tugging people from their homes and dragging them into the church. A jeep filled to the top with hay screeched to a halt and the driver and a comrade started bundling hay into the nave, tucking it under the wooden chairs and throwing it around the altar.

Joseph hid outside behind a tombstone and watched in horror as more families, some staggering with bullet wounds, were pushed into the church, small children being trampled underfoot. Soldiers marched in holding flaming wood torches which they held to the hay piles and the chairs until they caught fire. The terrible screaming of the wounded and the smell of scorched flesh filled the consecrated church nave like a scene from hell. Mothers were struggling to protect their children, flapping hopelessly as the flames grew higher and the acrid smoke denser. The heavy wooden doors were slammed shut and a wooden bar slotted into a metal bracket.

Joseph crept away between the tombstones. He couldn't help as soldiers were guarding the barred door. He could hear the people trapped inside banging helplessly on the door and endless screaming.

He crouched behind a hedge and shuffled along a ditch to the lane leading up to the woods. When he reached the hilltop, he knelt down and retched into the ditch, shivering with fear and horror. He had no idea how many villagers had been condemned to such a barbaric death. He picked a handful of damp grass and wiped his mouth and face but remained in a crouched position in the ditch, unable to move, feeling despair for his village.

He hid in the thickest part of the forest until dusk when he heard the military vehicles depart the village, the soldiers yelling their victory. He crept to where the forest thinned out on a rocky plateau and peered out at the desecrated village. Odorous columns of smoke were rising from the shattered buildings. Burnt bodies of humans and animals lay scattered in doorways and lanes. The beautiful ancient church was in ruins, its nave and bell tower crumbling and scorched. The stench was horrific. At first, he could see no signs of life until a child clothed in rags clambered over the burnt door of the *Boulangerie* and the heaps of stones into the *Place de la Mairie*. The child stood holding its arm which looked broken and gazed around at the desecration then sat down on a large stone. There was nobody else alive.

Joseph carefully descended the Roman lane, scanning his surroundings. He recognised the child as Rose-Marie, the daughter of Liliane and Jean-Jacques. He edged closer to the destroyed church until he was ten metres from her, then made a bird call. The child lifted her head and Joseph could see tears and dust clogged her eyelashes and her face. Her clothes were torn and scorched and she had no shoes. Joseph whistled again then crept across the *Place*. "Rose-Marie," he whispered, wiping his eyes. "*C'est Joseph. Ton bras est casse? Viens avec moi.*" He placed a gentle hand on the child's shoulder shocked by the rigidity of her body and the blank look in her eyes. He stood and picked her up in his arms, careful of the broken limb. He walked out of the village, taking the cobbled Roman road uphill to the safety of the forest. He found the old hunter's wooden hut, heaved open the warped wooden door and gently laid the child on the hay-covered bench. He found a tin cup and, kneeling in the soft leaves, dipped it into the well, and took it back into the hut.

Rose-Marie was lying prone on the bench with her clogged eyelids closed, shaking with fear and wincing in pain. Her broken arm hung from her side and Joseph could see burns on the fragile skin. He knelt by her, gently lifted her head and placed the cup of water at her mouth. "*Buvez, buvez, ma petite et apres je repare ton bras.*"

Rose-Marie opened her eyes, flinching at the effort and sipped from the cup, dribbling the excess over her delicate chin. "*J'ai beaucoup de peur. Ma mere et mon pere sont mort.*" She sobbed the words and clung with her good arm to Joseph's torn shirt. He helped her to sit up and held the child close to his chest, knowing he couldn't make her parents live but determined to protect this sole survivor of the village massacre.

That evening, the tall thin old man and the young girl stood, clothed in sooty rags on the edge of the forest and looked down at the destroyed village, its inhabitants, animals and buildings mingled in burnt piles. The ashes still glowed and small plumes of grey smoke rose into the balmy summer evening. It seemed sacrilegious that they were surrounded by the normal birdsong but the clanging of the ancient church bells had been brutally halted.

Aveyron Summer 1995

Memorial to Brutality

Laure Duprey parks her yellow Renault by the enamel memorial sign placed in a gravelled car park on the banks of the Aveyron River. It is late afternoon and the hot summer sun is sliding down the cloudless blue sky. She reads the sign with its description of German atrocity inflicted on the village of Broussac-sur-Aveyron. Her grandmother, Rose-Marie had survived the massacre, saved by Joseph, an old soldier of the Great War. Laure has taken an organised tour of Commonwealth War Cemeteries in northern France, then hired a car to drive south to the Aveyron and visit Broussac, burnt to the ground in retribution by the Germans for providing shelter, food and escape routes during World War II to the local *maquis*.

Laure holds a worn photo of a laughing dark-haired woman wearing a patterned overall and clogs. She's leaning against the wall of the *Boulangerie* and holds a bike with a wire basket attached to the handlebars filled with baguettes. A young girl is perched on the seat, bare legs dangling down to the pedals, her grandmother.

Laure looks up at the broken scorched buildings perched partway up the steep wooded hill and walks up the ancient cobbled road. Small unseen animals scurry through the leafy hawthorn hedge and wild violets nestling in the grassy verge. She admires the picturesque rural scene—the fields of rippling wheat and brilliant yellow sunflowers. She hears the muffled engine of a tractor harvesting a distant field and the soft hum of bees seeking pollen.

She walks through a thick oak forest and reaches a grassy clearing, surrounded by sweet chestnut trees. She's startled by a baby deer, a *bambi*, leaping through the trees. She sniffs the earthy odour of damp fallen leaves and looks up through the leaves to the blue sky. The organised tour had been interesting but the endless rows of crosses, each marking the remains of an unknown soldier, now placed in immaculately kept public gardens, felt overwhelmingly tragic. She knew the Aveyron *Departement* had designated the village of Broussac as a memorial to the tragedies of war and had left the ruins untouched until a decade ago when the French Government allowed tourists to visit. It was her mother's wish that her daughter, Laure, paid her respects to her courageous grandmother, Liliane, at the ruins of the Boulangerie in Broussac memorial. She turns left at the top following the signs and stops by the one saying, "Silence." She loves the perfumed dusk of a French summer, serenaded by blackbirds, robins, finches and pigeons.

She climbs the steps and smells the wild roses and honeysuckle spreading over the tumbled walls. She stops at the ruined church, its remaining arches in the nave split and scorched. The stone niches for saints are empty on the one wall still standing. There is a pale outline of a mural in the centre depicting the nativity scene. There are piles of stone covered in yellow lichen with tiny grey lizards lying on the warm rocks. The medieval stone tower still stands pointing at the sky like a finger, its carved wooden door is locked with a notice stating, *Interdit*.

Laure walks along grassy paths that had once been busy cobbled streets between family homes and shops. She stands in the *Place de la Mairie* where M'sieur Bertrand Danton had been shot as he tried to prevent the torching of the ancient church and the mass burning of his villagers. Few buildings have survived—the charred remains of wooden roof beams and furniture; a broken table leg.

Laure wanders down the silent main street looking at the desecrated ruins of the *Mairie, La Poste, the Boulangerie*, each building with a black coating of soot. A scorched bike leans against the wall of the *Boulangerie*, its frame twisted with the heat, the rubber tyres melted. She pauses to gaze at the arched brick roof of the bread oven and the charred remains of copper pans hanging from bent nails. This was where her grandparents had lived and perished. Her grandfather, Jean-Jacques Damour had been an artisan *Boulanger* and her grandmother, Liliane had used the bike to deliver fresh bread to the villagers and to the tiny hamlet of Villane-le-Foret nearby. She had courageously carried messages hidden in baguettes for local bands of *maquis*. Laure sits on a stone block overcome by emotion and the innate sadness of the place, sensing the uneasy ghosts of her family inhabiting the building.

She walks on to *La Poste* with its arched stone windows singed by the ferocity of the fire, the brass hinges for wooden shutters tarnished with age and soot. Madame Cantou ran *La Poste* and acted as a liaison point between the Resistance in the Aveyron and Lot and the local *maquis*. Next door is the *Mairie* reached by a set of tapered stone steps, its name is carved into the stone lintel above the charred remains of the wooden door. Two wide stone flowerpots by the door hold fresh flowers, their bright colours incongruous against the scorched grey stone walls.

Laure's grandmother had told amusing stories of official meetings of the popular *Maire*, conducted with several glasses of local wine, windows open to the fresh air allowing guffaws of laughter to echo round the village. The *Maire* was a staunch supporter of the *maquis* and championed the Resistance efforts.

Laure walks back to the *Boulangerie* and pulls the clinging ivy from the arched roof of the original bread oven which had collapsed inwards. She knows this was where her grandfather, Jean-Jacques had baked baguettes, cottage loaves and the patisserie he had been famous for. There is nothing left of the heavy wooden table on which he had rolled the dough or the trough in which he had mixed and kneaded it. She had another black and white photo tucked in her handbag of her grandfather handling the dough amidst the smoke from the wood-fired brick oven. He was plump with a bushy moustache and an apron tied round his stomach; his hands pale with flour. On the wall by the oven door was a wooden rack in which Jean-Jacques had placed the cooked loaves. All gone now—just a couple of rusty nails poking from the blackened stones.

Laure shakily sits down on the steps, resting her head on her bare arms. She feels overwhelmed with despair at this shocking evidence of the brutality of war. She raises her head and looks out of the village to the forests in the distance. In the silence, she can hear the splashing and gurgling of the river as it flows over a weir and the repetitive tap-tap-tap of a woodpecker in the woods up the hill beyond the village. A glossy blackbird lands on the charred statue of Jesus positioned at the far side of the *Place de la Mairie*. The dappled shade of a plane tree spreads across the cobblestones and she sniffs the heady perfume of climbing roses and honeysuckle waving in a gentle breeze.

Laure realises she must complete her visit before dusk darkens the lanes and visit the *cimetière* where her ancestors were buried. Ruined burnt buildings line the cobbled street, each one a cherished home. Her mother had talked to her about some of the village characters and she wonders where Madame Ricard and Madame Royal lived. She can see the shell of the *epicerie* across the *Place* and next door the stone footings of the café. Opposite is the large three-storied house which was the home of Josette with stone steps leading up to an empty entrance to the living area. The cellar at ground level is wide open sheltering a charred wooden cart and a rusty plough.

She crosses to the wide stone steps leading up to the shell of the chateau. The scorched ruins are softened by lichen and moss, the foundations loosened by saplings and undergrowth. It's built on an escarpment overlooking the fields and the glinting thread of the river in the valley. A small grey lizard sunbathes on a fallen piece of masonry originally part of the crenelated walkway in the north tower. Through the crumbling arch of a window, Laure glimpses in the far distance the outline of the Pyrenees mountains, one crag with a layer of snow highlighted by the sinking sun. She shields her eyes with one hand and spies several more peaks. She climbs a twisted stone staircase, the light filtering through broken roof beams and enters the main hall. She can see carved stone roof trusses poking out from the stone wall and several rectangular niches, presumably window seats. Two imposing fireplaces remain, their bases thick with powdered ash and charred logs. It was a melancholy place redolent of medieval power. She reads a metal sign that explains the chateau had provided a refuge for local *maquis* and refugee children in its extensive cellars. It had been a safe winter base for the local *Resistance* who stored arms and ammunition during the cold months of 1943-44. The chateau owners had escaped the savage

German reprisals with a few villagers, including her grandmother to the mountains of the Cevennes.

A few tears drifted down Laure's cheek as she remembers the stories her mother, Rose-Marie, had told about her parents, their meeting at Cahors market and the love affair that followed. Her eldest brother, Armand, had been tragically killed in an explosion in a German armaments' factory and Louis, the younger son had been shot as he tried to escape the forced enlistment, the STO authorised by Marshal Petain.

She reaches the *cimetière* and opens the wrought iron gate which swings on well-oiled hinges. There is no one visiting the graves but they are well tended with fresh and false flowers placed on the tombstones. There seems so many graves for a small village but she knows that over 300 hundred villagers were either shot or burnt alive on that horrific day in July 1944.

She finds her grandmother's family grave and kneels to place a large bouquet of flowers on the tombstone. Her knowledge of the French language is limited but she can decipher the words, *"mon bien-aime pere et ma bien-aimee mere."* After kneeling for a while at the grave, Louise gets up and walks to an iron bench placed in the shade of an oak tree.

Laure walks down the lane to the carpark and hears birds serenading the end of the day. She stops to watch a lone cow amble across the grassy field to join a group of cattle drinking from a metal water trough. She reaches her car and is opening the door when she sees a bent old woman with a stick driving a flock of waddling white geese into a grassy field. The geese are cackling and jostling as they munch the grass. The old lady unlatches a wire cage and stoops in to collect a handful of brown eggs, watched by a large gaudy cockerel. Swallows are swooping around the stone barn and chirping softly. A large pale owl flies out of the barn, lands on a post to look at the old lady and swoops off to a nearby oak tree. The woman feeds a bag of meat to the caged *chasse* dogs.

The old woman firmly shuts the cage doors, stumbles out of the yard and trudges up the hill to a dilapidated stone cottage. A smell of casserole drifts from the open door and a scrawny brown cat edges out to start its night-time hunting. The bells of a nearby village church ring the hour, the sounds echoing round the wooded hills. A red tractor rumbles down the lane pulling a trailer full of hay. A small boy is perched on the tractor seat clutching the shirt of an old man driving the vehicle. The child waves at her and shouts, *"Bonsoir, madame."*

She remains in her car and broods over her visit to Oradour-sur-Glane two months earlier. She remembers similar ruined streets and stark evidence of the fire that consumed the village and its inhabitants. She had walked to a café in the main square of the new town and sat at a metal table watching the sun sink in a blaze of red and orange over the forests. A radio was playing in the bar and she noticed a feeling of tension in the air. The other customers, mostly locals by their clothes, lifted their heads and listened in silence to a slow sad song. It is a lament about two lovers. An old lady at the next table tapped Laure on the shoulder and said in French, "*C'est le chanson de la tragedie du village.*" She sniffed a little and Laure replied, "*Merci.*" She noticed a couple at another table tightly holding hands and listening intently, tears shining in the faint sunlight. It felt like the whole café and the new town have stopped their activities to listen to the words of the song. Laure was deeply moved and decided to find the words translated into English.

Months later, she found a version with the English translation sung by Gerard Berliner who wrote the music, the lyrics written by Frank Thomas.

"The men were in the fields, the children in school
The baker in the oven, the carpenter in the wood
And the air was perfect for the birds…"

Vichy France Historical Notes

Broussac and the Aveyron

The location for my novel is the imaginary village of Broussac in the *Departement* of the *Aveyron*. My description of its buildings and history is based on actual villages and towns in the Aveyron area, including the hamlet in which I lived with my husband for ten years, participating in the cultural and historical events of a farming community. Our local doctor referred to it as '*un village tres sympatique*'. We made many friends and were supported through a few difficult periods. I have taken an author's liberty to include some locals in my story.

Broussac has several notable buildings, including a tiny thirteenth century chapel with a priest's house attached. In the central *Place de la Mairie* is the village well encased in a low stone wall with a heavy iron grille. On the outskirts are the ruins of a Crusader castle that have become a weed-infested heap of stones. The village had been on the pilgrimage route in the thirteenth century and briefly housed a Cathar sect in the same era. One of the old stone houses is reputed to be haunted by a badly wounded soldier of the Napoleonic wars.

The village church was built in the fourteenth century and has thick stone walls with a tall square tower used as a lookout during the wars between the French and the English. It houses a magnificent carved group of wooden figures behind the altar. At the crossroads outside the village is an ancient stone cross whose horizontal crosspiece is set in a shallow dip so it can be swivelled round to change direction. In medieval times, it was used to inform locals of the direction from which invading forces were coming, so they could hide in the fortified church. The tower was built for defence, so the villagers could hurl stones and flaming torches of pitch down to the enemy.

An ancient Roman road, also used as a pilgrim route in the Middle Ages leads to the church and the *Place de la Mairie.* The road has shaped stones embedded in the ground interspersed by grassy patches. It ascends through steeply wooded hills, over a rocky escarpment and drops into the river valley before heading north-west to Spain.

The *Aveyron Departement* is historically one of the poorest regions of France as it is remote and mountainous. The administrative centre and location of the *Prefecture* is Rodez, a town built in local pink-red limestone with a large medieval cathedral.

The former name of the province was *Rouergue*—land of red earth. The Massif Central provides a harsh eastern border for the Aveyron with the high plateaux of the Causses Sauveterre, Mejean and Larzac, and includes the limestone *causse* of *Cantal* (famous for its delicious hard cheese), *Aubrac* and *Monts-d'Auvergne*. To the north-west are the woods of the Segala region. To the south and south-west are the Monts de Lacaune and Mont Caroux.

The Aveyron River is 291 kilometres long and rises in the southern Massif Central near the town of *Severac-le-Chateau*. It flows through the historic towns of *Villefranche-de-Rouergue, Najac, Saint Antonin-Noble-Val, Bruniquel and Negrepelisse*. It is a diverse region with thick oak and chestnut forests, high rocky plains (*la causse*) and wooded gorges.

The picturesque Bastide towns and villages located on the river have a rich medieval history with fortified chateaux. Farms in the river valley grow wheat, hay, barley, rape and sunflowers in the heavy, rich red clay soil called *rougier*, which has a high oxide content laid over schist and limestone. This was used for building houses and churches. The steep hills leading to the *causse* (plateau) are densely forested but south-facing slopes have been terraced to provide maximum exposure to sunlight as the dry soils of schist and granite are ideal for vines.

German Reprisals

Indiscriminate reprisals were carried out in all parts of France. The *Musee de la Resistance* in Cahors in the Lot identifies examples of savage massacres carried out by Das Reich Division in May 1944. The Division was stationed in various towns in the *Departements* bordering the Aveyron—the Lot, Tarn, Tarn et Garonne. These included Montauban, Negrepelisse, Cahors, Figeac, Lauzerte, Montcuq, Limogne. Some reprisals were the outcome of denunciations, others were racial or political discrimination. Many were as a result of *maquis* attacks and sabotage or brave groups defending their village. Men were rounded up and either deported or killed, children were killed and many women arrested, interned in camps like the one at Gaillac in the Tarn and Montauban (Tarn et Garonne). The women were piled into cattle trucks and transported to Ravensbruck concentration camp. Few of them returned.

In Montpezat du Quercy in the Tarn, houses were burnt down and nameless atrocities carried out on the population. In Frayssinet-le-Gelat, all the exits were blocked, men were rounded up and houses set on fire. Women and children were locked in the church, women were hanged, men shot and mutilated. Women escaped to the woods and the men made to remove the bodies and place them in a common graveyard. The men were locked in the church from midnight while the SS indulged in uncontrolled looting and orgies.

In other villages, men were arrested and murdered, houses and barns set alight and cattle slaughtered, for example, in the villages of Planioles, Camburat, Lissac and St Bresson. St Terou was occupied for the second time and the village completely burnt down. Other examples are provided in the official brochure of the Museum of the Resistance, Deportation and Liberation of the Lot Department.

In the Aveyron region, reprisal attacks were equally savage. In Rynes, 26 inhabitants were massacred at different places in the village. In the region of Mont Muchet, other atrocities carried out, women and children pulled out of their homes and shot on their doorsteps despite the mayor in the village of Clavieres trying to reason with the German forces.

The STO Releve

On 11 November 1942, the Germans occupied the *zone sud* in response to the landing of the Allies in North Africa. Hitler ordered that the *Petain* regime should be retained and *Laval* should remain as Head of State. He stated, "French sovereignty would be maintained as long as it suited German interests." After the defeat of France, their army was disbanded and over a million and a half French soldiers were taken as prisoners of war by the German Reich. Most of northern France was devastated during World War 1 and there was increasing concentration on agriculture to provide food and crops. During the next twenty years, farming was mechanised using steam or petrol driven threshing machines.

From September 1942, Pierre Laval was forced to provide labour to Germany and introduced a system of voluntary labour service, *Service du Travail Obligatoire* (STO). Only workers engaged in vital war labour were exempt. This policy increased hostility by French officials to the Germans and their representatives in the Vichy Government as they were trapped between their fellow citizens and the occupier. The intent of the *STO* scheme was to recruit urban and industrialised workers whose skills had given them exemption from fighting in 1940. These would be traded for French prisoners of war. The workers were offered good wages and promised secure employment. The Vichy Government advertised the *STO* scheme as a moral and patriotic obligation. This resulted in resignations of officials and passive resistance.

STO Refractaires

Forty thousand unemployed men and 650,000 conscripts of the *STO* were sent to Germany. Thousands of French men were directly employed by the Germans. Large numbers of *STO* R*efractaires* (draft dodgers) forged false exemption certificates and went underground, often joining local *Maquis* groups. Laval established the French Militia in January 1943. The *Milice* was a force of volunteers whose responsibility was to maintain order and it absorbed local *gendarmeries*.

The Vichy Government redefined the duties of the *Prefects* in the *zone sud* to include close cooperation by the *gendarmes* in 'the arrest of German deserters and R*efractaires* and to pursue anyone engaged in attacks or acts of sabotage directed against the German presence'. Orders were given that all searches and arrests should be handled only by the French police, the *gendarmes*. By

December 1942, it was recorded, "The majority of people were hostile to the policy of collaboration."

The Maquis

By the end of 1941 and continuing in 1942 onwards, the *Maquis* evolved from rural groups carrying out isolated acts of defiance. They took the name of *Maquis* which means 'scrubland' as they operated covertly from unpopulated areas like the '*causse*' in the Aveyron and the Lot. Separate guerrilla groups formed of local volunteers who knew the countryside intimately including grocers, school teachers and policemen. In February 1943, when the Germans implemented the *Service du Travail Obligatoire* (STO) that forcibly drafted French young men to labour in Germany, many deserted (*les refractaires*) and joined *Maquis* groups.

The *Maquis* involved a mix of railway workers, postmen, gendarmerie, police and clergy. They had a strong sense of self-preservation honed over centuries of deprivation manipulated by powerful landowners. By the end of 1943, there were 43 Resistance groups operating independently in the *Departement* of the Lot. Their aim was to liberate their country. They ambushed lorries of corn, flour and livestock, especially German convoys which were loaded with produce requisitioned for the Germans.

The *maquis* soon learnt the advantages of easy mobility and speedy dispersal after their raids. They selected targets located away from their base camps and moved from one safe hiding place to another. They were dependant on the local population for supplies and shelter, including teachers, priests, restaurant owners and farmers. Local tradesmen also supported them—bakers, butchers, millers and garage mechanics. Village priests often worked closely with the *maquis*, for example, *Abbe Gauch* became their *cure* (priest) in the woods near the coal mining town of Carmaux in the *Departement* of the Tarn.

Many villages and isolated farms were suspected by the *Milice* of harbouring *maquis,* including the town of Decazeville and the village of Sucaillou in the Aveyron. The *maquis* learned through bitter experience to take account of differing local customs and animosities. Not all *paysannes* were in favour of the *maquis*. At Liberation, letters of denunciation were found at one Aveyron *Prefecture*. "I am a farmer in the Segala. I fought in the First World War and am a loyal French citizen. There is a *maquis* unit in the woods opposite my farm." It was signed with the writer's address.

By summer 1944, the *maquis* in the Tarn were turning away volunteers for lack of arms. News of the Allied landings had resulted in an eruption of people from all social classes choosing to leave their villages and towns and head for the forests and the plateau. Many were unused to the hard life and returned home within short periods.

Evacuation of Children from Paris

Destructive Allied air raids in 1943 on Paris and its suburbs forced the evacuation of local children out of bombed areas to the *Creuse*, a *Departement* to the south. They travelled in convoys by train and were housed with local people, supervised by the *Prefecture*. The children were accompanied by primary school teachers or priests. Groups of children had been separated from their families due to economic reasons or had left Paris in 1940 with their families during the mass civilian exodus when the Germans invaded Paris. In many circumstances, the father of the child was a prisoner of war having joined the French army in 1939 and the mother struggled to earn a living and look after the children.

The adopted children had experienced food shortages and hunger in Paris due to the German invasion and Allied bombing. Many were homeless and roamed the streets for food and shelter. As evacuees, they were placed with an adopted family and fed well on fresh country produce like cheese, vegetables and fruit.

According to published research carried out by the University of Huddersfield in the UK, refugee children stayed for different periods of time, adapting to rural life, enjoying the freedom of the fields and daily association with domestic animals. They experienced kindness and generosity as they attended local schools. Few children experienced a deep sense of displacement and emotional trauma.

Local Villages and Towns

Albi-UNESCO listed historical city on the Tarn, famous for being the centre of the medieval Cathar religion and its superb redbrick cathedral built by the Catholics after the persecution of the Cathars in thirteenth and fourteenth centuries. The birthplace of Toulouse-Lautrec, the artist and La Perouse, the explorer.

Cahors-Medieval market town located on the river Lot and the main train line from Paris to Toulouse. Administrative centre of the Department of the Lot. Famous for the medieval Pont du Valentre and beautiful cathedral.

Figeac-Medieval village situated on the river Lot.

Lalbenque-Large village situated on the train line between Cahors and Toulouse.

Le Quercy Noir-Dense forests.

Rodez-Administrative centre of the Aveyron Department located on a main railway line. A group of active *maquisards and FTP* were based in WW11.

Saint Antonin-Noble-Val-An important medieval town located on the river Aveyron. Its large weekly market is held in the *Place des Halles* and in several of the narrow streets. It is the location for two well-known films—*Charlotte Gray and The Hundred Foot Journey*.

St Martial (*imaginary*)-Ancient bastide village built on a prominent hill with houses adjoining each other. Encircled by medieval ramparts and archways, accessed by a medieval arched stone bridge over the river Aveyron.

Villane-le-Foret (*imaginary*)-Located two kilometres from Broussac in dense oak and chestnut forests.

Bibliography and References

Roger Price (2005) *A Concise History of France,* Cambridge University Press, 2nd Edition.

Robert Doisneau-several books of photographs

Kedward, H.R. (2003) *In Search of the Maquis; Rural Resistance in Southern France 1942–1944*, Oxford University Press.

Firelight and Woodsmoke; Applewood; Scent of Herbs. Omnibus Edition. Claude Michelet. 1995. Translation from French to English by Sheila Dickie. Orion Press.

Jean Edward Smith (2020) *Liberation of Paris,* Paperbacks.

Lindsey Dodd (2019) 'Wartime Rupture and Reconfiguration in French Family Life: Experience and Legacy', *History Workshop Journal*, 88, Oxford: University of Huddersfield.

Cathar Country, MSM 1992–2004.

Elsie Burch Donald (1995) *The French Farmhouse*, Little, Brown and Company.

Deportation and Liberation of the Lot Department (1993) The Museum of the Resistance, Official brochure.

Guide de Visite (November 2003) Musee de la Resistance, de la Deportation et Liberation of du Lot.

Rosine Lagier *Il y a Un Siècle…La France paysanne,* Edition Ouest-France.

Glossary French to English

Translation of common phrases and word I have used in my novel.

Allez—Go

Ami(s)—friend (s) or *Copains*—close friends, mates

Beaucoup—many, a lot

Cave—Cellar

Ca va?—how are you (informal)

Chasse—local hunt using certain breed of dog

Comme d'habitude—as usual

Comment allez vous—how are you (formal)

Depecher—to hurry

Les Nouvelles—some news

Epicerie—Grocer

Faux—False

Je vous remercie—thank you

Legumes—vegetables

N'inquiete pas—don't worry

Pas du tout—not at all

Potager—vegetable garden

Poule or poulet—chicken

Que'est que se passe?—What's happening

Salle de Fete—village hall

Sanglier—wild boar

Tarte tatin—Apple tart

Tout va bien—All's well.

Viens, venez—Come on.

Ingram Content Group UK Ltd.
Milton Keynes UK
UKHW020244250423
420704UK00002B/4